Acclaim for
THE PERSONAL HISTORY OF RACHEL DuPREE

**Winner of the Langum Prize in American Historical Fiction
Winner of the Texas Institute of Letters' Steven Turner
Award for Best Work of First Fiction**

"Deeply affecting . . . The title character, reminiscent of Celie in *The Color Purple,* is an unassuming heroine with true grit and deep-seated dignity."
—*San Antonio Express-News*

"An indelibly affecting teaching story: how unchecked selfish desires, regardless of their origins in historical cruelty and deprivation, lead inevitably to suffering. A suffering that can be alleviated only by the realization of a pure love for others greater than one's desires for self. Rachel and Isaac DuPree and their tiny, vulnerable family stand as monuments to the forgotten millions of brutal, spirit-deforming choices made and endured by so many brave and deeply wounded Americans."   —Alice Walker

"A captivating twist on the familiar pioneer story [that] is ambitious for a first novel, and it triumphs."   —*Richmond Times-Dispatch*

"An inspiring story . . . The flow and detail in the novel are to be admired. . . . It rolls along like a tumbleweed across the prairie. . . . So tough and tender is Ann Weisgarber's main character in *The Personal History of Rachel DuPree* that I lay awake one night worried about Rachel. . . . It is historical fiction worth getting caught up in."
—Samantha Stiles, *Austin American-Statesman*

"Ann Weisgarber tells the story of an African American family struggling to survive in the Dakota Badlands with a vividness and intensity by turns heartbreaking and thrilling. It is a story of human betrayal and human love, and a woman you will not soon forget."
—Robert Morgan, author of *Gap Creek*

"Emotionally enveloping . . . Reminiscent of the iconic Willa Cather and Laura Ingalls Wilder . . . The story is captivating, and will dig deep into the hearts of its readers."   —WOSU (Ohio NPR affiliate)

"A moving story about strength, perseverance, and maternal love in the face of dire adversity. Strong characterization along with evocative and hauntingly beautiful imagery fully engage the reader in this highly recommended debut novel."   —*The Historical Novels Review*

"A wonderful addition to the literature of the Great Plains. Ann Weisgarber not only locates a bright, clear voice in that vast, silent region but does so in a much-neglected part of its population. This is a brave, lovely novel."
—Larry Watson, author of *Montana 1948* and *Orchard*

"Heartbreaking . . . [A] quiet masterpiece . . . Book clubs looking for something new and original to discuss need look no further. . . . Weisgarber . . . captures perfectly the interior journey of a wife and mother, replete with unspoken hopes, fears, and resentments. I was reminded of Orleanna Price, the wife and mother in Barbara Kingsolver's haunting novel *The Poisonwood Bible*. . . . Take the opportunity to escape into *The Personal History of Rachel DuPree* for a few hours. It will be well worth the time."
—Diana Irvine, *Sacramento Book Review*

"This debut novel . . . offers taut writing and an unusual subject."
—*USA Today*

"I worried about Rachel for several days as I raced through this novel. Her story has never been told, and she is a singular heroine in a vivid and heartless world."
—Susan Straight, National Book Award finalist for *Highwire Moon*

"Beautifully done, rendered in spare, unshowy prose as denuded as the Dakota earth; while Rachel is a marvelously realized creation."
—*The Guardian*

"Compelling historical fiction at its best, with appeal factors similar to Charles Frazier's *Cold Mountain* or Breena Clark's *Stand the Storm*."
—*Library Journal* (starred review)

"An essential American story. Some will call this a novel of race, some will see the futility of the dust bowl settlement, some will believe it to be a tale of a strong woman. It's all of these and so much more—a grand achievement of the first rate."
—Jeffrey Lent, author of *In the Fall*

"Extraordinary . . . An unforgettable novel."
—*The Jackson Advocate*

"A shimmering novel of the sacrifice, hardship, and determination of a black family in the early twentieth-century settlement of the West."
—*Booklist*

"A stunning novel—so accomplished, insightful, and deeply affecting that it is hard to believe it is a debut. Rachel will capture your imagination, break your heart, and inflame your hope."
—Ellen Feldman, author of *Scottsboro* and *Lucy*

"Vintage Americana, as chilling as *Cold Mountain*."
—*Red*

"Striking . . . Admirably crisp . . . Weisgarber's style is Alice Walker by way of Kent Haruf."
—*Kirkus Reviews*

"Ann Weisgarber has written an astonishing novel of the pioneering West —a novel as beautiful, profound, and unsentimental as those of Rolvaag and Cather. And yet her story feels brand new, its insights into race in America poignant and timely. *The Personal History of Rachel DuPree* is the finest novel I've read this year. I can't wait to read her next one."
—Lin Enger, author of *Undiscovered Country*

"A gem . . . Pride and prejudice are the prevalent themes running through this book. From the dramatic first chapter it's a powerful story of courage in the face of adversity."
—*Irish Examiner*

"By writing a novel that no one else has thought to write yet, Weisgarber has pushed a frontier herself [and] changes a key point in a quintessentially American narrative—a narrative that, up until now, has centered almost exclusively on the experiences of white people."
—*Bookslut*

"An exciting, fast-moving novel about courage in the face of the terrible truth. You will inhabit the lives of these characters as you read the novel, and long after you're done, the characters will inhabit your life."
—Thomas Cobb, author of *Crazy Heart* and *Shavetail*

"A personal history of a woman that you will not forget."
—Watermark Books

"A story best experienced firsthand with fingers pressed to the pages and an uninterrupted stretch of time. . . . Without a doubt, Rachel DuPree will take her place among America's literary heroines. Weisgarber captures the otherworldly landscape and harsh climate expertly—so much so that you can feel the grit under your fingernails and the dryness in your mouth long after you close the book. This is a poignant tale that will move you in unexpected ways. . . . Not only did this shoot to the top of my list of all-time favorites in historical fiction, but it easily takes a spot among my favorites of any genre. If I'm asked to recommend one must-read book for the year, *The Personal History of Rachel DuPree* is definitely it."
—N. Gemini Sasson, *My Dog Ate My Manuscript*

"Emotionally arresting . . . Vivid and expressive . . . A compelling story that at times will leave the reader breathless. . . . One would never guess this is a debut novel for Ann Weisgarber. Her prose has a sophisticated flow to it that, in combination with the story, immediately draws the reader in. There's no showboating or silly tricks, just the raw truth of her fictional characters' lives. . . . The writing is superb, leaving this reader looking forward to whatever Weisgarber comes up with next."
—Jessica Harrison, *Deseret News*

ABOUT THE AUTHOR

CHRISTINE MEEKER

Ann Weisgarber was born and raised in Kettering, Ohio. She holds a master's degree in sociology and has worked as a social worker and has taught high school and college. She has lived in Boston and Des Moines and now divides her time between Sugar Land and Galveston, Texas.

The Personal History of Rachel DuPree is Ann Weisgarber's first novel. It was longlisted for the Orange Prize, was a finalist for the Orange Award for New Writers, and won the Langum Prize in American Historical Fiction and the Texas Institute of Letters' Steven Turner Award for Best Work of First Fiction.

To access Penguin Readers Guides online, visit our Web sites at www.penguin.com or www.vpbookclub.com.

THE PERSONAL HISTORY
OF RACHEL DuPREE

ANN WEISGARBER

A Weisgarber

10/24/19

Center for the
Great Plains
Studies

PENGUIN BOOKS

PENGUIN BOOKS

Published by the Penguin Group

Penguin Group (USA) Inc., 375 Hudson Street,
New York, New York 10014, U.S.A.

Penguin Group (Canada), 90 Eglinton Avenue East, Suite 700,
Toronto, Ontario, Canada M4P 2Y3
(a division of Pearson Penguin Canada Inc.)

Penguin Books Ltd, 80 Strand, London WC2R 0RL, England

Penguin Ireland, 25 St. Stephen's Green, Dublin 2, Ireland
(a division of Penguin Books Ltd)

Penguin Books Australia Ltd, 250 Camberwell Road, Camberwell,
Victoria 3124, Australia
(a division of Pearson Australia Group Pty Ltd)

Penguin Books India Pvt Ltd, 11 Community Centre, Panchsheel Park,
New Delhi – 110 017, India

Penguin Group (NZ), 67 Apollo Drive, Rosedale, Auckland 0632,
New Zealand (a division of Pearson New Zealand Ltd)

Penguin Books (South Africa) (Pty) Ltd, 24 Sturdee Avenue,
Rosebank, Johannesburg 2196, South Africa

Penguin Books Ltd, Registered Offices:
80 Strand, London WC2R 0RL, England

First published in the United States of America by Viking Penguin,
a member of Penguin Group (USA) Inc. 2010
Published in Penguin Books 2011

1 3 5 7 9 10 8 6 4 2

Publisher's Note
This is a work of fiction. Names, characters, places, and incidents either are the product
of the author's imagination or are used fictitiously, and any resemblance to actual persons,
living or dead, business establishments, events, or locales is entirely coincidental.

THE LIBRARY OF CONGRESS HAS CATALOGED THE HARDCOVER EDITION AS FOLLOWS:
Weisgarber, Ann.
The personal history of Rachel DuPree : a novel / Ann Weisgarber.
p.   cm.
ISBN 978-0-670-02201-4 (hc.)
ISBN 978-0-14-311948-7 (pbk.)
1. African American women—Fiction.   2. Ranchers—South Dakota—Fiction.
3. African American veterans—Fiction.   4. Badlands—South Dakota—Fiction.
5. South Dakota—History—20th century—Fiction.   I. Title.
PS3623.E4537P47   2010
813'.6—dc22   2010004713

Printed in the United States of America
Set in Warnock Pro   Designed by Alissa Amell

For my husband, Robert L. Weisgarber

CONTENTS

1. THE BADLANDS   1

2. LIZ   11

3. MRS. DuPREE   29

4. SERGEANT DuPREE   37

5. ROUNDER   67

6. MRS. FILLS THE PIPE   81

7. ISAAC   105

8. INDIANS   119

9. IDA B. WELLS-BARNETT   133

10. JERSEYBELL   155

11. AL AND MINDY MCKEE   175

12. JOHNNY   191

13. MARY   205

14. THE MANDOLIN PLAYER   229

15. EMMA   237

16. MARY AND JOHN   247

17. PAUL LAURENCE DUNBAR   261

18. WANAGI CANKU   283

19. RACHEL   299

ACKNOWLEDGMENTS   323

We Can; We Will

—Motto of the Ninth Cavalry

Again, I think it would be somewhat different if it weren't for the wind. It blows and blows until it makes me feel lonesome and so far away from . . . Illinois.

—Oscar Micheaux,
South Dakota Homesteader

THE BADLANDS

I still see her, our Liz, sitting on a plank, dangling over that well. She held on to the rope that hung from the pulley, her bare feet pressed together so tight that the points on her ankle bones were nearly white. She was six. She had on her brother's cast-off pants, and earlier, when I'd given them to her, she'd asked if wearing pants made her a boy. I'd told her we'd wait and see, and that had made her giggle.

The plank Liz sat on swayed and twisted in a wind that blew stinging grit. Her bandanna covered her nose and mouth. The rope around her waist was knotted to the one that held the plank. Isaac, my husband, called it a harness. He said it'd keep her from falling off.

"We're right here," I said to her. "Daddy's got you."

She looked at me, her coppery face frozen up with fear. The wind gusted, and Liz flinched, her eyes slits. Isaac and our oldest girl, Mary, stood side by side as they gripped the well handle. They dug in their legs and pushed the handle up.

The rope jerked. Liz dropped a handful of inches. She sucked in some air and then let out a sharp, piercing cry.

My knees buckled, but I steadied myself against the well.

"You're our brave girl," I called as she sank into it, her eyes closed.

The sunlight caught the top of her head. Her brown braids tied up with scrap rags went rusty red. Her shoulders shook. She made a gurgling sound and then she was gone.

I wasn't one for calling on Jesus and asking for favors. But that day I did. *Merciful Jesus. Sweet merciful Jesus. Be in this well with my child.*

Isaac and Mary held on to the well handle, turning it, keeping it steady as their neck and arm muscles bunched and shook. John, our ten-year-old son, did what I couldn't bring myself to do. He leaned over the top of the well and watched Liz. Above him, hanging on a second pulley—a makeshift one that Isaac had put up that morning—was a bucket. Four others were on the ground by the base of the well.

I coughed and spit out some dust. I tightened the knot in the back of my hair kerchief and then pulled my bandanna back up to cover my mouth and nose. I'd pushed it down earlier; I wanted Liz to have a good look at my face. I didn't want her thinking her mama was hiding behind a ragged piece of cloth.

Hold her hand, sweet Jesus. Hold her tight.

Yesterday the water pump by the house blew nothing but air. Later, Isaac tried the well at the barn. The bucket came up empty, but the bottom was wet. When I saw Isaac knotting a plank to the well rope, my blood ran cold.

"Not that," I told him. "Not that."

"Have to," he said.

"But the White River's still running. Can't you—"

"It's down to a trickle."

I looked at him.

"Liz," he said as if I had asked.

"Lord."

"She'll be all right."

"You could drop her."

"I won't."

"Don't do this thing."

Muscles pulled around his mouth. "I have to."

"No," I said, "no," but there was nothing behind my words and Isaac knew it.

"At ease," he said to Mary now, their hands still gripping the well handle. The rope was played out; Liz was at the bottom. Mary let go of the handle and shook out her hands and shoulders. She ran her palms down the sides of her skirt. She was almost thirteen and tall for her age. She took after Isaac that way, but like me, she was dark. When Isaac had told her that he couldn't turn the handle without her, her back straightened and her chin went high. Isaac could do that to a person. He could give a person the worst chore and make that person feel honored to be chosen. I'd had fourteen years to try to understand this about Isaac, about how he made this happen. This was what I'd come up with. It was because his eyes admired you for bearing up, and when he looked at you that way, there was nothing finer. And there was this, too, about Isaac. He didn't shy away from any chore. He knew what had to be done, and he did it.

Being Isaac's wife, I knew this better than anybody.

"Send the bucket," Isaac told John. "Slow. Call down, tell her it's coming."

John did and then, his cracked lips tight, began turning the makeshift handle. The wind tossed the bucket, sending it in circles. The metal cup inside the bucket clinked from side to side.

In the well, the rope holding Liz hung taut, turning some. Isaac, though I guessed that he didn't need to, kept his hands on the handle. Off in the north pasturelands a dust devil whirled and skipped, picking up stray clumps of tumbleweed. Cows, knotted up by the barbwire fence, flattened their ears as the funnel blew past them. I watched all this but it was our Liz I saw in the darkness, ladling water into the bucket cup by cup.

The Lord is my shepherd; I shall not want.

But I did. It was my greed, my pride, my love of my wood house that drove us to do this. And land, that was part of this too. Land was everything to Isaac. Isaac. I was willing to do anything he wanted. Anything.

He maketh me to lie down in green pastures.

The dust devil buckled like a bedsheet on a clothesline, gathered itself, and made for the house. It blew up onto the roofless front porch and then petered out, tumbleweeds sticking to the windows and the door.

He leadeth me beside the still waters. He restoreth my soul.

Tears burned the backs of my eyes. The South Dakota Badlands wore everything down, even children. But I had my wood house. Just two years old and already it was scraped raw. Sprouts of prairie grass grew on the roof where the tin plates shifted and dirt had blown in. Dust sifted through the edges of the glass windows and the door, and no matter how many times in a day I swept, I couldn't keep the grit out. Now there was this tumbleweed mashed up against our house, making it look shabby, like nobody lived there.

He leadeth me in the paths of righteousness for His name's sake.

Sweat ran from Isaac's hair even though his hands were loose on the well handle. Dripping circles darkened the front of his shirt. It was so hot I was sure I felt the hard earth cracking under my feet. My mouth was swelled up as if I'd been eating grit. The cottonwood tree over by the dried-out wash swayed, most of its leaves already gone. My hand went to the back of my neck, knowing the ache that must be pinching Liz's arms and shoulders as she scooped water.

Lord Jesus, have mercy. Lord Jesus, have pity.

A low-slung cloud, flat on the bottom and puffed at the top, slid under the sun. Its shadow spread out on the ground, darkening the house, the barn, and the well. The coolness brought by the shadow set my heart pounding even faster. It'd been over two months since it'd rained; we were long past due. I waited, hoping, knowing I was foolish to expect anything from this cloud. It passed on, opening up again the hard-edged glare of the sun.

"Dad-dy," a faint voice called.

"Pull it up," Isaac said to John. "Help him, Mary. Keep it steady."

When the bucket was up, I willed the shaking out of my hands. I undid the knot and then tied the rope to the second bucket. John sent it down to his sister.

I let Rounder, our cattle dog, have a gulp before pushing him away. John said, "What about me? Don't I get some?"

"No," Isaac said. "Not yet."

Yea, though I walk through the valley of the shadow of—

I turned away from the well and looked up at our house.

It had been the winter of 1915 when Isaac figured it was time to build us a wood house. For twelve years I had kept house, and before it was all over, I had birthed seven children—Isaac Two and Baby Henry were laid out in the cemetery—in a four-room dugout. Its walls were nothing but squares of sod. The ceilings sagged. The floors were dirt. Summers, grass grew on the inside walls and I'd take a match and burn the shoots to keep the prairie from staking a claim on the inside of our home.

Most folks in the Badlands that stayed longer than three years built themselves wood houses. These houses weren't grand, far from it. Most of the houses were low to the ground and not all that much bigger than a dugout. But Isaac held off for twelve years, not wanting to spend money on lumber. I imagined that gave folks around here something to talk about. But likely they talked anyway. We were the only Negroes in these parts.

I will fear no evil for thou art with me.

The second bucket came up out of the well, and John sent the third one down. That morning he had begged to go down in the well. He was the boy, he'd said to Isaac. No, Isaac said. You're too big, son. I can't hold you. And the rope might break.

Mary came over and stood beside me. She took my hand.

Thy rod and thy staff they comfort me.

It had taken me and Isaac all spring, summer, fall, and part of the winter to build our wood house. We did it between tending to the wheat crop and the garden and seeing to the cattle. When time allowed, Al McKee and Ned Walker, neighbor men, came by to help. That July, Emma was born. It was an easy birth, not like some of the others. Four days later I was back helping Isaac. I held the lumber steady as he sawed and hammered our house into place. Mary and John handed nails and held tools for us. We tied Liz and Alise to the cottonwood so they wouldn't wander off and get hurt somehow. When baby Emma fussed long and hard, I sat under the cottonwood and gave her my breast. Sitting in the shade with my children, I watched Isaac and the other men, if they were there. It made me lift my chin. Our house was rising up at a place where once there had only been a rolling stretch of prairie grasses.

The fourth bucket came up and the fifth one went down. Dusty wind flapped our shirts, skirts, and pants, making hollow flat sounds. I pressed my bandanna close to my mouth. Grit vexed my eyes, but I wanted it to. I deserved far worse for doing this to Liz.

"Air," I said to Isaac. "Is there enough down there?"

"She's all right."

It had to stink down there. Anything that deep in the ground always did.

Thou preparest a table before me in the presence of mine enemies.

When we were building our wood house, there was nothing better than the smell of the fresh-cut lumber. Isaac had gone all the way into the Black Hills, figuring lumber prices were better there than in Rapid City. I'd never smelled anything finer than that wood. Growing up in Louisiana, my family lived in the shack where my father had been born a slave. That shack lost its wood smell years back. When we moved to Chicago, there was nothing to smell but the sooty stink of the slaughterhouses. But our Black

Hills wood was filled with a raw crispness that made a person think about the goodness of the earth. I used to put my nose right up to that lumber and fill my lungs with its smell.

Thou anointest my head with oil.

The fifth bucket came up. It wasn't even half full. "No more," I said to Isaac. "Please. No more."

"All right," Isaac said.

Bearing down, him and Mary pushed the handle up, fighting to keep it steady when it turned down. Mary's toes curled and gripped the earth. Isaac's face glistened with sweat.

Sweet Jesus, sweet Jesus, sweet Jesus.

The top of Liz's head showed, then her face—grayer than I had ever seen her—and finally the rest of her. There was a long, jagged rip in her left sleeve, and the hem of her pants dripped water. Her knuckles were scraped raw, and one of her toes was bleeding. Her eyes were squinted shut against the sun, but that didn't stop the tears.

"Mama," she said, the plank turning in the wind.

John and I reached out, caught the plank, and pulled Liz to us.

My cup runneth over.

I worked at the harness's knot, my fingers all thumbs. When at last it came loose, me and John got her off the plank and onto the ground. Isaac and Mary let go of the handle, and it spun wildly as the plank dropped to the bottom, making a cracking splash.

Liz pressed her face into my swelled-up belly and cried. I let her. I wondered if she was thinking how she'd done this thing for us—for Mary, for John, and for her two little sisters latched in their bedroom. I wondered if she knew there was a baby inside of me needing that water too. I wondered if she'd ever forgive us. I believed that she wouldn't.

Isaac and Mary slumped on the ground, their backs against the well, their legs out before them. Isaac glanced up at me, then looked away.

"What?" I said.

He didn't say anything. But I knew. He would do this again to Liz. We all would. Every day until the drought broke. Or until there was no water left to scoop.

I closed my eyes for a moment, wanting to put a stop to this, wanting to say, "Isaac. We've got to think of something better." But I had to save it for later. It wasn't our way to talk over worries when the children were listening.

I pulled out my handkerchief that I kept tucked in my dress sleeve. Liz blew her nose. When she was done, Isaac got to his feet and put out his arms to her. She ran to him, and he held her high.

"You're a DuPree, Liz," he said. "Through and through. You too, John and Mary."

Liz's arms were tight around Isaac's neck, her face pressed into his shoulder.

"She's bleeding," I said. Isaac put his hand around her toes, the blood smearing on his fingers. Then he put her down.

"Let's get you fixed up," I said to Liz. "Get you out of those wet things." I looked at Isaac. "How much is for us?" I said.

"Two buckets."

The rest was for the four horses, the milk cow, and the one hen still living. I said, "Mary, you bring up one. John, get the other." And then, I'm sorry to say, my voice turned hard. "And don't you spill a drop, you hear me, young man?"

"Yes, ma'am." John licked his lips and looked at the buckets, the question showing on his face.

I glanced at Isaac. He shook his head but said, "One finger. Stick one finger in and lick it. That'll hold you till supper." Mary, John, and Liz each put a finger in one of the buckets and then, their cheeks pulling, they sucked their fingers dry.

"All right now," I said. "There's dinner to get on." What there was of it, I thought. I took Liz's hand; she gripped it tight. I looked at Isaac, but he was heading off to the corral carrying two of the buckets. There the horses stood near the railing, their nostrils quivering like they knew water was coming.

"Come on," I said to the children, and we began the climb up the rise to our wood house, Mary and John with the buckets, Liz holding on to me while Isaac went the other way.

2

LIZ

It was later that day when Isaac came into the kitchen; he'd been out in the east pasture. His shirt, wet with sweat, stuck to his back. The heat had worked on my nerves, making my skin prickle and my feet swell up. I was peevish with the children. They kept asking for water and for something to eat. I told them to sit down, quit all that whining, supper was coming in due time. Then I swatted Emma's bottom. She was two, and I was in no mood for her fussiness.

Putting Liz in the well was wrong. I should have stopped Isaac from doing it, I should have stood up to him. But I hadn't, and that shamed me. The only time I'd ever stood up to him was before we were married. Now, when I believed he was wrong, when Liz needed me to stand my ground, I had forgotten how.

Isaac came into the kitchen and hung his wide-brimmed hat on a peg. My shame kept me from looking at him. "Six more dead," he told me, his voice low. I gave him a rag to wipe the white dust from his face and hands. The children were just a step away, lined up on the benches along the table, napkins tucked into their collars. I had scared them into being quiet. They were peeking at me and Isaac, listening. "Pneumonia," Isaac said.

I'd lost track of how many cows that made altogether. "Sixty-seven," he said, like he had read my mind.

The first time we lost a cow to a sickness, I figured we'd butcher it and make steaks. It'd see us through for a good long time. But Isaac wouldn't do it; he'd heard of people dying that way. He didn't trust the meat, and I always went along with him. Today, I wasn't so sure. Today, I would have been willing to chance it. The thought of steaks made my mouth water.

Steaks were for city folks, though, not for us. In the Badlands, a rancher what butchered a healthy cow for his own family was thought a foolish man. It didn't matter if his children were hungry. Cows were that man's livelihood, and to eat one was the same as eating dollar bills by the handful.

Breathing deep, Isaac looked into the iron pot simmering on the cookstove. There wasn't much to look at, just stringy meat from the scrawny red and brown hen the children had called Miss Bossy up until then. That and a few brown-edged shreds of cabbage.

Isaac wiped his forehead with the rag, then looked into the pitcher. "Jerseybell's not giving much milk."

I stirred the stew, scraping the bottom of the pot where it was sticking some. "I know it," I said.

"Still have a fair amount of tobacco saved," he said. "Al McKee might be willing to swap for a can of milk." Still stirring, I nodded to show I was listening. There was only one short row of tin cans on the cupboard shelf that hung off to the side of the cookstove. Isaac picked up one of the tins—pears, I thought it was. He ran his finger around the rim as he looked at the shelf. I hoped Isaac was seeing how bad things were in the kitchen. I hoped he was working out a plan that was bigger than a can of milk. He put the tin back. "All right," he said. "I'll go to town, see about getting in supplies."

I'd been waiting to hear those words for a week. I said, "I'll get a list together."

"I'm not going to Interior," Isaac said. "Last time Johnston's prices were sky high. Hard times is no excuse to gouge honest people. I'd rather go to Scenic. Prices can't be any worse there."

That meant he'd be gone overnight, but I'd get by. The baby was probably two weeks off, give or take a day or so. But even if the baby was just a few days away, I wouldn't have stopped him, not with supplies running out and five children to feed. I tied rags on the pot's handles and said, "You'll go tomorrow?"

"First thing."

"I'll cut your hair after supper then." I tried not to think about all the money it would take to buy supplies. I carried the pot of stew to the head of the table where the children were quiet, still smarting, I figured, from my sharp tongue.

"Now come on and eat," I said to Isaac.

He gave his neck one more wipe with the rag as he looked at the children. Then all at once, he pulled in a deep breath, put his shoulders back and his head up. He clicked his heels together and snapped a salute to me.

"Troops, supper's being served. Bow your heads."

They all giggled. Except for Liz.

It was still full light when supper was over, but most always you could count on the day's work easing up after the dishes were washed and put up on the cupboard shelf. Out on the porch, Alise and Emma played on the floor with their rag dolls. Liz was there too, but she wasn't playing. She just sat, her head down, her knees drawn up under her chin. Nearby, Isaac was on the kitchen stool he had carried out. I put a cloth around his broad shoulders and began combing his hair, working out the grit and knots. Usually, I took pleasure in cutting his hair; it wasn't anything like mine. His was wavy and brown, and only his sideburns showed white. Mine was just the other way: springy, tight, and black with gray showing up in too many places. But tonight I couldn't stop looking over at Liz. It was wrong what we'd done.

Isaac said, "Up there on the barn roof, over on the east corner. Looks like a few shingles are working loose. The wind catches them wrong and they'll be gone. I'll fix them as soon as I get back."

"Always something," I said, working the scissors around one of his ears, but in my mind I was seeing Liz tied to the plank, the wind blowing her over the open well. We needed the water, but that didn't make it right. Still, we did it and there was no going back.

"Rachel," Isaac said. "You all right?"

Put your mind to your work, I told myself. "Yes," I said. "It's the light—it's hard to see."

I worked at the back of his neck. Mary took the girls—Liz, Alise, and Emma—to the outhouse, and when they got back, Mary went off to the barn to tend to the milk cow. Caring for Jerseybell was her favorite chore. Mary had been two when Isaac got Jerseybell. She liked the cow right off, and when she got bigger, Isaac told her the cow was hers to care for. Mary took that to heart. She was the one what did the milking and she was the one what fed and watered Jerseybell. When Jerseybell's stall needed cleaning, Mary did that too.

I blew the cut hair off of Isaac's neck and shook out the cloth I'd put around his shoulders. I gathered up the comb and scissors and took the girls inside. Liz and four-year-old Alise unhooked each other's dresses, stepped out of them, and hung them up on the wall pegs. I undressed Emma, but I couldn't keep from watching Liz. Her eyes were too wide, giving her a startled look. She was afraid to close them, I realized all at once. The well had made her scared of the dark.

I stood the girls in a row and dusted the grit from their hands and faces with a dry rag. They sat on the edge of their low bed and stuck out their legs so I could get to the bottoms of their calloused feet. That done, they stood and put their arms straight up. I pulled their white nightdresses down over their heads; they wrestled their arms through the openings.

In bed, the three little girls laid flat on their backs, Emma in the middle. Liz and Alise each had a leg over her to keep her in place. It was hot, but that was how they did, summer and winter. Most usually it made me smile, but that night I didn't have a smile in me. Liz's eyes were flat like she couldn't see.

"Mama?" Alise said.

"What?"

"Our story."

"Oh," I said. It had slipped my mind. I could hardly think straight for worrying about Liz.

I lit a kerosene lamp and got the book of fairy tales from the parlor. I admired the feel of a book. The cover on this one was worn; Isaac's mother sent it when our first son, Isaac Two, was born. That was eleven years this past February. I opened the book and held it to each girl's nose. I always believed that smelling the pages of a book took a person into the story.

"Go on. Say it," I said, figuring this would do Liz some good.

Alise and Emma wiggled a little, grinning with excitement. "Fee, fie, foe, fum, I smell the blood of an Englishman," Alise sang with Emma a word or two behind her. Liz didn't, though. She kept her mouth pressed.

Alise turned her head on the pillow. "What's the matter, Liz?"

Liz stuck out her bottom lip.

I shuffled through the book, page after page of make-believe about kings wanting sons, poor men seeking gold, and beautiful young women waiting to be rescued by princes.

"Honey," I said, looking at Liz, "you got a story you'd like to hear?"

She shook her head but said, "Rapunzel."

I found the story and held the book as close to the lamp as I could. My reading eyes were fading on me. Isaac used a magnifying glass to read by, but I couldn't bring myself to use it. I already felt like an old woman. I'd rather guess at the words. I knew the stories well enough to do that.

Squinting some, I read. The girls listened as if the story might be different this time or as if they had never heard of Rapunzel, the girl with the long fine hair like spun gold who lived locked in a tower pining for her handsome prince.

"Prayers," I said when the story ended, and together we thanked Jesus for looking after us and keeping us safe. "Sleep tight," I told them and kissed each one on the cheek. I picked up the lamp.

"Mama?" Liz said.

I turned back.

"Mama, there was a snake. In the well."

Alise and Emma looked at Liz, then looked at me. I put the lamp on the dresser and felt Liz's forehead. I said to her, "You aren't scared of snakes, are you? You've never been before."

Liz gripped my hand. "It was in the well and it came at me."

"Did it hurt you, honey?"

"It tried to. I kicked it and it hissed me."

Alise and Emma sucked in their cheeks.

I said, "But you got it?"

Liz shook her head. "It went behind a rock but I saw its eyes. They were red. It's waiting to get me, Mama."

Emma's face screwed up. I put my fingertips on her lips and patted them, hoping to keep her from crying. "A red-eyed snake, why, that's the best kind," I said. "That's a good snake, just surprised to see you, Liz, that's all. Not used to seeing a child in the well. Probably just curious."

Liz puckered her forehead. She wanted to believe me, I thought, but was finding it hard to do.

"A friendly snake?" Alise said.

"Like a bull snake," I said. "Now go on to sleep."

I pried Liz's hand from mine and kissed the back of it. I wanted to take away her fear. I did. But that wasn't how it worked.

She had to carry it all by herself. Like we all had to. But looking at her in her bed, I knew I had to stop that fear from getting bigger.

I said, "Think about Rapunzel with all that yellow hair."

Liz nodded.

"I'll leave the lamp."

Isaac was outside on the porch in his rocking chair. His pencil was behind his ear and his accounts book was on the plank floor by his left-hand side. Like always in the evening, he'd been recording the day. It was his way to keep a constant tally on the cattle, the weather, and any money spent and any money earned. I wondered if he had made mention of Liz in the well. I wondered if he recorded that I didn't like it, and that it took Mary to help him. I figured I'd never know. The book was Isaac's. It wasn't mine to read.

The wind had settled into a breeze, and we didn't need our bandannas. I sat down beside him in the other rocker and put my mending basket on the floor. Isaac put his head back to study the sky. When we built the house, I had hoped for a porch with a roof, but we ran out of wood. "Next year," Isaac had said at the time. Over my knees, I flattened the shirt that Liz had worn and studied the rip, wanting to set it right.

Liz was a lot like Isaac. She could take on a shine like something funny had just crossed her mind, and like Isaac, she could take the most everyday thing and turn it into a story worth hearing. But she didn't look the least bit like him even though she was almost as light as him. Like me, she was little-boned and short.

Squinting, I jabbed the thread at the needle's eye a few times.

Isaac said, "Look there." He pointed northward across a stretch of prairie land that swelled up into small hills and dipped into easy valleys. Just past was a craggy string of sandstone buttes. Their stony points were stark against the softening sky. I knotted the thread and poked the needle back into the pincushion. The biggest butte, the one close to the middle of the range, was called Grindstone Butte. The western sun had caught it just right—it shimmered like a storybook castle of gold with handfuls of diamonds tossed here and there.

"Still something, isn't it?" Isaac said.

I pushed together the sides of the tear in the shirt and pinned it with my straight pins. The baby gave a little kick; I shifted some in my chair. I said, "What we did today was bad."

"I didn't take any pleasure in it either."

"Liz is scared."

"She's all right."

"She's gone all quiet. Her eyes have a bad look."

"She'll be all right."

"We can't do it to her again. We can't."

"Damn it. What do you want me to do?"

"I—"

"Snap my fingers? Do some kind of rain dance? Is that what you have in mind?"

I winced. "No."

"Lose the horses? Jerseybell? Let the children go without?"

My resolve crumbled.

"What then?"

"I don't know." I stared off at the Grindstone without really seeing it. Years back I had learned this. Isaac was smart; he knew what to do. Then there was this. A man and his wife fell apart when they fought. Even when they didn't see eye to eye, they had to put their shoulders together and push in the same direction. Folks who didn't, didn't stand a chance. Not in the Badlands.

"I'm sorry," I said. "You're doing what you have to, I know that. Just wish there was another way."

He didn't say anything. He sat in his rocker, stiff and unmoving as he stared off to where the sun was meeting up with the horizon. Grindstone and the other buttes were orange by then, and their long shadows darkened the pastureland. The dried stalks of prairie grasses swished in the breeze. Far off, cattle bellowed their hunger and thirst. It was a sound I had come to hate. It was the kind of sound that made my chest tighten. It was the kind of sound that made me want to put my hands over my ears.

Isaac stood up, put two fingers in his mouth, and whistled.

"Coming," John called back. His voice was far away—he must be behind the barn. Then Mary called back too, sounding just as far off. I wanted Isaac to say something to me. I wanted him to say he forgave me for questioning his judgment. But he didn't say it. He just stared off, watching Mary and John climb the rise, Rounder lagging behind as he nosed through the grass.

Mary and John were halfway up the rise by then, the dried-out grasses crackling under their feet. Strangers might say that Mary and John didn't look to be related—the girl so dark and the boy a mild shade of brown. But the dimples on their left cheeks were the same; all our children carried that gift. It came from me.

"Nothing," John said when he got closer. Like every night, he'd been checking his rabbit traps.

"Maybe tomorrow," Isaac said.

"Daddy," Mary said, "Jerseybell's puny. She's got the runs."

"I know it."

Mary and John stepped back, the sudden sharpness in Isaac's voice surprising them. "Now go on to bed," he said to them, "and stop worrying me about that cow."

"Five pages, Mary," I said to ease the hurt showing in their eyes. "No more. And just two sips of water. Sips. Understand, both of you?"

"Yes, ma'am."

After they went inside, Isaac leaned forward in his rocker, his arms on his legs. He crossed his wrists and let his hands dangle over the sides of his knees. There was a small tear in the knee of his left pant leg. That was one more thing that needed fixing. I'd do it after Isaac went to bed. I folded my mending and closed my sewing basket. I wished he'd say something—anything. From the corner of my eye, I saw him studying the country spread out all around us. He looked tired, the lines around his eyes deep. A wash of tenderness came over me. It was hard on a man when his family had to go without. I wished I could reach out and smooth his worries away.

Until this summer, we had had good luck. Our wheat was suited to the Badlands, and we didn't have much trouble with grasshoppers. Isaac had an eye for buying cattle that bred easily and stood the winters. Our first spring here, he bought a threshing machine from a homesteader what was selling out. Isaac rented it to other ranchers, and in two years, it paid for itself. As for me, I knew a little something about gardening. On Saturdays, before we had so many children, we got up in the dark and took our produce, eggs too, into Interior and sold them to homesteaders on their way west to Wyoming. There were times we were so worn out we were asleep before dark. But we had twenty-five hundred acres to show for all the work.

"There's all kinds of ways to earn respect," Isaac was given to saying. "Owning land's one of them. A man can't ever have too much. Especially if that man's black."

Maybe that was true. I wasn't always so sure, although for the most part, folks around here treated us fair. But there was no denying that Isaac was proud of the Circle D. That was what he'd named the ranch after he staked our claims. I was proud too. The first time, though, when I saw where our homestead was, it scared me.

"Where's everybody?" I asked Isaac that day fourteen years ago when he stopped the wagon in the middle of nothing, jumped down, and said we were home.

He turned in a big circle, taking it all in. "The Walkers are that way," he said, pointing east. "And Carl Janik is just beyond those buttes."

I stared until my eyes blurred. There wasn't the first house, barn, or person. There were only knee-high prairie grasses, buttes too steep to climb, and canyons that split open the earth.

It was so big. All that land and sky, all that openness; there was no end to any of it. It made me feel small. It gave me a bad feeling. I didn't belong; this place called for bigger things than me. If for one second I lost sight of Isaac, I'd be alone and lost in this country that didn't have any edges. I said to him, "Will we be all right here?"

"I told you this wasn't anything like Chicago."

"I know you did, but this . . ." I couldn't find the right words to say what I meant.

"Don't worry about it. The Indians were put down years back," and that gave me something new to be scared about. The first year I kept a close watch, always expecting half-naked men to rise out of the grasses, streaks of red paint on their faces, scalping knives in hand. I had heard about Indians when I was growing up, and I had paid close attention when Isaac talked about his army days at Fort Robinson, Nebraska. But I never told Isaac I was scared. I even kept still when I saw my first Indians—a flinty-eyed, sneaky squaw with her little boy. I'd never wanted to give Isaac any reason to question my grit. I didn't want him sending me back to Chicago.

Years later, the Badlands was still big. Big in its dryness. Big in its need to turn everything to dust.

Through the open door I heard Mary reading *Swiss Family Robinson* to John. It was his favorite book; Isaac's mother had sent it when he was born. It occurred to me that we weren't so different from those people shipwrecked on an island. Like them, there was nobody but us to pull us through. It called for hard work and determination. But money would be a help. Things would be easier if all our money hadn't gone for Ned Walker's land. Isaac had bought it this past spring when the drought was just a small worry. It was an opportunity, he had told me then. Just like it had been when he bought the Peterson ranch seven years ago and then Carl Janik's land a few years later.

Off in the distance, the buttes turned dusky, their edges fading in the twilight. I wanted to make things right with Isaac; I wanted to get rid of the uneasy silence that sat between us. "Tomorrow," I said, "I appreciate you going to town. I know you wanted to move the cattle."

He leaned back in his rocker. "I'll move them as soon as I get back. John and Mary'll help."

I eased back too. The sharpness was gone from Isaac's voice. He was like that. His words could cut the meat off of a person's bones, but just as quick, he could forgive and forget.

Above us, the darkening sky was wide and open, stretching farther than a person could see. There was a half-moon; it was low. Below it and a little off to the side, a star bigger than all the others shined bright.

"Wouldn't surprise me," Isaac said, "if the train's bringing water in for folks. I've heard that they did that before, a few years before we got here."

I waited, my hands on top of my swelled-up belly.

"While I'm in town I'll ask around, see if there's any."

Relieved, I blew out some air.

"Still have to water the horses in the morning. Can't risk losing them."

I tensed.

"I'll be gone more than a day. The children have to have water. You do too."

Liz, I thought.

Isaac laid his hand on the arm of my rocker. "I'll get us through this, Rachel. I always have."

"I know that." I sank back into my rocker. I had let Liz down.

I couldn't sleep that night from the worry of it all. I dreaded morning when we'd put Liz back in the well. In the dark, I laid on my side in our narrow, low-slung bed, Isaac's back pressed up against mine. His breath came out in short puffs as he slept. I imagined Liz's eyes staring at me. My mind skipped from that to worrying about money, about how we didn't have any. I worried about all the cattle that were dying, and I worried about the price worn-out cattle would get at market next month. I worried about the coming winter, and I worried about the baby what was just a few weeks off. Then I got to worrying about water, and that turned my mouth even drier. I thought about having a long drink of cool water, and that set the baby off, pushing on me. I got up and went outside.

I liked to think my feet had eyes—they were that good about getting me around in the star-bright darkness. They carried me over the rocky ground and around the empty prairie-dog holes that were deep enough to snap an ankle if you stepped just a little bit wrong.

I went in the outhouse. There, I did what I'd been doing for the past two weeks. I unbuttoned the top half of my nightdress. I put my hands to my bosom and like before, a chill caught ahold of me. There wasn't enough swelling; I was going to have trouble feeding this baby.

I stroked my belly for a moment, then fixed my nightdress.

I left the outhouse and for some reason I couldn't explain, I turned the other way and went down the rise to the well by the barn. From the way the moonlight hit it, the well looked to be shining. The wood-slatted cover was over the opening. The plank, tied to the pulley rope, swung back and forth in the breeze. I put my hand to it to stop it.

Folks in Chicago had running water in their houses.

And just like that, I was homesick. That quick, my chest started aching. I missed how me and Mama and Sue, my sister, used to sew together on Sunday afternoons, talking over the past week. I missed Johnny, my brother, and how we used to do our lessons together at the kitchen table. I missed how Dad came for me at the boardinghouse where I worked and how he walked me home at the end of each day.

I put my hand back up on the plank hanging over the well. In Chicago, open crates showing off crisp, shiny apples filled market windows. I gave the plank a hard push. In Chicago, men delivered bottles of milk to people's back stoops. I caught the twirling plank. In Chicago, I had a job; I had a little money in my purse. In Chicago, Isaac's mother had money. Has money. My hand tightened its hold on the plank. My pulse hurried.

I pictured Mrs. DuPree, squatty shaped and her mouth always turned down. She owned three boardinghouses. I pictured the boarders and all the money they handed her week after week. Me and Isaac wouldn't ask for much, just a little. It'd be for the children—Mrs. DuPree's only grandchildren. We'd pay her back. It'd been years. Maybe she was a changed woman, maybe she had softened some. Maybe she had forgiven us.

I gave a short laugh. Isaac would never ask his mother for money. He'd eat dirt before he'd stoop to begging.

I gripped the plank and gave it a hard push. This time it went spinning so high that it whacked the pulley. It was a gratifying noise. It was so gratifying that I did it again.

3

MRS. DuPREE

Isaac's mother, Mrs. Elizabeth DuPree, owner of the DuPree Boardinghouse for Negro Men in Chicago, had standards. She took only the men what worked the day shift at the slaughterhouses. She said they were a better class than the ones what worked nights. No drinking, no swearing, no women visitors in the rooms—those were a few of Mrs. DuPree's rules.

"My responsibility is to do my part in advancing the respectability of hardworking Negroes," she told the men when she collected the rent every Saturday. "We've got to be as good, even a little better, than white folks if we're ever going to get ahead."

That was how Mrs. DuPree talked.

The men listened to her, showing their respect by nodding when Mrs. DuPree fixed them with a sharp look. What they said, though, when she wasn't around, was that they stayed on, paid the extra dollar on the week, and put up with her fancy standards all because of the fine meals I cooked. Not that Mrs. DuPree would admit to that. She was forever pointing out that her boardinghouse was the cleanest in the city. Her house was quality; it was on the far edge of the stockyard district. Quality and cleanliness— that was why her rooms were full. No one said different. The bedclothes were changed every other Monday, and the outhouse shined like a new Indian-head penny. But it was the food the men admired out loud.

Six days a week for nearly eight years, I cooked at Mrs. DuPree's. Every morning, long before dawn, I let myself in the back door, put on a fresh apron, and fired up the coal cookstove. I was at home in that kitchen with its canisters of flour and sugar on the shelf, the coffee grinder bolted to the edge of the wooden counter, and the icebox by the cellar door. In that kitchen that wasn't really mine at all, I baked rows and rows of buttery biscuits. My bacon was crisp, and I fried the eggs until the edges curled up and browned just a tad. That was how the men liked them. I perked the coffee deep and strong. After breakfast, I sent the men off to the slaughterhouses with ham sandwiches wrapped in waxed paper. When the dishes were washed, I baked my pies, sometimes butterscotch cream, other times apple or cherry, depending on the season. On Saturdays the men counted on me to make a cake, maybe gingerbread or chocolate or sometimes a white cake.

"What's for dinner, Miss Reeves?" the men asked me most every morning. "Fried chicken or maybe pork? Roast beef?"

"That sounds good," I liked to say, teasing. I wasn't going to tell them, and they knew it. Those men hated their work at the slaughterhouses. They deserved one good surprise in a day's time.

Early evenings, the men showed up in the alley behind the boardinghouse, their shoulders bent and their heads down. They had washed at the slaughterhouses and left their overalls and boots stiff with blood there. But being of a particular nature, Mrs. DuPree made them wash with soap at the backyard pump before coming inside. I watched them from the kitchen window. In the winter these washings were hurried, the men shaking in the icy wind. In the summer, though, the men scrubbed their hands, faces, and necks hard, doing their best to rid themselves of the animal grease that worked its way into their skin. But even the best scrubbing couldn't clean spirits worn down by the butchering of screaming animals.

I liked to think my dinners perked up the men some. They sat elbow to elbow on the two benches along the dining table and joshed, bragging about having the dirtiest jobs or about having the meanest bosses. This went on until I served their pie. Those men loved pie, but for some reason it changed their talk. Maybe it was because pie made them think about their people back home. Maybe it took them back to when they were boys and how they watched their mamas roll the crust. I didn't know. But when I served pie, the men's voices got deeper and the joshing quieted down.

One of these days, the men said after licking their forks clean, they'd quit their stinking jobs and go back home, cash in their pockets. Looking back, they said, thinking about it now, they weren't sure why they ever left. If someone had told them what it was like in the slaughterhouses, they would have stayed put.

It was the money that brought them to the city, that's what it was. But who could save money in a place like Chicago where nothing was free? Back home, now that was a different story. Neighbors were friendly, bosses were fair, and the girls were the prettiest in the world. Home, the men said, stretching the word long. Home. Someday, they'd go on back home.

I listened to the men while I scrubbed dried-up, crusty pans in the kitchen. This dining-room talk was nothing new. I had been working for Mrs. DuPree since I was seventeen.

When the coffeepot was empty and their plates scraped clean, most of the men went upstairs. Some of them played cards in their rooms or wrote letters home. Others moseyed into the kitchen. I'd come to expect this from the ones what didn't have wives or sweethearts waiting for them in some far-off place like Louisiana or Alabama.

At first, Mrs. DuPree didn't allow the men in the kitchen, but by the time I was twenty-five, she pretended not to notice. Likely she thought I was an old maid and that the men looked at me as nothing more than an older sister. But maybe there was a spot of kindness buried somewhere in her heart. She had a son of her own far away from home. Maybe she understood that a man needed to lean against a kitchen wall. Watching a woman tidy up was good for easing homesickness.

But not all of the men saw me as a sister. Some of them tried to court me.

One particular evening it was Thomas Lee Patterson who spoke up. Four other men ringed the kitchen. "Miss Reeves," he said. "That strawberry pie was right tasty."

"Crust didn't do like it should," I said, drying the last pan.

"Puts my grandma's to shame, it was that good."

"Better not let her hear that."

He grinned, straightened up, and looked at the other men. I felt their eyes telling him to go on, give it a try. I shook my head a little to warn him off. Thomas Lee didn't seem to see. Instead, he took a steadying breath. "What say, Miss Reeves? How about me walking you on home tonight?"

The air tensed.

"Oh my," I said. I tilted my head, acting like I was considering the offer. But I wasn't. Thomas Lee was as good as the next slaughterhouse man, but that was what he was: a slaughterhouse man. I had lived in the district since I was eleven and knew all there was to know about such men. Dad was one until he slipped and fell in a mess of hog guts and blood, knocking himself senseless for a night and a day. When he came to, his face drooped, his left hand dangled by his side, and one of his legs didn't do like it should. He never was able to work again.

There was something about slaughterhouse work that soured a man; even my mother said so. He could start off all right, but if he stayed more than a year, the work laid him low. Killing animals for a living broke a man's dreams, turned him bitter and mean. Or turned him to drink. That wasn't the kind of man I wanted. I wanted a man what aimed to better himself, what wasn't afraid to look inside a book, and was willing to save his money for something grander than a pint of beer.

Thomas Lee Patterson was a handsome man. But he'd been in the slaughterhouse for nearly three years. He'd never get out.

"Much obliged," I said to him, "but you know my father. Most likely he's out there now, on the stoop, waiting for me." That was because, I could have added, Dad didn't want anybody courting me, he didn't want me getting married. Him and Mama counted on my wages.

"Yes, ma'am, I do. Men back home, that's how they do for

their daughters. It's just that your daddy, he drags that leg of his so bad, thought maybe it'd go easier for him if somebody else was seeing to you."

"Where you from, Mr. Patterson?"

"Huntsville, Alabama."

"Well then. You're a Southern gentleman just like Dad." I took off my apron and put it in a laundry basket for Trudy, the housemaid, to launder. "Now out of my kitchen," I said, flapping my hands. "All of you. Out."

"But—," Thomas Lee said.

"Out," I said as if I didn't know his meaning. One of the other men laughed. I shot him a hard look, shushing him. Thomas Lee's head drooped. I stepped close to him, wanting to make him feel better. "It's my father. He's old-fashioned," I whispered, shrugging my shoulders as if to say that otherwise it'd be different. He drew in some air and gave me a quick glance as he left. He didn't believe me but pride kept him from pressing. Pride, I also knew, would keep Thomas Lee out of the kitchen from then on. He'd have to find something else to do to fill the lonesome evening hours, and that made me feel bad. But not bad enough to change my mind.

Alone in the kitchen, I hung up the last frying pan and put the footstool back in the corner. I set the dining table for the morning, and then, after giving the kitchen one last look to make sure everything was in its place, I turned off the electric lights.

Outside in the crisp April evening, Dad leaned hard on his cane and heaved himself up off the top step of the back stoop. He tossed his glowing cigarette butt at a rat. He missed.

"Ready?" he said. Then, seeing the cloth sack in my hand, Dad pointed. "Something I like? Fried pork, maybe?"

———

One afternoon not long after, I was stoking up the cookstove fire, getting it hot enough to bake my bread, when Mrs. DuPree swooped into the kitchen, her round body making the room feel too tight for the both of us. It wasn't like her to bother with me in the middle of the day. Afternoons were when Mrs. DuPree liked to go over her accounts and order supplies for the house. Either that or call on friends, sit in their parlors, sip tea from fine bone china, and exchange ideas about how best to advance the Negro race.

"Rachel," Mrs. DuPree said that day, "I want you to help Trudy with the cleaning. You'll have to stay late a few evenings."

"Oh," I said, surprised. We'd just done spring cleaning last month.

"My son's coming home. He'll be on leave, expects to be here for several weeks."

My heart fluttered.

Mrs. DuPree waved an opened envelope. She put on her eyeglasses, pulled out the letter, and read it to herself, her lips putting shape to each word. "He's to arrive next Wednesday. That's if the trains run on time." She peered out the kitchen window. Elevated railroad tracks crisscrossed every which way two blocks over. "Still surprises me to think they have trains out there in Nebraska."

"Nebraska," I said, but I wasn't thinking about that. I was thinking about Isaac DuPree. I had met him once before when Mrs. DuPree took sick with pneumonia and the doctor declared her on death's doorstep. Isaac rushed home; he was just back from winning the war in Cuba. That had been five years ago. I had given up on ever seeing him again.

Mrs. DuPree pushed her eyeglasses back up and studied the letter like the words might say something new. She was a hard one to know, I thought. Most widows would be smiling with joy to see their only child. But that wasn't Mrs. DuPree's way, at least not in front of the help. But all the same, Mrs. DuPree was excited. Her heartbeat showed in her neck. I hoped my own heartbeat wasn't so easy to read.

"I want this house shining," Mrs. DuPree said, "every pot, every pan, every inch of it shining. Even behind the cookstove. He's been out in the wilderness so long I'm afraid he's forgotten how civilized people live."

"Oh yes, ma'am."

"And I want the food to be good. I'll make up a list of his favorites."

I smiled. "I'll do my best."

"See that you do." She eyed me. My smile was too big to suit her. I made it go away. She said, "Start with the floors—get the marks up. And I want the silver polished and the sideboard waxed." I nodded and she left.

I waited until I couldn't hear her footsteps. Then I drew up my skirt, held it above my ankles, and did a little waltz around the kitchen. *Isaac DuPree*, I sang to myself. *Isaac DuPree was coming home. Coming home.*

4

SERGEANT DuPREE

Isaac DuPree was a man set apart. Maybe it was because of his blue army uniform with the gold buttons on his collar and the broad yellow stripes on his left sleeve. Or maybe it was because he was tall and even fairer than his mother. But I thought it was more than all those things. Isaac carried himself with pride. When he met the boarders, he looked each man in the eye and shook their hands. When he saw me and Trudy, the housemaid, in the kitchen doorway, he gave a little bow like a gentleman would and that made us smile.

Isaac hadn't been home but a handful of hours when he wheedled his mother into letting him eat dinner with the boarders. "I'm used to eating with my men," I overheard him say. "Give me a couple days of civilian life and then we'll eat in the parlor. Just the two of us. How about it, Mother?"

He had a way with Mrs. DuPree; anybody could see that. I set the platter of sliced roast beef before him on the dining-room table. Mrs. DuPree might have a rule about fraternizing—as she called it—with the men, but there she was, sitting at the same table with them, her at one end, Isaac at the other. She was all dressed up in her black satin skirt and her cream blouse that had so many pleats and layers of lace that it took Trudy a full hour to press it.

"Tell the boys about army life, Isaac," Mrs. DuPree said as I went back into the kitchen. "Tell them where all you've served."

"Mother," Isaac said, a grin in his voice, "let the fellows eat in peace."

"Come on, man," one of the boarders said. Bill Miller. "Tell us about the army. Never seen a colored man in uniform before."

This was new dining-room talk. I opened the kitchen door a little wider so I could hear while I heaped mashed potatoes into three serving bowls.

"Wyoming," Isaac was saying. "Now that's fine country. That's where the Yellowstone flows. But it's the Teton Mountains I'll never forget, how they rise up out of the flats, bold and mean looking against the bluest sky I've ever seen."

I admired his voice. It was smooth, and as I listened while getting dinner on the table, his voice carried me out of the kitchen so that I was someplace else altogether. I was a soldier with Isaac in the Ninth Cavalry. We were winding our way on horseback along the narrow rim of a Badlands canyon tracking a band of renegade Sioux. I was on the Powder River in Wyoming, then I was in Butte, Montana, keeping an eye out for union men wanting to break the railroads. I was on a naval ship sailing for Cuba, ready to back Teddy Roosevelt's Rough Riders. Never before had I met a man whose everyday life was filled with such fine adventures.

After I finished serving the coconut cream pie, I stood tucked in the kitchen doorway, taking care to avoid Mrs. DuPree's eye.

"How long you been in the army?" Robert Bailey said. "You've got a mighty good show of stripes there."

"Thirteen years."

Mrs. DuPree said, "Isaac joined the day after he got his diploma. From high school. My son is an example for all of you."

"Mother."

"He's the kind of Negro man who'd make Mr. Booker T. Washington and President Lincoln proud. My son is more than a soldier. He works at the army hospital, side by side with the doctor."

"Mother."

"No need to be so modest, son." Mrs. DuPree's back was ramrod straight, she was that proud. She looked at the men. "Isaac's father was a physician—Isaac grew up in a house of medicine. A few years ago the fort didn't have a doctor, but they didn't need one. Not with Isaac there." She paused. "He even delivered a baby."

"Baby?" Bill Miller said. "There's women out there?"

Isaac shifted his attention from his mother to Bill Miller. "Sure. Some of the soldiers are married."

"But what about Indians?" Robert Bailey said. "Seen any?"

"Hell, yes," and then Isaac held up his hands. "Sorry, Mother." The men all laughed, but not too loud. Mrs. DuPree did not abide swearing, and if she caught anybody doing it, she always had something sharp to say. This time, though, she only pressed her lips.

"You ever seen any scalping?" Robert Bailey said.

"No, those days were before my time."

"But there's still Indians out there?"

"Plenty, but not like before. They're dying off. But they were everywhere when I first got to Fort Robinson the fall of '90. A few years later we moved them up to Pine Ridge, but before that, you couldn't turn around without tripping over one." He gave a short laugh. "Warriors. That's what they call themselves, and maybe that's true for the old ones. But now they're nothing but agency Indians."

"What's that?" Bill Miller said.

"Just about the lowest kind of Indian, that's what. Worthless drunks with their hands out. Every month the U.S. government passes out free food to them. Barrels of flour, sugar, meat on the hoof. Free. Every bit of it free. Not to mention all that reservation land. Free food, free land. Can you believe that, men?"

They couldn't. They shook their heads.

"Allotment day," Isaac said. "Now that's a sight to sour your stomach. That's when the squaws line up at the agency door waiting for their handouts. But it's the men, they're useless. Most of them stink of whiskey and on the days when the government gives them their livestock, they sit on their horses outside the stockyard waiting for the cattle to get turned loose, greasepaint all over their faces like it's some kind of buffalo hunt. Or like they're a war party." He shook his head. "Half the time they end up shooting each other."

"Dear me," Mrs. DuPree said.

"After the men shoot up the cattle, the squaws show up, bloodthirsty, just itching to get on with the butchering. Damn. The agency smells for days. But those Indians, especially the squaws, they like the stink of blood." The slaughterhouse men eyed each other. The benches squeaked and cracked as they shifted in their seats.

"The only thing Indians like better than blood is liquor," Isaac said.

Just then, a train two blocks over rattled through, the conductor riding the horn. I thought about old newspaper accounts that told of red savages what drank the blood of little white children. That was after they'd scalped them, after they'd driven hatchets into the hearts of their fathers and ruined the honor of their mothers.

The train's racket dimmed into the distance. Mrs. DuPree scooted her chair a few inches away from the table. That was her way of saying dinner was over. But Isaac wasn't finished. He said, "It doesn't sit well, not with me, all that reservation land, thousands of acres going to waste. Agency Indians don't know anything about ranching. But men, there's still a few acres left for the rest of us."

"What d'you mean?" Henry Ossian said.

"I mean the Homestead Act. You men know about that?"

They shook their heads. I went to get the coffeepot warming on the stove, hoping there was enough for another serving. When I got back to the dining room, Isaac was pulling a newspaper clipping from his breast pocket.

I picked up his plate, clearing his place. Isaac smiled his thanks, and my heart gave a little leap. His plate in one hand, I poured his coffee, my hands a little unsteady from the pleasure of standing close to him.

He smoothed out the paper with his long fingers.

"Right here," Isaac said, pointing to the words, "it talks about the Homestead Act that was passed by the United States Government. Back in 1862."

Henry Ossian said, "Maybe I have heard something about that. Always figured there had to be some kind of catch."

I poured Mrs. DuPree's coffee.

"No, sir. Any man, even an unmarried woman, says so right here, can claim a hundred and sixty acres of public land."

"That don't mean it's open to Negroes," Henry Ossian said.

"That's where you've been misled. There's Negroes homesteading all over out west. The Homestead Act doesn't care about the color of a man's skin. A man's a man in the West."

"Come on, you're pulling my leg."

"Get me a stack of Baptist Bibles, Mother. This man doesn't believe me." Then Isaac's face sobered. The boarders leaned forward. I stopped pouring the men's coffee.

"It's right here in black and white, men. Can't get much truer than that. Here's how it works. You stake out the one sixty, give them eighteen dollars at the nearest land office—they call that a filing fee—and then you put up a house and farm five acres. Live on it for three years and it's all yours."

Thomas Lee Patterson whistled low and soft. "I knew there was a reason why I was hanging on to my money."

"None better," Isaac said. He took a folded map from the same pocket as before and spread it out, smoothing the creases. A few of the men got up and stood around Isaac for a better look.

"This is South Dakota, just north of Nebraska. Some of the fellows and I have been cowboying at the fort—we're taking care of the army's livestock. Practicing, you might say. That Nebraska land's good. Wish I could get my hands on a few acres of it, but it's all claimed." He gave his mother a quick look; she narrowed her eyes. Isaac ran his finger near the lowest crease in the map, stopped, and tapped his finger two times. "But this wasn't, not this section right here."

Mrs. DuPree sucked in air between her teeth.

"I'm ranching just as soon as I'm discharged come June."

"No," she said. "Not that."

Nobody seemed to hear her but me. The boarders stared at Isaac, open mouthed. A Negro with a hundred and sixty acres of land, that's what they were thinking. They had never heard of such. Then, all at once, the men recovered their senses and began talking, their words rushing and overlapping about what they would do if they had a homestead. Their wheat fields would stretch from here to the horizon. They'd have too many cattle to count. No hogs though, they hated hogs. With a hundred and sixty acres they could have big spread-out houses, room after room, and each would have a fireplace. And horses, why, they would drive pairs of high-stepping honey-colored mares and their buggies would be fit for President Theodore Roosevelt himself.

Isaac, his mouth tight, looked down the table at his mother.

"No," she said above the talk. "Not farming, not that."

"Ranching," he said.

"I won't have it."

Isaac's eyes cut away from hers. He looked at each of the men standing and sitting at the table, all of them talking over each other, their faces lit up with the excitement of going to South Dakota. "Corn," I heard one of the men say. "Sweet corn, that's what I'll plant." Someone else said, "What about tobacco?" and somebody laughed and said, "That's Kentucky. We're talking about South Dakota here."

Isaac looked at Mrs. DuPree and held her hard stare. He didn't care the least little bit, I saw, what his mother thought. He was a man made of determination; he was going to have his ranch, and that made me admire him all the more.

"Gentlemen," Isaac said. "It's been a pleasure. Now if you'll excuse us, Mother and I have some catching up to do." Only a few men looked his way—they were too busy with their hundred and sixty acres. He got up and pulled out Mrs. DuPree's chair. As he did, he looked my way. I shook my head to warn him about his mother. She has a sharp tongue, I tried to tell him with my eyes. You've been gone a long time; likely you've forgotten.

Mrs. DuPree got up, her chin high, her eyes glittering. She stepped past Isaac, not looking at him, and left the dining room, her skirt crackling, the heels of her shoes telling her displeasure. Isaac's mouth twitched; he put a finger above his top lip as if to keep from smiling. He looked again at me. I widened my eyes to show I knew he was in for it. But Isaac wasn't worried. Instead, he winked—lazy-like—as if we shared a joke. Startled, I laughed right out loud, and that was when I fell hard in love with Sergeant DuPree.

From then on there was nobody for me but Isaac DuPree. I woke up thinking about him. I'd think about cooking eggs and bacon for him, I'd think about pleasing him at dinner with the best cuts of meat and the creamiest mashed potatoes ever. But it didn't work out that way, not for dinner. Invitations came from Mrs. DuPree's friends asking her and Sergeant DuPree to luncheons and dinners, all given in his honor. Every day the two of them went out together, Mrs. DuPree dressed in her Sunday best and Isaac in his uniform. Trudy, who lived in the boardinghouse cellar, said they never got home much before eleven at night, sometimes closer on to midnight.

The house was quiet when Trudy told me about Mrs. DuPree's plans. It was the third day of Isaac's leave, and I was sitting in the dining room having a little coffee before starting dinner for the boarders. The newspaper was spread out before me. I stared at the print, but I was thinking about Isaac's smile that came so easy, and how his fingernails were always clean, and how his hair had a soft wave to it.

"Mrs. DuPree's trying to find him a wife," Trudy said as she swept the floor. "That's what these socials are for."

I looked up. Trudy was older than me by a few years. She was tall and skinny, and her skin was a deeper black than mine.

"Lydia Prather this, Lydia Prather that. That's who Mrs. DuPree's picked out for him. Her and the sergeant had an awful row last night. Tried not to listen, but I couldn't help it. They must've been sitting right by the parlor vent. Woke me up, they were that loud."

A wife. I put my hands flat on the table to steady myself.

Trudy said, "Mrs. DuPree doesn't have one good word to say about this ranch the sergeant's got fixed in his mind. She wants him to help her look after the business. That's what she called it. The business. She's got money for another boardinghouse, only this one's going to be for out-of-town visitors. High-class people, that's what she called them. Doctors and professors and such-like. Once he's quit of the army, she wants him to run it. Him and his wife. Lydia Prather. She went on and on about it, how rich they'll get and she'll buy more and more till she owns every Negro boardinghouse in Chicago." Trudy stopped to catch her breath. "She wants grandbabies too."

Married. To Lydia Prather. Or someone like her.

"But no, ma'am," Trudy said. "Sergeant DuPree wasn't having no part of it. Said he was his own man, he didn't want to depend on his mother. Said he has to stand on his own two feet. The army's been taking care of him all these years, time to go out on his own." Bending, Trudy swept a pile of bread crumbs into her dustpan.

She shook the crumbs into the garbage pail, then looked at me funny. "You all right?"

I nodded and because she was still looking at me, I said, "He's sure got nerve."

"I'll say, standing up to his mama like that. The things he said. 'Didn't you raise me to be an independent man?' That's what he said. He said, 'Think about it, Mother. A hundred and sixty acres. This is an opportunity. Father would want me to do it.'" Trudy upended the broom and knocked down a cobweb in the corner. "I'll tell you what. That set her off, crying and wailing like a baby with a filled-up diaper."

I shook my head; it was all I could manage. It pained me to think of Isaac married. But it grieved me even more to think of him giving in to his mother. I wanted him to be different from the slaughterhouse men. I wanted him to be more than just talk. I wanted Isaac DuPree to have his ranch.

Trudy was saying, "It's not like me to feel sorry for a man, but I sure do for this one."

I looked at her.

"You ever know Mrs. DuPree to come out second? After all these years of working for her? No, ma'am. She's not going to give up this easy; she'll get him one way or the other. The sergeant might as well go on and marry Lydia Prather and do what his mama wants. If you ask me, he'll save himself a heap of wear and tear if he gives up now." Trudy plucked the cobweb from the broom's bristles. "Lydia Prather sure will have her hands full. Mrs. DuPree will run her life, just you wait and see. Well, good luck I say. I say that to any woman what marries Mrs. DuPree's son." She rolled the cobweb into a little ball and threw it into the garbage pail.

I turned away and pinched the inside corners of my eyes to keep from crying.

Every morning during his leave Isaac was up early, his eyes puffy from all those late nights, just so he could have his bacon and eggs with the boarders. It was like he missed the company of men and how they talked when their women weren't around. Each day he sent the men off to the slaughterhouses with more stories about the West and how there, most anything was possible if a person was willing to work. The land of opportunity, Isaac called it. The land of opportunity.

After the men had gone off to the slaughterhouses, Isaac settled into the habit of wandering into the kitchen. He wore a gray suit and a black tie—civilian clothes, he called them. I liked him as much in his suit as I did in his blue uniform. The first two mornings Isaac sat on the kitchen stool and watched me work. We talked about nothing much, usually the weather, or maybe the news from the daily paper. Sometimes Trudy was there washing down the walls or dusting the floorboards. By the fourth morning, he was lending a hand, drying the dishes and emptying the pan of dirty dishwater out back. He never talked about Lydia Prather, and I was glad for that. I didn't want her in the kitchen with us.

On the fifth morning, Isaac told me about his father, a man I didn't know much about other than he'd been a doctor.

"Father never turned a sick person away," Isaac said. "He practiced at Provident Hospital, helped start the nursing school there. Had this house built for Mother when they got married. It wasn't so close to the slaughterhouses then or the railroad tracks. But everything changed when Father died. I was fifteen. Cancer of the lungs. He was sick a long time, and Mother spent all their savings trying to find a cure. Borrowed against the house. He knew it wasn't any use, but you know Mother."

That made me feel bad for Isaac; a boy of fifteen needed his father. But there was something else that made me feel even worse: the groove that ran between us. Isaac's father was educated and had done important things; mine had been a slaughterhouse man. Isaac had finished high school; I had to quit after the eighth grade. He was fair; I was dark. Outside of this kitchen, Isaac would never look twice at a woman like me.

The thing he talked most about, though, was land. "Don't get me wrong," Isaac told me and Trudy on the seventh morning of his leave. "I'm not taking anything away from Booker T. Washington." He sat on the kitchen stool, a cup of coffee in his hand. The kitchen smelled rich. The coffee was fresh, and there was raisin bread rising in the oven.

"Good thing," Trudy said. She put linens to soak in a pan on the counter. "Your mama thinks the world of that man."

"And so she should. But being a tradesman isn't good enough, not for everybody. Booker T. Washington needs to understand that. A man's got to have land. I've staked my hundred and sixty and nobody's ever taking it from me." Isaac paused. "Nobody."

"Don't think anybody'd dare," I said. I was washing two mixing bowls. "But it's the weather; it all comes down to the weather. I was raised on a farm and that's what I most remember. Worrying about the weather."

"Your father's a farmer?"

"Was. Back in Louisiana before coming here. Sugarcane."

Trudy said, "How come you never told me that?"

"How many acres?" Isaac said.

"Can't say. I never heard. Dad tenant farmed."

"How'd a tenant farmer from Louisiana end up here?"

"It was something Dad always talked about, coming north, how it'd be so much better. Everybody did. We lived on a plantation down there." I picked up the coffeepot. Isaac held out his cup to show that he'd enjoy a little more. I poured it for him. I said, "The plantation was Mr. Stockton's, and when he passed, his daughter didn't want the place. It was falling apart, so she sold it. Mama called the new people white trash with money and said no good ever comes from mixing with that kind. We took a train bound for the North. Chicago was the last stop, and Dad said it was as far from Louisiana as we needed to go." I put the coffeepot back on the stove and turned down the heat. "Dad figured it'd be better in a big city like Chicago."

"Is it?"

"In some ways."

Trudy said, "You couldn't give me a hundred dollars for the South." She kneaded the wet linens, working on a stain.

Isaac blew on his coffee, then had a taste of it. Thinking about Isaac's question, I opened the oven door and stuck a toothpick in the center of the first loaf. The toothpick came out moist; the bread needed a few more minutes.

My school in Chicago, I recalled, was better than the one in Louisiana—there were more books. Jobs were easier to come by in Chicago, but rent was high. Still, a person could make a decent living. But the stink, it was bad. No matter which way the wind blew there was no getting away from the smell that came from the stockyards. Day and night, slaughterhouse fires burned carcasses. Black clouds of soot blocked the sun and there were no stars at night. For all that, though, I was glad to be here. Chicago was where I'd met Isaac.

I turned to him, smiling.

Our eyes met, and just like that, everything went still. The trains, Trudy sloshing the linens in the basin, the creaks in the house, it all stopped. Isaac's eyes took me in. I stood before him, letting him admire me, me looking back at him, me taking pleasure in it all.

"Your bread," Trudy said. "Mind your bread," and that quick, it was over. Isaac took a long drink of his coffee, and me—my heart racing—I didn't do anything. "Your bread," Trudy said.

"Yes," I said. I opened the oven, drawing in deep breaths of the hot air, feeling woozy. Isaac had seen me in a new way. I fumbled with the hot pads, my hands shaking as I took out the three loaves. I ran a knife along the insides of the pans, then flipped them upside down onto the cooling rack. I felt Isaac watching me; I wanted to go to him. I wanted him to put his arms around me; I wanted his lips on mine.

I tapped the bottoms of the bread pans with the knife. The metal made a sharp sound. The bread loosened and dropped. Something had passed between Isaac and me. I kept on tapping, needing the noise to fill the kitchen.

Trudy wrung out a section of her wash. "Yes, sir, Sergeant DuPree," she said. "The boarders sure do admire you."

He put his cup on the counter. "That so?"

"You're all they talk about," Trudy said. "You and that homestead of yours, it's turned their heads. And you," she snapped at me. "Stop that tapping."

Startled, I dropped the knife. It fell on the floor, clattering. I stared at it, heat rising in my cheeks. Still sitting, Isaac slid the knife toward him with the toe of his boot and picked it up.

"Give it here," Trudy said. He handed it to her, the handle pointed out. "Now go on," she said. "We've got work to do."

"I can see that," Isaac said, smiling some. Then he glanced at me and in that instant, I believed I saw a shine of admiration.

He wasn't gone but a second when Trudy turned on me. "What's wrong with you? Making eyes at that man. You're nothing but the help and he knows it. You'll get yourself in trouble this way, throwing yourself at him. He'll forget you before he's even through with you, and didn't I tell you about Lydia Prather? There's talk of a June wedding." Trudy pointed a finger at me. "Watch yourself, that's all I've got to say."

I closed my eyes against it.

On the tenth morning of Isaac's leave, he came to breakfast wearing his uniform. I'd been the one what had rubbed out the spots and set the creases right even though laundry was Trudy's job. I had insisted, telling Trudy that I had spare time while she had so much to do. In truth, I wasn't thinking about Trudy. I wanted to run my hands over Isaac's clothes and breathe in his smell. Trudy knew that; I could tell by the way she clicked her tongue when she handed me his uniform. But what harm could it do? I saw her thinking that too. Isaac was leaving on the 9:45 A.M. for Nebraska.

It was hot for early May. The kitchen window was up, and between trains the birds sang. The robins were all back, and usually the sight of those summer birds made me smile. But that day, the day of Isaac's leaving, tears blurred my eyes as I cooked breakfast. I was so sad and my heart so heavy that it was a wonder I was upright.

I wasn't the only one grieving. Mrs. DuPree was in her bed, claiming a sick headache.

After breakfast, Isaac went with the men to the back alley and shook their hands good-bye. I watched from the kitchen window as I washed dishes. Jingling horse bells broke through my sadness. It was the coal man bringing his wagon from the other end of the alley. "Trudy," I called out, my voice dull in my ears. "Mr. Jackson."

In the alley, the boarders slapped Isaac on the back, and I imagined them telling him that they'd all meet up soon in South Dakota. He held his hand high in a wave as he watched them walk down the gravel road, their lunch pails swinging a little with their steps. When the men were gone, Isaac called out something to Mr. Jackson, the coal man, who said something back. Then Isaac came through the yard, stopped for a few moments as if unsure of his way, and came on toward the kitchen stoop.

My heart thumping, I dried my hands on my apron. The last two mornings he'd kept away. Trudy told me I should be glad; Isaac DuPree was doing me a favor, so I'd best stop looking so puny. For all of Mrs. DuPree's faults, Trudy said, she had raised her son to know right from wrong, even if I had puffed myself up like a brazen woman. He knew to stay away from the help. His last morning home, though, he was heading to the back steps. He was coming to see me.

In the open kitchen door, Isaac stopped and looked again at the alley. "Poor bastards," I heard him say to himself.

He didn't know the half of it. Eleven days ago Isaac DuPree had walked into the boardinghouse, and without giving it a thought, he'd made every one of us want something big. The boarders wanted land of their own, Isaac's mother wanted to keep him here with her, and me—I dreamed of making a home with him in South Dakota.

Mr. Jackson had his wagon in the backyard now. Trudy hurried through the kitchen to meet him, but not before throwing me a knowing glance when she saw Isaac at the kitchen back door. He stepped aside for her to pass, and that put him an arm's length away from me.

My breathing turned ragged. I held out the sack lunch of biscuits and boiled eggs that I'd packed.

"What's this?" Isaac said.

"A little something to tide you over."

"Obliged."

His eyes flickered over me as he took the sack lunch. I drew in my breath. He liked what he saw. Because I believed this—wanted to believe that his eyes shined for me—I said, "I'm proud to know you."

Isaac raised an eyebrow.

"A man with land. That's a proud thing."

"So it is."

"There's talk."

Isaac cocked his head.

"Talk that you're getting married."

"Gossip," he said.

"To Lydia Prather."

"Lydia Prather wouldn't last a day in the Badlands."

I bit my lip to keep from smiling. In the side yard, Trudy said something about Mr. Jackson making a mess the last time he was there. "That's the nature of coal," he said back. Then they both fell to squabbling, each saying the other needed to learn how to mind his own business. It came to me that a year from now, five years, ten, I'd be still in Mrs. DuPree's kitchen, still looking out the same window, still listening to the same bickering. Mr. Jackson started up with his shovel. It made a raw scraping sound as it scooped up coal. I pulled myself up. Coal clunked down the chute that ran along the side of the kitchen.

"Likely not," I said to Isaac about Lydia Prather. "But you'll want a woman out there. In South Dakota."

Isaac stared at me.

I looked him right in the eye. "One to cook for you, do up your laundry." I smiled. "One to help in the fields."

"No," he said. "Not me. I'm doing this alone. I don't need Lydia Prather. I don't need anybody."

"I—"

"You're as bad as my mother."

I'd made him angry; his muscles pulled at his mouth. Before I could make it right, he was gone, leaving nothing but his footsteps on the wood floors as he went through the dining room and then the parlor. The front door opened and closed. My ears rang and my heart flopped around in a strange way high in my chest. I hoped it meant to kill me quick.

I stumbled into a corner, knocking over the kitchen stool. Holding my apron to my face, I tried to cry. I wanted to cry from the shame and the disgrace and the misery of having thrown myself at a man what didn't want me. I tried, I gave a little wail, but I couldn't cry. The hurt was too big.

Somebody coughed. I spun around. Isaac. Heat flooded my cheeks. He'd come back to humiliate me even more. "Please," I said, putting my apron up to my face again. "Go away."

He cleared his throat.

"Go away."

"Now this is why women are such a mystery."

I didn't say anything.

"God made women just to keep us a little off balance."

I looked at him over my apron.

He was leaning against the pie safe, a little smile pulling at the corners of his mouth, but there was a hardness in his eyes. He said, "You might have something. The right kind of woman could come in handy. Another pair of hands. You do know your way around a kitchen, and like you said before, you grew up on a farm." Isaac paused. "You were talking about yourself, weren't you?"

My heart skipped.

He said, "A single woman can stake a claim."

My mind stumbled over the words.

"That'd give me three hundred and twenty acres."

I put a hand on the counter.

"I'll have you write out a statement saying you intend to homestead. That way I'll get the claim now. Land's going fast. The agent'll expect a little extra; you're supposed to be there in person. But there's ways around that."

His face blurred.

"It'll be hard work. You'll have to pull your share. It'll wear you thin. There'll be days you'll curse me, you'll curse yourself for leaving Chicago."

"No," I said.

"You say that now, but it's not Chicago. There's no electric lights out there, or running water, not where I'm going."

Everything was suddenly very clear.

"Three hundred and twenty acres," he was saying. "I can raise a fair number of cattle on that, wheat too. It'll get me off to a quicker start."

I said, "I expect to be married."

Surprise flashed across his face. "You can't be. A woman has to be single to stake a claim."

"Then stake it now," I said. "Like you said. In my name. Then come back and marry me. If you want that land."

His lips disappeared into a thin line. He hadn't expected this, not from me, the kitchen help. I hadn't expected it either; I didn't know where the words came from. But now that I had said them, I made myself stand square to Isaac.

He said, "What's in it for you?"

A chance to be in your arms. A chance to have something that counted. I said, "My own home."

"That so?"

"Yes."

He turned away and looked out the back door, and I guessed that he wasn't seeing Mr. Jackson driving his coal wagon out of the yard. He wasn't seeing the alley and he wasn't seeing the back sides of the next row of houses. Isaac was seeing, I believed, three hundred and twenty acres of land filled up with cattle and wheat.

"I wasn't looking to get married," he said, still looking out the door.

"Three hundred and twenty acres," I said.

"Hell." Then he squared his shoulders. "All right," he said, turning to face me. "But there's one condition. We'll give it six months. That's enough time to get me started, get me through planting season. Then we'll end it. You'll come back home. There'll be talk, but gossip never bothered me. We both get what we want. You'll have been married, and I'll have the land."

I wanted Isaac to say that I meant something to him, that he'd be proud to take me as his wife. Instead, I felt cheap. This wasn't how I wanted it to be. I had sold myself for a hundred and sixty acres of land. But it didn't have to stay that way. I'd work hard. I'd prove myself. Isaac wouldn't be able to do without me.

He might come to like being married. I said, "A year. I want a year."

His eyebrows rose.

I said, "A year. Four seasons."

"You drive a hard bargain."

I didn't say anything.

"Most women don't last that long homesteading, but all right. A year. I'll come for you mid-June. Have your things ready."

"I want a preacher."

"I figured that."

He opened his gold pocket watch. "I've got just enough time to tell Mother." He snapped the watch closed and put it back in his pants pocket. "But first your statement for the claim."

"That's right," I said. "My claim." A chill ran through me. "And your mother."

I waited in the kitchen while Isaac was upstairs telling his mother about our plans. Waiting turned my nerves bad. I went out back to get some air. Mr. Jackson, the coal man, had driven his wagon into the alley and was calling to his horses to keep moving. Trudy stood on the back stoop watching him, her hands on her hips.

"Trudy," I said. "He's marrying me."

"What're you talking about?"

"Isaac DuPree. He's coming for me mid-June."

She narrowed her eyes. "What'd you do to get him?"

"Nothing. He just came out and asked me. Mid-June, that's when."

"Lordy. You must have done something."

"Can't you be glad for me?" I turned away and went back into the kitchen. She followed me. "Rachel," she said. "I didn't mean it that way."

I started to say that she did mean it, but then I put my hand up. Isaac was coming down the stairs; he was coming to tell me what his mother said. His footsteps echoed through the parlor. I held my breath. The front door opened, then closed. The house was quiet.

Trudy looked at me. "There goes your groom."

"Tramp," Mrs. DuPree said to me. "Get out." She stood in the kitchen in her nightdress and bed jacket, her face heavy with rage. Isaac hadn't been gone over ten minutes.

Stunned, I shook out my wet hands and left the frying pan I'd been scrubbing in the washbasin. "Tramp," Mrs. DuPree said louder, as if I hadn't heard her the first time. I fumbled with the knot in my apron strings, my hands still wet. "That's how you got him," she said. Trudy came in from the dining room holding her broom.

I hung up my apron and got my cloth bag.

"Give it to me," Mrs. DuPree said, pointing at my bag. "Some of my silver's missing." I gave it to her; I was used to obeying her. She emptied it onto the floor.

"Lordie, Lordie," Trudy said.

Mrs. DuPree shot her a warning look. With the toe of her shoe she pushed at my things—my tapestry coin purse, my pocket mirror and comb, my handkerchief, some pieces of hard candy in silver foil. My cheeks burned.

"Mrs. DuPree," Trudy said. "You know Rachel. She wouldn't steal."

She glared at Trudy, shushing her. She pointed at me. "Get out, right now. Get out of my house." I stuffed my things back into my bag, all thumbs and jittery. I struggled with the door and then I was outside and almost to the alley when she opened the door and yelled at me to get back in the kitchen, the dishes weren't finished, and there was dinner to cook this afternoon. I didn't think twice. I turned around and went back. Mrs. DuPree was gone.

"What's the matter with you?" Trudy said. "You got what you wanted. You got her son, a man with land. Where's your pride?"

Traveling on a train to Nebraska, I thought. I had to come back. Isaac didn't know where I lived. If I wasn't at the boarding-house when he came for me, he might not try all that hard to find me. But that wasn't the kind of thing I was willing to say out loud. I said, "I need the money. I'll stay as long as she'll let me in the door."

Trudy shrugged her shoulders. "It's your funeral."

Mrs. DuPree placed a newspaper advertisement for my job. That brought all kinds of women to the back door, but none of them suited Mrs. DuPree. "Too nervous. She'll break every dish I own," she told Trudy about one woman. "Hands shake. She probably drinks." Of another she said, "Shifty. That one will steal me blind." One woman, still nursing, wanted to bring her baby with her.

Once a gray-headed white woman showed up begging for the job. "Poor white trash," Mrs. DuPree said. "Won't have her kind in my house."

Trudy thought Mrs. DuPree turned away all those women just so she could keep on tormenting me.

"You think you're marrying a rich man," Mrs. DuPree said on those days when she was so angry I believed I could smell her bitterness. "You better think again, you conniving little cheap tramp. I know your kind, coming up from the South, looking for easy money. Think you're marrying up, a dark girl like you snagging my son. Well, think again, missy. Marry my son and he'll never see a penny of my money. You'll be the ruin of him. You mark my words, you'll bring him down."

Other days though, Mrs. DuPree talked to me only through Trudy. "She's wanting you to stay late again," Trudy would say. "Wants the oven scoured and polished all over again. Told her you just did it yesterday, but that wasn't good enough. Said you were sloppy." Or, "Now she's got you cooking for her friends, wants you to make chicken and dumplings for Preacher Teller. Mercy, Rachel. I don't know how you're standing it, her being so nasty. Why don't you go on and quit, you don't need this job."

But I did. I was buying for my own home now—cooking pots, a frying pan, and dishes and cups for two. One by one I packed each thing in the traveling trunk Mama bought second-hand for me. I was not going empty-handed into this marriage.

Mid-June came and went.

At first I worried that Isaac had been killed, scalped by Indians. But then a letter addressed to Mrs. DuPree came from Nebraska and she turned even meaner.

"He didn't write you, did he?" Mrs. DuPree said to me.

I tried to smile.

"Of course he didn't. He's forgotten all about you. But Lydia Prather, he hasn't forgotten her. He's quite taken with her."

I tried to ignore Mrs. DuPree. I did my best to keep my hopes up. Isaac was an army man; he was a man of his word. But he hadn't written; he hadn't tried to explain why mid-June had come and gone. In my heart, I believed the worst. He had my statement for the claim. He didn't need me.

Days passed. Heartsore, I cooked for the boarders and kept still when Mrs. DuPree talked about Lydia Prather. Each night I went to bed beside my sister Sue, worn out but too hurt to sleep. On the last of June, Mama said it was time to put Isaac DuPree behind me. She patted my hand when she said this. She and Dad didn't like it that I'd agreed to marry a man they hadn't met. But Mama liked it even less that Isaac DuPree had hurt me. The next day, the first of July, me and Sue carried the traveling trunk with its pots and pans up to the attic.

Mama thought I should do the same with my plum-colored wedding dress. She thought I'd never forget Isaac DuPree as long as the dress hung from a peg in my room. She was right, but I couldn't bring myself to put it up in the attic. I wanted the dress near me. I wanted to admire the lace collar and to be able to touch the pearl-shaped buttons that ran down the back. I wanted to think how it would feel for Isaac to take that smooth satin dress off of me.

"No," I told Mama. "Not yet."

She covered it with an old bedsheet, telling me that would keep it fresh until the right man came along. But I knew different.

The right man had already come along. For me, it was Isaac Du-Pree or nobody.

It was the seventh of July, just before dinner, when Isaac showed up at Mrs. DuPree's back door, I froze right up, unable to move or say a word. "You're still here," he said. I didn't know what to make of that. He said, "We'll leave in two days. Wednesday morning," and I was so thankful that he had come for me, that he hadn't forgotten, that I burst into tears, embarrassing myself before him.

"What's this?" he said. "You didn't think I'd back out of our deal, did you?"

I pulled myself together and shook my head.

"I was up in South Dakota, staking your claim. That, and other business, took a little longer than I expected. But just wait until you see it. Three hundred and twenty acres all told. Prettiest piece of country I've ever seen."

That was the last night I cooked dinner in Mrs. DuPree's boardinghouse. Isaac sat at the head of the table with the boarders. His mother was shut up in her bedroom, spitting mad that he had come for me. The men begged for more stories about the army and about Isaac's homestead, and he was glad to oblige them. Feeling light on my feet, I served bowls of fried chicken, snap green beans, and sweet yams. I thought I saw pride in Isaac's eyes as he watched me. When it was all on the table, I went back to the kitchen. There, Trudy said she'd do the dishes—that was her wedding present to me. Tears in my voice, I promised her I'd write; she said she'd come visit. "I'll look for you," I said as I hung up my apron for the last time. I took off my hair kerchief. I went back to the dining table, my bag in hand. One by one, I said good-bye to the boarders. I saw the envy in their eyes, but they wished me well, even Thomas Lee Patterson, the man I had snubbed not all that long ago. When I came to Isaac, he gave me a quick nod. I expected him to say something but he didn't.

I turned back to the kitchen. "Not that way," Isaac said. I didn't know what he meant. He got up and took my arm. I stumbled as a shock bolted through me. It was the first time he had touched me. I felt woozy and weak. He tightened his hold. The boarders watched. A few of them grinned. To my surprise, Isaac led me through the parlor to the front door. We stood there not sure what to say to each other. Finally he said, "Wednesday morning. Eight o'clock. I'll meet you at Preacher Teller's church. The train leaves at 10:10 A.M."

"I have a trunk," I managed to say.

"Have it sent to the station."

"How?"

He hesitated. In that moment I saw that he understood what he was getting: a woman what didn't know anything about the world. He said, "Bring your trunk to the preacher's then."

He let go of my arm and opened the screen door for me. I went out, hearing the door slap closed behind me. I looked over my shoulder. Isaac was gone. All the same, I held up my hand as if he were there to see me wave good-bye.

Forcing a smile, I stepped off of the front porch and went along the gravel walkway to the walk that followed the street. I hardly knew where I was. The alley was my way home, not this.

Old oak trees lined the walk. Their thick, twisted roots buckled the surface. I picked my way over the roots, sure that I was going to fall. My legs felt loose and my ears rang. My skin was clammy like I was coming down with something. Nerves, I thought. I stopped and steadied myself, pulling in some air. It was then that I saw that the houses on the street were shabby. They wanted paint, and the yards needed trimming. All but Mrs. Du-Pree's. The neighborhood had once been the home of Chicago's educated Negroes, but that was before the slaughterhouses got so close. That was when Mrs. DuPree had been the wife of a doctor. That was before her husband died and she was forced to take in boarders. The neighborhood once was grand. But now Mrs. Du-Pree's son was marrying the help, and that help had just left by the front door.

I started walking again, picking my way over the broken sidewalk, my chin high. Mrs. DuPree might have the money for a second boardinghouse, but this neighborhood was where she lived. Mrs. DuPree was on her way down, I told myself, but the next Mrs. DuPree—me—was on her way up.

On my wedding day, Dad hired a horse cab and took me to Preacher Teller's. My mother and Sue had to work. So did church friends and neighbors, Trudy too. But standing in the front row of the church was Johnny, my older brother. I was so happy to see him that I nearly laughed. He worked nights playing piano in a saloon, and it had been years, I figured, since he had seen this side of eight o'clock. His eyes were streaked red and the smell of ciga-rettes clung to his suit. But his face was fresh shaved and it light-ened my heart to have him there.

He was proud of me for marrying Isaac. He'd said so from the start. "You're making something of yourself. Didn't I always say that you would?" he had said. "You're the smart one—you're getting out of this stinking city."

"You will too," I said.

After the ceremony, I kissed Dad good-bye. "I'm proud of you, girl," he said, and this brought tears to my eyes. Up until that day, he had made out like he was glad Isaac hadn't come for me. He hadn't had anything good to say about Isaac DuPree. He didn't care that Isaac DuPree came from a good family. In his day, Dad had said more than once, a man paid at least one visit to a woman's parents before proposing marriage.

I kissed Dad again. When I hugged Johnny, I whispered, "Come see me—us—in South Dakota."

"When you get yourself a piano in your parlor," he said, "I'll be on the next train out. I'll play for the cows."

"See you real soon then."

An hour later me and Isaac boarded the 10:10 A.M. and began our journey to South Dakota.

5

ROUNDER

South Dakota. The land of opportunity. But that was before the drought, that was before me and Isaac put a child in the well. That was before we did it the second time. The second time, Liz screamed when Isaac told her he needed her. She screamed until I put my hand over her mouth and held her lips together. It was wrong what we were doing to her, but Isaac was right about the horses and Jerseybell. They had to be watered.

Like before, I latched Alise and Emma in their room. I went with the others to the well, none of us saying anything as we walked against the wind. Isaac carried Liz, who cried into his shoulder, her arms around his neck. At the well we knew what to do, we knew what to expect, and that made it all the worse. We were getting used to doing this thing. We were giving in to it.

Afterward, Isaac watered our four horses and then hitched two of them, Bucky and Beaut, to the wagon. He was holding true to his promise to get supplies, and John was going with him.

Me and the girls—I had to make Liz—went down the rise to the barn to see them off. John waited on the buckboard, all grins. It had been a good while since he'd been to Scenic; it had been Mary's turn the last time. I gave Isaac a small cloth bag. "Soda biscuits and a can of pears," I said. "It's all I've got."

"It's enough." He quickly touched my arm and then he hoisted himself to the top of the wheel. The wagon rocking some, Isaac settled on the buckboard, finding the worn spots where he always sat. He took the reins from John and giddyupped the horses. Creaking, the wagon lurched, and they pulled away, Rounder lagging behind them likely as hot, thirsty, and hungry as any of us.

Me and the girls stood watching on the hard dirt road that ran along the bottom of the rise. We wore our bandannas tight over our noses. The wind blew so hard that the three little girls fastened themselves to my legs to stay upright. Even Mary leaned into me. Isaac sent Rounder back home, and we waved good-bye until the wagon and horses were nothing but an unsettled cloud of dust.

Standing on the road, I felt peculiar and unseated. During our first years in the Badlands I always went to town with Isaac. I didn't want to be left by myself. I went even after Mary and Isaac Two were born. But when John came along it was too much to pack up the children and travel all those miles. The road was rough and pitted and made the babies cry. So I stayed home and worried. I'd worry that Isaac'd get caught up in a storm, or that a horse would kick him in the head, or that he'd get lost somehow and I would never see him again. I missed him so much that I'd cry over the least little thing. A meadowlark's song left me crying in my apron. In the winter when the sun lit up the snow like diamonds in a Chicago jewelry store, sudden tears choked my throat.

But today wasn't like that. I wasn't all that much worried about Isaac or John; they'd be all right. It was Liz's screams from this morning that had me this way. I couldn't shake the sound. Maybe I never would.

"You coming, Mama?" Mary called. She and the girls were halfway up the rise to the house.

"I'm coming," I called back.

I wanted my mother—that was a part of my peculiar feeling. I always wanted her with me when our babies were being born. That was natural. And three years ago, when Mama wrote me that Dad had died from the influenza, I grieved something awful that I wasn't there for his burial. But this was different. This was the same feeling I had had last night. I was homesick for the people I'd left behind in Chicago.

Jerseybell, the milk cow, caught my attention. She was tethered to a stake by the root cellar where a patch of grass grew in the shade. Her back was humped like it pained her, and she wasn't chewing, just drooling. Panic fluttered in my belly. Jerseybell had been dry this morning when Mary tried milking her.

Put one foot in front of the other, I told myself. *Put your mind to your chores.* That was the best cure for worry and homesickness. Back in the house, I put on a pot of the last of the pinto beans and swept out the kitchen. I sent out everybody but two-year-old Emma to pick up cow chips. A home couldn't ever have enough cow chips. They kept the fire going in the cookstove, and they kept the furnace hot in the winter.

Emma at my feet, I found the wooden baby cradle in the barn, and later, when its padding had aired on the clothesline, I stuffed the saggy parts with Miss Bossy's feathers. Midmorning I put Emma down for a nap. Mary let Star and High Stepper, our other horses, out of the corral to free range. The girls all came in from the fields, and it wasn't long after that when a four-foot snake twisted its way out from behind the cookstove. Liz, who chanced to be in the kitchen at the time, screamed, waking up Emma. Mary and Alise ran in from the porch in time to see me chop off the snake's head with Isaac's bowie knife.

"It's nothing but a bull snake," I told Liz, who stood frozen by the kitchen table. Mary took Liz by the hand and got her out on the porch. I quieted down Emma, and then I dragged the snake out. It was still twisting some. Liz covered her eyes, saying how it was the one in the well, how it'd come to get her.

"That's good," Mary said. "'Cause it's dead. Can't get you now."

Me and Mary each took one end of the snake. Liz pressed herself flat against the outside wall of the house. We carried it to the barn for Mary to skin. It would be supper.

Back at the house, I had Liz come inside with me. I got the three little girls' rag dolls for them to play with under the kitchen table. I put the iron on the cookstove to heat and set up my ironing board. Alise and Emma played a game of pretend, but Liz just laid on the wood floor, holding her doll to her chest. I couldn't see her eyes but I imagined that the hollowness was still there.

There had to be water in town, I thought. *Isaac had to bring some home. No matter what it cost, he just had to.*

The iron was hot now. I hadn't washed our clothes and bed linens in weeks, but that didn't mean they couldn't be pressed. Mama was probably busy ironing too, in the laundry room at the Chicago Palmer Hotel. I pictured her hands—tough, scarred, and her knuckles big from so many years of handling hot irons. Sue worked at the Palmer too; she would be one ironing board over from Mama. Sue was light and airy and nothing ever bothered her, not even the stink from the slaughterhouses. She was smart, though. She could spell. Me and my brother Johnny used to play a game with her. We'd pick out the biggest words we could find in the newspaper. We'd show them to her real quick, then spin her around in a circle. Spell *clamorous*, we'd say. Spell *diplomatic*. Try *harbinger*. She always got them right. She had a gift.

I shook out Isaac's shirt, then laid one of the sleeves on my ironing board, my hands stretching the cotton material, working out some of the wrinkles. I picked up my iron. Two months after I married Isaac, Sue married Paul Anders. He'd been asking her to marry him since she was sixteen. Now they had two boys and two girls. That was enough, Sue wrote, after the last one was born. As for Johnny, it was harder to picture him. Three years ago he'd married Pearl Williams, a slaughterhouse widow with a baby girl not quite two years old at the time. Mama thought Johnny could've done better, and it shamed her all the more that Pearl was showing when Johnny finally got around to marrying her. Their son was born a few months later. When I heard all that, I felt bad. Johnny would never get out of Chicago. But he surprised me. Last year him and Pearl took the children to East St. Louis. Johnny made good money there, Sue wrote. He had a job playing the piano six nights a week at a downtown theater.

As for Isaac's mother, I knew she was doing just fine. People like her always were. Two letters ago Mama wrote that Mrs. Du-Pree had three boardinghouses now. Likely she was sitting pretty with all those boarders to preach to and all that hired help to boss around. And all her money, I couldn't stop thinking about all her money and how just a little of it would be a big help to us. Isaac should think of it; he should put his pride aside and ask.

My throat tightened. Home. I wanted to go home.

I looked at the little girls under the kitchen table as I put the iron back on the stove. *This was their home,* I told myself. Our home. Not Chicago. I was lucky to have so much. I had a house, a wood house. I was the only one in my family able to say that. A person didn't just walk away from her house, not even when times were bad.

Something inside of me bucked at that. This drought was driving out homesteaders right and left. I used to feel sorry for them, but not anymore. At least the drought was over for them. Their mouths weren't dried up like they'd been chewing grit. They weren't watching their cattle die, and they weren't dropping their children into water wells.

But they had other worries, I told myself. *Most everybody did. Things were going to get better here. They had to—it couldn't stay dry forever. So stop feeling sorry for yourself and put your mind to your work.*

Later that day, when the sun was burning its hottest and the wind blowing its strongest, me and the girls sat down to a noon dinner of beans and half-filled cups of lukewarm water. The girls all made faces. I had strained the water but it still clouded up with silt. The beans were nothing without fat or salt, but they were filling and we were hungry. Even Liz ate. When we finished, I gave Rounder a spoonful of beans I'd put aside for him.

"Time for the outhouse," I said to Alise and Emma, expecting

Mary to dry-wipe the dishes clean. Liz gave me a questioning look. "You too," I told her. I picked up Emma, put her on my hip. She stretched a leg across the top of my belly, resting it there, and that made me smile a little.

Alise whined on the way to the outhouse, Rounder following, but I tried not to listen to her complain about her mouth being all dried up. The Palmer Hotel in Chicago had indoor plumbing. All a person had to do to get water was turn a faucet at the kitchen sink. The hotel even had indoor bathrooms. Mama once wrote that she figured someday all the houses in Chicago would have them too, even the ones in the Black Belt.

When Mary was almost two and Isaac Two a new baby, Isaac made the outhouse bigger. He dug a second hole and cut and sanded a new wood seat that had two round openings. One seat was small for Mary and her brother for when he'd be out of diapers. The other was larger for us. The outhouse was good size, but too small to hold me with my swelled-up belly and three children. "Wait outside," I told Liz. "Don't you go off anywhere."

I held Emma steady while she sat on the smaller hole. "Stinks," Alise said, pointing at her.

"Hush," I said.

Mama loved to tell stories about the Palmer Hotel. It was ten stories high and had a long view of the lake. Shiny black horse cabs waited out front to take the white gentlemen guests to the downtown skyscrapers. Sometimes it was their wives, wrapped in furs, what rode in the cabs. These women shopped in the department stores and when they wore themselves out doing that, they had afternoon tea in the hotel dining room. Dinners on silver

trays were delivered to their rooms at seven, and later the gentlemen and their wives left together, that time wearing evening
clothes for the theater.

When we moved to Chicago, it took Mama just one day to
find her job at the Palmer. After Sue finished the tenth grade, she
went to work with Mama deep in the basement far below the
guest rooms. Not me. I had to have windows. My first job was
rolling pie crusts in a Michigan Avenue bakery. I was almost fourteen. But before I had to quit school, I liked meeting Mama at the
end of the day so we could walk home together. I waited for her
beside the department store catty-corner to the hotel. In the winter, I hunched up inside my wool coat and pulled my hands high
up into my sleeves. There, I watched the doorman in his red vel-
vet cape sweep guests in and out of the hotel's yellow-gilded tall
front doors.

"Liz," I called as the three of us left the outhouse. "Your turn."
She was nowhere to be seen. I called again. Still no answer. That
rubbed me wrong. Liz knew better than to go off without telling
me. The Badlands was a dangerous place for children. They could
lose their bearings and get lost, they could fall into a narrow slit
in the earth, or they could, like our Isaac Two, slip from a low
boulder.

"Where's Liz?" Alise said. The look she gave me said she
hoped Liz would get a spanking. She wouldn't be disappointed.

I looked around as we walked up to the house. Star and High
Stepper had wandered to the cottonwood and stood switching
their tails at flies. Jerseybell was gone; Liz must have gone off to
help Mary move her to another patch of grass. She was always
trailing after Mary. Maybe Liz had called through the outhouse

door asking permission, and I hadn't heard her. Maybe she hadn't had to use the outhouse after all. No matter. She was still going to hear about it.

Alise and Emma went back to playing with their rag dolls under the table. I stirred what was left of the beans, not wanting any of them to stick to the bottom of the pot. I looked out the window and my heart nearly stopped. Mary was in the near west pasture putting cow chips in the wheelbarrow. I pressed closer to the window. Mary was alone.

I went outside and waved her in.

"Isn't she with you?" Mary said when I asked about Liz.

My chest seized up. "Look in the barn and the root cellar. I'll look in the dugout and the outhouse."

I went back into the house, told Alise and Emma to get their dolls and come with me. "Why?" Alise said.

I said, "Never mind, just do it." I yanked them up by their arms, hurried them into their room, told them to be good. I was scaring them but I didn't care. Without another word, I latched them in and rushed off to the dugout the next rise over. Likely that was where Liz was. In good years, during planting and harvest seasons, Isaac hired a few of the boys what rode the train west to find work, and we put them up in the dugout. We kept beds there, and Liz was probably hiding under one of them.

Halfway up the rise, I had to slow down. Winded, I tried to pull in some air, but I couldn't get much. The baby took up all the space in my belly and chest. My breath came out in short puffs.

"Liz?" I called when I finally got to the dugout. Nothing. I knew she couldn't be there—the cobwebs in the doorway hadn't been torn—but I went in anyway. She could have gotten in some-

how. I called again as I looked in the kitchen and in the two bedrooms. She wasn't there.

I hurried out of the dugout. She better not be hiding in the
outhouse thinking that'd be the last place I'd look. The little girls
knew they weren't allowed in there alone. The larger hole wasn't
all that big, but if a child got to playing and stood up, she could
slip and lose her balance. Liz wasn't all that much bigger than
four-year-old Alise, but she was old enough to know better. If she
was hiding there, and something told me she was, she was going
to hear from me and my big wooden spoon.

The outhouse door banged in the wind. My mouth went
even drier. We always kept it latched.

Holding my belly, feeling like I was carrying a twenty-pound
sack of flour, I ran.

The outhouse was empty, but I couldn't shake the bad feeling. I put my ear to the larger toilet hole. Sharp lime fumes stung
my nose and eyes. Wind whistled in the deep, dark tunnel.

Straightening, I thought I heard a cry. I put my ear back to
the toilet. "Liz!" I screamed into the hole.

Nothing.

Wild thoughts took ahold of me. In Chicago's slaughterhouse
district, children were forever falling into open sewer holes, grown
folks too, if they were tipsy from drink. I gripped one end of the
wood plank that made the seat and pulled. When those bodies
were pulled out, they were swelled up and gray, not looking anything like human beings. I pulled again. The plank gave a little.

I pulled harder. One of the boards cracked, splintering
around the nails. "Liz," I screamed into the pit. "Hold on, I'm getting a rope."

I backed out of the outhouse and nearly fell, stumbling over Rounder. He barked at me.

"Liiii-zzzz!" Mary called from somewhere behind the barn.

I ran to the barn for the rope. This was all my doing. I'd been daydreaming, thinking about Mama and the Palmer Hotel with its indoor plumbing, and now something bad had happened to Liz. But some of this was her fault; I couldn't help thinking that too. She'd run off on purpose; she wanted to make me sorry for putting her in the well.

Inside the barn I slowed down, my eyes adjusting to the gloom as I made my way to the wall where we hung the rope. My breathing was loud and quick. Rounder circled tight, hemming me in, meaning to stop me. "Get away," I shouted. I found the rope and hurried out but stopped, blinded all at once by the sudden glare of the sun. Squinting, I put a hand up to shade my eyes.

Rounder bumped up against my leg, nervous, and without thinking, I patted his neck to calm him. His tongue darted out and licked my fingers. Panting, Rounder tightened his circles around me, and suddenly I understood his meaning. "Liz!" I said. He barked, put his ears flat, and raced off to the wash, a narrow cut in the earth by the cottonwood.

"Mary!" I called, dropping the rope, running.

She came from the trash heap behind the house. I pointed at Rounder, and Mary went after him.

Rounder went down into the part of the wash that was the depth of a grown man. Mary followed him into it, sliding on her bottom, gray dirt tumbling down behind her, dust swirling. I ran, breathing hard, my fingers spread out under my belly. A cramp shot through my side; I hunched up. Isaac Two had slipped from a low boulder. A pointy-edged rock had pierced through his right temple when he landed, killing him. He'd only been five years old.

My legs wobbled; I caught myself.

"Mama! I found her!"

My knees buckled and my legs gave way one part at a time and before I knew how, I was sitting on the ground, my legs folded up under me.

"She's all right!"

I didn't try to get up. I sat there thinking how I was going to give Liz a tongue-lashing that child wouldn't forget anytime soon. But all at once she was throwing herself on me and I didn't care that she nearly knocked the air out of me. Her arms were around my neck, and I rocked her, back and forth, both of us crying, and that was when I knew that I hated the Badlands.

The shock of this thought stopped my tears. I hated the Badlands. For years I had hated it; I just didn't know it until then.

"Mama," Mary said, her voice low. She knelt beside me. "Mama." Her face was pinched with worry.

I hated the Badlands, I hated everything about it—the bigness of it, the never-endingness of it, the lonesomeness of it. The weight of my hate bore down on me. I wanted to lie down in the dirt and cry.

"You're bleeding," Mary whispered. "Your hands."

Over Liz's shoulder, I held them up. One fingernail was partly torn off. There were splinters in other fingertips. There were tears and scratches in my palms. It took me a moment to understand it was from pulling at the outhouse seat. Blood ran down my hands; it was on my sleeves. It was on Liz's dress, and all I could think about was the long soaking it would take to get the stains out and how there wasn't any water. The blood was going to set, and me and Liz would have to wear these marked dresses.

Rounder circled the three of us, panting, his tongue too swollen for his mouth. Mine felt the same. I pulled myself together and told myself I didn't hate the Badlands, I couldn't. It was the place where me and Isaac made a home, it was the place where I birthed our children. The scare of losing Liz had played fast with my nerves; I couldn't hate my home.

"Mama?" Mary said, holding out the handkerchief that I kept tucked in my sleeve. She wiped Liz's eyes, and then she wiped mine.

So easy to lose a child. It could happen anywhere. It could happen to any child, to any mother. But God was watching even if I wasn't. God and Rounder.

"Why'd you do this, Liz?" I said. "Why'd you hide like that, scaring us this way?"

Liz hid her face in my neck. She didn't have to say it. She had run away from the well. And from me. I said, "Don't you ever do this again. You hear me? Don't you ever."

"Yes, ma'am."

I thought of Alise and Emma in their room and a flutter of panic rose in my chest. I couldn't take any more lost children. "Let go of me, honey," I said to Liz. "Can't get up if you don't let go." Mary unwrapped Liz's arms from my neck and pulled her up. Somehow, then, Mary got me to my feet.

I stood there a moment looking down into the wash. In good times it had water in it.

I turned my back on it. "Come on," I said. "Let's see to your sisters."

6

MRS. FILLS THE PIPE

Alise and Emma were crying when we got up to the house—
me hurrying them into their room had scared them bad.
They weren't the only ones. My dress was soaked clear through—
that was what losing Liz had done to me. After me and Mary
got the little girls settled, I wrapped up my torn fingernail, and
Mary used a needle to pick the splinters from my hands. I put on
my other dress and hung the damp one with its bloody spots on
the clothesline to dry. I wanted a bath in the worst way. I imagined sitting in a tub of clear water, the grit floating off of me. I
wanted a cool drink of water to take the swelling out of my tongue.
The girls were every bit as thirsty; Emma got to crying from it. We
settled for a few sips each of lukewarm water, Rounder too.

My ironing was waiting for me. The outhouse seat needed
fixing, but like the ironing, it was just going to have to wait. What
we needed was a little rest on the porch. Mary gathered up the
girls' rag dolls, and I spread out our red Indian blanket for the
girls to play on. Mary and Liz sat on the top porch step, the wind
tugging at their bandannas. For something to do, Mary tried to
play school. "What's two plus two?" she asked Liz. "Two plus
three? Three plus two?" Liz acted like she didn't hear Mary; she
just looked down at her fingers spread out on her knees. When

Mary gave up, I told her and Liz to move Jerseybell to a fresh patch of shade, and after that they needed to pick up more cow chips.

Alise and Emma rested on the blanket, their dolls hugged to their chests. Likely they were too thirsty to play much. Off to my left, Rounder laid on his side, his eyes half closed so that the whites showed. It wasn't my way to sit idle in the afternoons, but for once I didn't care about my chores. I wanted to rest. I wanted to step away from the hard feeling I had about the Badlands. I wanted to not think.

The southern wind blew hot. There was so much grit in the air that from a distance Grindstone Butte's sharp points had faded into a hazy white. In a month or so, when the weather shifted, we'd wish for that southern wind. Usually I didn't mind winter all that much. Chores changed in the winter. That was when I quilted; that was when I sewed a new dress for Mary and for me, and new shirts for Isaac and John. But on that hot September day, the thought of winter chilled me. The garden had dried up weeks ago, and I didn't have the first thing canned for winter.

Don't think about it, I told myself. Isaac was bringing water. Him and John would be coming on home tomorrow. I put my head on the back of the rocker and let my legs go out before me.

The two porch rockers came from Mabel Walker. When she sold her ranch to us in the spring, she told Isaac it came with the rockers. She couldn't bear the chairs anymore, she said. She couldn't sit in one without her husband Ned in the other. He had died without warning. On Christmas Day morning, Ned had sighted a deer and meant to get it for winter provisions. Mabel said she knew something bad had happened when he didn't show

up for Christmas dinner. She and her daughter Norma didn't
find him until the next afternoon. He had fallen in a heap on the
ground; there wasn't the first sign of wounds or blood. A thin
layer of snow had drifted over him, and the coat he was wearing
was frozen to the ground. Norma came to us for help, saying
it looked like Ned's heart had quit on him. Isaac chopped Ned
free and brought him to our barn so Mabel and Norma wouldn't
have to look at him while they waited for a spring thaw to loosen
the ground.

I felt sorry for Mabel losing Ned that way. He was a good
enough man. But in some ways she was lucky. She'd gone back to
Missouri, the place where she had family. She got out before the
drought, and she had our money.

Our money.

Gliding shadows of turkey vultures crisscrossed the earth.
Put it behind you, I told myself. Buying the Walker ranch looked
like the smart thing to do. That was how Isaac saw it. Nearby, a
vulture swooped close to the ground, its black eyes hard and un-
blinking. I hated those birds and what they meant. But I'd always
given them their due. No others rode the breezes in such grand
style, their black wings spread, the silver in them flashing as they
dipped and banked and soared.

When Mabel Walker sold off, I didn't know if I could do like
her and let people have our belongings. But if it meant earning a
little money, I guessed that I could. Some things would hurt more
than others, like our bed's headboard with the oak leaves carved
into it. Isaac got that nearly ten years ago when Carl Bergson's
bride took one look at the Badlands and turned right around and
went back home to Sioux Falls. It'd be just as hard to give up the

two red upholstered parlor chairs that we got when we bought the Peterson place seven years back. Those chairs still made me proud; I never figured on having anything so pretty.

All at once, Rounder barked, sharp and shrill. Startled, I jumped. Mary and Liz were running up the rise, their skirts held high above their bare knees, pointing and yelling about somebody coming. I squinted. Shimmers of heat, wavy, rose from the earth. I pushed myself up out of my rocker and went to the edge of the porch to look eastward. A fair-sized dust cloud was rounding a bend in the road near a row of low boulders. I couldn't make out a thing, not even a wagon. Couldn't be Isaac and John. They'd be coming from the west, and anyway, I wasn't looking for them until tomorrow.

Alise and Emma sat up and watched the dust cloud. It made my nerves jumpy. I didn't like it when people, especially men, came by when Isaac was gone. But maybe these travelers were in a hurry. Maybe they were just passing through and wouldn't stop any longer than to say, "Any rain these parts?" Maybe they wouldn't expect to stay for supper. It shamed me that I didn't have anything better to fix than snake meat. I hoped they wouldn't stop at all. I hoped they'd just wave and keep going.

I put my hand on Rounder's neck, felt the standing fur. I was glad he was here.

Mary and Liz were on the porch now, and the five of us waited, straining our eyes. We heard the wagon before we saw it, the wheels creaking, the wagon cracking as it likely swayed from side to side. We heard the horses, their slow, heavy hooves on the dirt road, and I imagined that I heard them tossing their heads, snorting, blowing grit from their noses. Shapes of people riding on the wagon began to appear.

"Mary?" I said. She had the best eyes in the family. Isaac liked to say she could spot a stilled rabbit a half mile off.

She stood on her tiptoes, her eyes almost squeezed shut. "Mrs. Fills the Pipe," she said, her words coming slow. "Those are her horses. Three people up front, and I think maybe one's a boy. Somebody's in the back. He's leaning over the side."

"You sure it's Mrs. Fills the Pipe?" I said.

"I'm sure."

A woman. And one what wouldn't expect to stay for supper. Indians never did.

"Been awhile since she's been by," I said. "Don't know when."

"This spring," Mary said. "The cottonwood was just leafing."

"That's right, it was."

Mrs. Fills the Pipe lived at Pine Ridge Reservation, a two-day journey southwest of our ranch. I recalled how on that day when the cottonwood leaves were a fresh green, Mrs. Fills the Pipe had been on her way northeast. She was going to her brother's at the Rosebud Reservation to care for her sister-in-law sick with tuberculosis. Since then I hadn't given her a thought; Indians came and went along the road every week or so. Before the drought, when Indians stopped to rest under the cottonwood, I'd go down, or send Mary or John, and tell them they were welcome to drink from the well behind the barn. But it wasn't always that way. When I first came to the Badlands, the Indians scared me silly. When I saw them on the road, I hid in the dugout and latched the door.

"They're harmless," Isaac had told me then, "but keep a sharp eye. If there's a pebble on the ground they think you might want, it'll be in their back pocket."

"Where're they going?" I asked him. "All this traveling."

"Who knows? Probably to another reservation. They're all related to each other in some complicated way. Only God knows how. Clans and tribes and bands."

"Why don't they all live on the same reservation then? That's what I'd do."

"Army split them up awhile back," Isaac said. "Keeps them docile."

Isaac was right. The Indians were harmless. I had even gotten to know the names of some of them.

Mary rocked up on the balls of her feet. "Think that's Inez with her, but I don't know the boys." She stretched her neck. "But that's Inez and her mama all right. Maybe the others are kin."

Kin. The word was like a spark. Excitement rose in my chest, covering up my tiredness. Mrs. Fills the Pipe wasn't kin, far from it. But she was a woman, and all at once, I wanted in the worst way to be in the company of a woman. I longed for a visit. I longed for a chance to talk and to share worries. Mrs. Fills the Pipe was a squaw, but she was a woman and she was handy.

"Liz," I said. My skin nearly tingled, I was that perked up. "Get Rounder in the barn; his barking'll scare them off. Alise, you stay with me. Mary, go meet them on the road. Ask them up for a visit."

Mary looked at me, her eyebrows puckered. I knew what she was thinking: Daddy wasn't going to like this.

"Never mind that," I said. "Go on now."

She gave me one last doubting look before turning to go. Then I thought of something. "Wait," I said. "You too, Liz." They turned back, Liz's hand on Rounder's collar. "Don't—" I stopped. I could hardly find the words for what I had to say. The girls looked at me, puzzled. I couldn't meet their eyes. "Don't ask for anything," I said.

"Like what?" Alise said.

"I'm talking about refreshments. Like how folks do in Chicago."

"Refreshments?" Mary said, and I felt foolish. This was not Chicago.

I said, "Like how we always do when company comes. Something to eat and drink." There was no easy way to put it. "There's not enough for everybody. You can have a little water, but that's all. Don't ask, and don't take even when others are having. Company's served first."

"Water?" Liz said. "You're giving them our water?"

"They're company."

"That's our water."

"Liz. That's enough."

"But Indians?" Mary said.

I ignored her. Nothing was going to stop me from having my visit. My longing had turned into desperation. I needed to talk to a woman what understood about children getting lost, what understood how hard it was to make food stretch, and what might even know something about living with a man with a stubborn streak.

"Hurry up," I said. "Go meet Mrs. Fills the Pipe and get Rounder in the barn." I turned to Alise and Emma and made them come inside with me.

In the kitchen, excitement rose up again in my chest. Thank goodness yesterday there had been enough flour to make a half batch of soda biscuits. I carefully wiped the dust off my china plate with the hand-painted pink roses. I laid out four soda biscuits, one each for my guests. Four biscuits looked skimpy, but I couldn't spare any more. I broke the four into halves, making eight. Likely nobody'd be fooled, but a person had to at least try to keep up appearances. Once you stopped caring about that, you might as well quit living.

There were a couple of pinches of chokeberry tea in the bottom of the canister. It was just enough to make a few cups if nobody minded it thin. I blew on the smoldering cow chips in the cookstove, stoking the fire. I put a little water in the teakettle. Guilt twisted my heart. *I wasn't using all that much water,* I told myself. *Isaac would be back tomorrow with plenty more. It was all right.*

I looked out the parlor window. Mary was on her way to meet the wagon, and Liz was hurrying to catch up. Pushing my guilt to the side, I got out two of our good blue porcelain cups. Tea. All at once I felt like singing. I was serving tea.

The wagon, I saw now, was stopping under the cottonwood. I pulled off my hair kerchief, licked my palms, and patted my hair into place. I got my straw sun hat from the bedroom and checked myself in the parlor mirror as I tied the ribbons. I looked out the window.

The boy on the buckboard jumped down. He was tall and his

shoulders had breadth to them. He wasn't full grown but close. He put his hands around Mrs. Fills the Pipe's waist as she backed one foot onto the high side step, and he lifted her like she was a child. Once on solid ground, she shook out her shoulders and stomped her feet to bring the life back to them.

The boy helped Inez down. On the ground, Inez took off her duster, folded it, and gave it to the boy to put in a basket on the floorboard. The child in the back of the wagon jumped—flying, more like—over the tailboard but landed on his feet, his knees bent and his arms out before him to hold himself steady like he was daring the wind to push him over.

I couldn't remember the last time I was this pleased to see company.

I hurried and put away my ironing board. I glanced into the parlor, thinking how Mrs. Fills the Pipe had probably never been in such a fine room. Not that I had any intention of inviting her inside; Isaac would never stand for that. I brushed the grit off the front of my dress, and then me, Alise, and Emma went out on the porch to wait for our company.

I put my hand up in greeting as the Indians and the girls walked up the rise. Mrs. Fills the Pipe raised her hand to me. She looked older and slower than she had in the spring. Her back was bent with a little hump, reminding me how women folded in on themselves when their childbearing years had passed. I straightened my own shoulders.

Air caught in my throat. I couldn't believe my eyes. Inez looked like a young lady—a white lady—the kind you see in catalog advertisements. She was fresh and clean as if the wind was not full of grit. Her dress was cream colored, and there was a wide

pink sash gathered around her narrow waist. The dress was short,
a good six inches above her ankles, showing off her white stock-
ings. Her sheer pink head scarf was tied with a big bow angled to
one side of her chin.

Was this, I thought, *what the government was passing out to
Indians while hardworking, honest ranchers were making do on
next to nothing?*

At least Mrs. Fills the Pipe looked the way an Indian should;
that took some of the sting out of Inez's city dress. Like always,
she wore a patched-over cotton dress and beaded ankle-high
moccasins. Her butternut headscarf, knotted by a firm hand, covered her hair, but all the same, strands of gray blew loose from her
long braid. The skin around her black eyes was wrinkled and
thin.

Except for their hair, the boys could be sons of ranchers in
their blue cotton shirts, the hems fraying some in their too-short
pants. The older boy, the one what was almost grown up, had a
ponytail pulled back with a strip of leather. The little boy's hair
was cut so close that it stood up in peaks. He looked to be about
John's age.

"Mrs. Fills the Pipe," I said, smiling. "Hello."

"Mrs. DuPree." She wasn't smiling.

"Please sit down. I just happened to put some tea on. You
can stay, can't you?"

"Tea?"

My smile froze. Water from the well was all I had ever offered Mrs. Fills the Pipe. Tea? At the house? Lord, what had I
done? No wonder she was frowning, Inez too. *You're right, Mrs.
Fills the Pipe,* I wanted to say. *Why don't you just turn around and*

go on home. Ranchers and Indians don't mix. Everybody knows that.

But it was too late to say such a thing. "Please," I said, pointing at the rockers. "Stay awhile. If you can."

Mrs. Fills the Pipe hesitated for a moment and then nodded. Like me, she knew it was too late to turn around and go back to her wagon. Lifting her skirt a little, she stepped up onto the porch and sat down in one of the rockers.

"Mary," I said, "get the other rocker for Inez."

After that everything went by in a big hurry. Mary carried out my bedroom rocker and pulled the three rockers close to the house to catch the shade. I brought out a pitcher with a little water in it and, giving Liz a warning look, I told her to pass the cup around to the boys what stood stiffly at one end of the porch. Liz was just as stiff. She glared at them as they took long drinks from the cup. I offered the biscuits to the boys. Mrs. Fills the Pipe said to take only one. I told my girls to take the boys down to the cottonwood where there was a touch of shade. I could tell Mary wanted to stay on the porch with us; she was staring at Inez, admiring her city clothes. I shook Mary off, telling her with my eyes that Inez was all grown up now and that she wasn't.

"Let Rounder out of the barn," I said to the girls. "If you think he'll behave. It's too hot in there."

The teakettle whistled. In the kitchen I got out my third porcelain cup for Inez. There was a dried-up spider in the bottom; I turned the cup over, then dusted it out with my apron.

"Beautiful plate," Mrs. Fills the Pipe said a few minutes later when I passed her the biscuits. She took one. Inez did too.

"Why, thank you," I said, my heart puffed up with pride. "It was a wedding present." I eased myself into the rocker on the other side of Mrs. Fills the Pipe. The three of us were lined up in a row, the sun on our knees but our laps and our faces in the shade. "It's from my brother, Johnny. He lives near St. Louis now."

Inez caught my eye. She was on the other side of her mother and had crossed her legs at the ankles like a lady does. But it was her shoes I couldn't stop looking at. They were the color of a new-born tan calf and they fit as tight as kid gloves. A row of cloth-covered buttons started at the instep and ran clear to the top, just a few inches above Inez's anklebone.

That must be what fashionable women were wearing in Chicago. Folks there would take one look at me in my shapeless brown dress covering my big belly, see my scuffed, dusty work boots, and take me for a backward country woman. And they'd be right.

I blinked back the tears of shame that came up from no-where. Through the blur of them, I watched the string of children as they meandered to the cottonwood, Mary going out of her way to stop and pat Jerseybell, tethered by the root cellar.

Mrs. Fills the Pipe blew on her tea, then took a sip. She nod-ded her pleasure. "Chokeberry tea."

"Oh," I said, coming back to myself and remembering my manners. "Chokeberry's my favorite. Glad you like it too." I put my hand over the mouth of my cup; my water was plain. "Wish I had something cold to offer. Wouldn't it be something if we could stretch some of that winter ice clear through summer? The last of ours ran out mid-July. A cold drink of water would be such a treat on a day like this."

"I would not take it," Mrs. Fills the Pipe said, "when there's chokeberry tea."

"Oh. Me neither, I don't suppose." *That was polite of Mrs. Fills the Pipe,* I thought. I gave her a sideways smile. She smiled back. I took a small sip of water. As I did, I saw that her moccasins were decorated with red, blue, and white beads. Around the ankles, the beads were in the shape of zigzags, making me think of lightning, making me think of courage. To my surprise I said, "I'm so glad you could stop, that you weren't in too much of a hurry."

"My cousin's place is between here and home. We will get there before dark."

"How nice," I said, relieved that Mrs. Fills the Pipe knew this invitation to tea did not mean staying on for supper. "You'll get to visit with family."

"That's right. This is Inez's last time home before she leaves." There was pride in her voice. "She will be gone two years."

"Mercy, Inez. Where you going?"

"Minneapolis," Inez said. "The nuns have a place for me there."

"You're going to be a nun?"

"No. Nursing school. They want me to be a nurse."

"Why, my goodness."

"It's not my idea. I want to go to California. Hollywood, California."

Mrs. Fills the Pipe clicked her tongue. "Doesn't matter what she wants," she said to me like Inez wasn't sitting right there. "The nuns are giving her an opportunity."

Opportunity. The word set me back. That was the very thing Isaac had said about coming to South Dakota. Now here was Mrs. Fills the Pipe, a Sioux, sending her daughter east. Suddenly I ached with envy. I wanted to be able to send my daughters east to school. I wanted my daughters to become beautiful young women in fashionable clothes. Where did Mrs. Fills the Pipe get the money to do so much for her daughter? Must be another hand-out, I decided. Just like free land and free food. But instead of the government, this time it was the Catholics.

A gust of wind caught and lifted our skirts. We each pressed them back into place before they could bellow even bigger, but in that one instant, I saw a mended tear in Inez's right stocking just above her knee.

Something about that made me feel better, and I had to look away to keep from smiling. A little way off from the cottonwood the older boy had a long strand of rope knotted into a lariat. Our horses stood nearby. The boy twirled the rope near his feet. Then he played it out a little and let it loop big and loose over his head.

"Showing off," Mrs. Fills the Pipe said, also watching the children.

Envy was the devil's work, that was what my mother used to say about that. I told myself to put it behind me. The dress was a handout. I put my teacup to my lips and blew on it, giving me time to push away the envy. Everything the Indians had was a handout. Me and Isaac would never stand for such a thing.

I said, "How's your sister-in-law? Is she feeling some better?"

"If she stays in out of the wind, stops eating the dust. My

brother does not see to Eleanor right." She pointed her chin at the children. "Those two are his. Franklin and Little Luther."

"I'm sorry my boy John isn't here. He'd like your nephews."

Mrs. Fills the Pipe smiled. "Boys."

"Aren't they something?"

Mrs. Fills the Pipe nodded at my belly. "That one's a boy."

I couldn't keep from smiling. "Nothing would please my husband more."

"Men," Mrs. Fills the Pipe said.

I laughed, surprising myself.

Side by side the three of us sat, each of us thinking, I supposed, our own thoughts. Our rockers creaked over the wood-planked floor as we rolled our feet, ball to heel, back and forth. The wind, caught on the south corner of the dugout, howled low.

I said, "When you came by last, you had that quilt you'd made for your sister-in-law. It was so pretty. She must be proud of it."

Mrs. Fills the Pipe smiled, accepting the compliment. "My brother's neighbor, Sadie Horn Cloud, has a new pattern. There's a sun in the center, rising. Each square has its own sun. Some are coming up, some are higher, others are in between. It's pretty. But it makes me hot to look at it."

"I can just imagine. But come winter, all those suns will do a world of good."

Inez said, "It never gets cold in California."

Mrs. Fills the Pipe ignored this. "The nurse at the clinic gave my sister-in-law cream for the dryness in her skin. It helps in the winter."

"That'd come in handy." I ran the tip of my tongue over my cracked lips. "That reminds me. For Christmas my sister Sue—she lives in Chicago—she sent me a big bottle of something called aspirin. It's a little white pill. It takes the heat out of a fever. Do you know it?"

"Yes. Cures headaches too."

"Is that right?"

"So many good medicines," Mrs. Fills the Pipes said. "But . . . then there is my cousin, Margaret Two Bulls, old enough to know better, looking for the fountain of youth. Thinks it comes in a bottle. Keeps ordering tonics from big-city catalogs."

"The fountain of youth, mercy. Has she found it?"

Mrs. Fills the Pipe flapped her hand in the air. "A younger man, that is the fountain she needs."

Inez laughed, and then I did too. How good it was to talk woman talk.

By the cottonwood, Mary was spinning the lariat now. She was a good roper and would practice for hours on end if it weren't for chores. She threw the rope and caught Liz around the waist. Liz squealed, untangled herself, and then everyone took off running before Mary could rope the next person. It lightened my heart to see Liz play.

"Please," I said, holding out the china plate. "Have another biscuit."

Mrs. Fills the Pipe shook her head no, but Inez helped herself to another piece. Mrs. Fills the Pipe shot her a warning look.

I said, "The drought's something else again, isn't it?"

"Bad," Mrs. Fills the Pipe said.

"I miss the meadowlarks. Can't hardly wake up without their singing."

"One of the elders claims they are all at the Missouri."

"Is that right? I wondered what happened to them. I was afraid they were all dead."

Franklin, the older boy, had the rope now. He spun it fast. It whipped through the air and lassoed Mary. Franklin reeled her in. Mary laughed.

I said, "How's the water table at your place?"

"Low, but still filling the bucket."

I almost told Mrs. Fills the Pipe about our well and how two times now we'd had to send Liz down. But I couldn't bring myself to do it. It wasn't the kind of thing a person talked about. I said, "Sometimes I think about moving to the city." I stopped, embarrassed by what I'd just said. "I mean to Interior. Or maybe Scenic."

Mrs. Fills the Pipe glanced at my belly. "Neighbors," she said.

"I could stand a few." Then, because that sounded like a complaint against my home, I said, "As soon as it rains, I'm doing my wash. I'm going to let my wash soak for days. Get all this grit out. Scrub down the house, my hair too."

Mrs. Fills the Pipe agreed. "Half the Badlands is in my house."

"The wind never stops."

"This is a hard place. Hard to take, hard to like."

I looked at her in surprise. I said, "But aren't you from here?"

"No."

"Oh." I waited for her to tell me where she'd been born and bred. When she didn't, I said, "I was born in Louisiana."

Mrs. Fills the Pipe put her hand to her chest. "The Platte," she said.

"The Platte River?"

"In Nebraska," she said. "That's my home."

"My goodness," I said. "My husband soldiered there."

There was a small hesitation, then, "Did he?"

"At Fort Robinson."

Mrs. Fills the Pipe's rocker went still.

"Mother," Inez said. "Don't."

Startled, I looked at the two of them. Mrs. Fills the Pipe stared straight ahead, her mouth set in a hard line. Inez's hand was on her mother's arm. Wind whipped around the house, making a shrieking sound. At the cottonwood, the children laughed as Rounder barked and pounced on the rope that Little Luther flicked back and forth in the dried grass. But on the porch a sudden heavy tension wrapped itself around the three of us.

Mrs. Fills the Pipe said, "This is the home of an army man?"

"Well, yes, but he's been out a long time."

"I was there. Fort Robinson."

"Mother."

I said, "Well, then, you—"

"They rounded us up, held guns to us."

My breath caught.

"Said the Platte was theirs now. Made us live at the fort. It stank. Then they moved us here. Good enough for Indians, they said. Nobody else would want this land."

Sweat broke out on my forehead. Mrs. Fills the Pipe was an agency Indian, the kind of Indian what Isaac hated. Agency Indians were worthless drunks; agency Indians were bloodthirsty. They stood in line, their palms up, all too willing to take government handouts. Agency Indians were the worst kind of Indians, and I had two of them sitting on my porch.

Mrs. Fills the Pipe said, "I remember those army men."

A chill ran up my spine. Bloodthirsty. I had to get rid of Mrs. Fills the Pipe and her daughter and those boys what were playing rope with my daughters. "My ironing," I said, my nerves talking. "It just never goes away. That's what I was doing. Even when there isn't any washing, there's always ironing."

She didn't seem to hear me. She stared off toward the children what were running, laughing, tagging one another. From the corner of my eye I looked over at Inez. She watched her mother, a wary look on her face. She had uncrossed her ankles and had her feet square on the floor. She leaned forward slightly as if she were ready to leave.

"Wounded Knee Creek," Mrs. Fills the Pipe said.

My skin crawled. Soldiers had been killed there.

"Buffalo soldiers," Mrs. Fills the Pipe said. "Saturdays around dark. I remember that too."

"Mother."

"It wasn't enough that they killed us. They had to have our women too."

Her words pinned me to my chair. Hot liquid rose up from my chest, burning my throat. I swallowed. "No," I said.

She put her porcelain cup on the floor and stood up; Inez did too. I tried to get up but my belly held me down and my hands were filled up with my cup and the china plate with two half biscuits. By the time I scooted to the edge of the rocker, by the time I put my cup and plate on the floor, Mrs. Fills the Pipe and Inez were off the porch and halfway down the rise, the wind pulling at their skirts from all four directions.

At the wagon, Mrs. Fills the Pipe whistled once, sharp and shrill. Little Luther, Liz, and Alise popped out of the low end of the wash, Rounder zigzagging around their legs.

Inez pulled herself up onto the wagon's side step, and once on the buckboard, she gave her mother a hand up. Little Luther climbed up behind her, and from the high buckboard he jumped flat-footed into the bed of the wagon, rocking it. His trick made Liz and Alise giggle. Mrs. Fills the Pipe whirled around and said something to him. He sat down.

Mrs. Fills the Pipe whistled again. Inez put on her duster. Minutes passed before Franklin and Mary came running from the wash, Emma bouncing in Franklin's arms. He shifted her to Mary and when he did, I saw how his hand stayed on Mary's arm while he said something to her. Then he jumped up onto the wagon. He cracked the reins and the wagon jerked forward. The girls ran beside it, waving and calling good-bye.

Mrs. Fills the Pipe and Inez did not wave back. Neither did they look up at me. All at once furious, I was on my feet, hollering, "And don't you ever come around here again!" The wind blew my words back at me. They couldn't hear, and that gave me courage. "You're nothing but Indians! Agency Indians!" Suddenly spent, I sank back into the rocker.

"Mama!" Liz and Alise had turned back from the wagon and

were running up the rise, their dresses tangling around their knees, yelling about all the fun they'd had. I closed my eyes, cursing myself for inviting squaws to tea, cursing myself for giving them water and food. And Isaac. I didn't want to think what he was going to say about all this.

The girls jumped up onto the porch steps, shaking the floor, jarring my nerves, and making my head hurt. "Hush up," I snapped. "I hear you just fine." They were too worked up to pay me any mind.

"Luther was funny," Liz said. "He was doing somersaults in the wash. You should've seen him. Grit was sticking all over his shirt. His hair too! He shook himself off like Rounder does after rolling."

On the porch, Alise crouched low and tucked her head between her knees, eager to try a somersault. Liz gave her push and Alise flopped on her side, giggling. I loosened my sun-hat ribbons, hoping that would ease the headache that had come up from nowhere. Just like the memory that flashed through my mind.

Fourteen summers ago, I suddenly recalled, a squaw and her half-breed boy had showed up at our homestead. She had come looking for something. I tried to remember what it was, but as the memory began to take shape in my mind, I saw Mary coming up the rise. I leaned forward some. There was something new about her. She was all light and airy even though she carried Emma, squirming, on her hip.

"Mary?" I said, when she came up onto the porch.

She didn't answer. She smiled in a loose kind of way like she had come across a secret that pleased her. Or like she had just been walking with a boy.

"Mary."

"Ma'am?" There was a faraway look in her dark eyes.

"What's gotten into you?"

"Nothing." She kissed Emma on the forehead and giggled as she swung her to the ground.

"What'd you and that boy talk about?"

"Franklin? Oh, nothing much. Just about school, mainly. He'll be going back in ten days. He goes to the same boarding school as Inez. Or where she used to go. Inez just graduated; smartest girl in her class. She's so pretty, don't you think, Mama?" Mary didn't wait for my answer. "Franklin sleeps in a dormitory there with forty-nine other boys. In bunk beds. So does Luther. I think that would be so much fun, but he says it's not, not really."

"How old is he?"

"Fifteen. Just turned in July."

Isaac would have a fit.

Just then the memory of the squaw and her half-breed boy came back to me. The boy's face had chilled me. The squaw was swelled up with a baby. Isaac had run them off but they hadn't gone far. They showed up the next day.

"Mama, I'm hungry," Alise said.

"Me too, me too," Liz said, Emma joining in with her, their high-pitched voices making me wince from the pain in my head.

"Enough," I snapped. The girls stopped, pressing their lips to swallow their whines. I rubbed my forehead. I never wanted to see Mrs. Fills the Pipe again. She had insulted me in my own home; she had brought up ugly memories.

"Mary," I said. "Go corral the horses."

She smiled, her eyes still far off. *Her mind was on that boy,* I thought, *that Indian boy.* I narrowed my eyes at her. "Enough of that," I said, startling Mary, bringing her back to herself.

At least empty bellies were a familiar worry.

7

ISAAC

It was the next afternoon when another wagon—coming from the west—stirred up a dust cloud. This time it wasn't Indians; it was Isaac and John.

It should have been a homecoming to lift my heart. They were bringing water and supplies. But my nerves were in a knot. Mrs. Fills the Pipe and her ugly words about buffalo soldiers kept circling in my mind. So did the squaw what showed up at the homestead years back with her half-breed boy. But most of all, I thought about Isaac. He wasn't going to like it when he heard about Indians sitting on our porch, and he wasn't going to like it when he found out that I'd done the inviting.

The girls and Rounder went to the barn to meet Isaac and John, and I followed, not moving near as fast. There, Isaac brought the wagon to a stop and he and John jumped down. "What'd you bring, Daddy?" Alise said. "Candy?" and that started the excitement and the clamor that was always part of a homecoming. Mary and Alise got to guessing about what was in the supply boxes, and I was glad for all the noise. Maybe nobody'd think to mention Mrs. Fills the Pipe's visit.

Liz clutched my leg. Her eyes were wide and stared at nothing. "Isaac," I said, my hand going to the top of Liz's head. John was standing near him. "Did you get water?"

"Buckets of it," Isaac said, directing his words to Liz. "More than enough to wet your whistle."

John grumbled something under his breath. I frowned at him. He frowned back. "Mind yourself," I said, my voice low. John's eyes darted to Isaac, and Isaac gave him a hard, steadying look. John ducked his head but he was angry. His fists were knotted up. A chill walked up my backbone.

"How was town?" I said, not knowing what to make of any of this.

"Like usual," Isaac said. "For the most part." He and John locked eyes for a moment before John turned away and went over by the hitched horses. Isaac said, "Folks aren't themselves right now. This drought's bringing out the worst in some."

Behind Isaac, Mary lifted Alise to the top of one of the wagon wheels. "Careful now," I called out. Alise's feet slipped. Mary caught her and pushed her up and over and into the wagon bed. At my side, Emma had a fistful of Liz's skirt balled up in her hand as she tottered on the rocky ground.

I turned back to Isaac. "What do you mean? Was it John? Did he misbehave?"

"No."

"What then?"

"I told you. People aren't themselves," he said, his voice as low as mine.

"Something happened. I can tell."

"Nothing did." Then he said, "Mrs. Svenson."

"You had business at the post office?"

"No."

Mrs. Svenson was the postmistress, and her husband was the ticket agent for the railroad. He wasn't so bad, but Mrs. Svenson didn't like us, and because we had never given her cause, I always figured it was because we were Negroes. When I used to go to Scenic with Isaac and needed postage to send a letter home, Mrs. Svenson sold it to me without speaking. Instead she stared at me, her blue eyes narrowed as if she expected me to try to steal the stamp. She had a way of curling her lips that showed her yellow teeth. I'd never seen her clean. The front of her dress was always soiled with spots of food. Mrs. DuPree, Isaac's mother, would have called her poor white trash. My mother would have gone along with that.

"What'd she do?" I said to Isaac.

"Doesn't matter. We got the water."

I glanced at John. He had his left hand up on Bucky's withers, but his eyes were fixed on Mary and Alise what were in the wagon bed. He made like he was listening to all their chatter about the food supplies but I knew different. John was listening to me and Isaac.

I lowered my voice even more. "Did she say something to John?"

"No." The muscles around his mouth were tight. "It was me, if you have to know. She and I had a few words. At the depot. That's where they're keeping the water brought by the train. It's being rationed. You buy it from Anderson at his store, pick it up at the depot."

I waited.

"She claimed all the water was spoken for."

My eyes flickered to the wagon's bed. "But—"

John said, "She called Daddy 'boy.'"

"Lord," I said, putting my hand out toward Isaac.

"Forget it," he said. "I got the water."

I pictured the train depot, seeing in my mind a handful of townsmen and a few ranchers too, all there to get water. I imagined Isaac and John standing with them near the water tower, the tracks to their backs. The men talked about the drought, shaking their heads over all the families what had been driven out by the hard times. Isaac was a man with twenty-five hundred acres, and so far he had managed to hang on to every bit of it. In the Badlands— even in the best of times—that earned respect. I imagined how his easy manner with the other men riled Mrs. Svenson.

"Trash," I said. "She's nothing but trash."

"I said forget it. I have." Isaac turned around to the wagon. His back stiffened. Mary and Alise stood in the bed, quiet, their eyes wide, staring at us. They had heard, and I saw that they were puzzled, they didn't understand. Isaac was a grown man, not a boy.

"Move," Isaac said to Mary and Alise. The harshness in his voice made them jump away and they stumbled as the wagon rocked. He reached over the side of the wagon and pulled a box to him. All at once, John looked ready to cry. He rubbed at his mouth, tugging at the corners. I wanted to spit out more ugly words about Mrs. Svenson but before I could, Isaac whistled out some air. He let go of the box that he'd pulled to him. He stepped away from the wagon, facing us. He forced a grin that came out lopsided, and then he cleared his throat. "John and I had ourselves quite an adventure on the road. Just a mile or so from here."

Nobody said anything. They all—even Liz—looked to be still turning over in their minds what had happened in town. "You did?" I finally said.

"Yes, ma'am. We had ourselves an adventure."

"What happened?" Mary said.

Isaac gave Mary a quick look of appreciation. "We were just minding our own business, heading home. John had the reins." A sparkle worked its way into Isaac's eyes. "I believe we were talking about how well he handled the horses when all of a sudden he said, 'Look over there—it's a tornado!'" Isaac had the children's attention now; even Liz was listening. He let his voice turn serious. "It was a surprise, I'll tell you. The sun's shining and here comes a tornado. Right for us. Spinning faster and faster. 'Take cover,' John yelled, and you never saw two men move as fast as we did getting under the wagon. We covered our heads—we were ready. But girls, that tornado stopped right in front of our very eyes and turned into a—" He paused. "John, you tell them."

John frowned, shaking his head.

"What was it?" Alise said.

Isaac looked to the left, then he looked to the right. Alise hunched down in the flatbed. Liz tightened her hold on my leg. Isaac cleared his throat, shaking his head. "No, can't tell you. It's too scary. But I'll say this. It had a tail that stretched from here to the house."

The girls' eyes widened.

Bucky blew and sputtered, shaking flies from his eyes, startling the girls. "What was it?" Liz whispered. Isaac looked over his shoulder and then back at Liz and Alise.

"A dragon!" Isaac said, his voice booming. The girls all jumped, screaming. Mary laughed and then Alise and Liz did too. Not John, though. His head was down, hurt, I knew, by what had happened in town. Hurt too, maybe, that Isaac looked to be making light of it. But Isaac had to. A man was a man in the West, that was what he believed. It didn't matter if that man was black or white. Work hard, pull your fair share, and people couldn't help but respect you. Isaac, I knew, couldn't bear it any other way.

By then, Isaac was reaching for one of the supply boxes. It scraped like sandpaper as he pulled it along the bottom of the wagon's bed. Groaning some, he hoisted the box to his shoulder. Nothing more, I knew, would be said about Mrs. Svenson. I could ask Isaac from now until midnight about the particulars of what had happened, but he'd only shake me off saying how it amounted to nothing. Mrs. Svenson, Isaac might say, didn't get along with anybody, not even her husband.

Maybe. All the same, it happened to Isaac. I said, "Let's get these groceries in."

It wasn't until the two wooden boxes were unpacked that I realized there were just enough supplies for four weeks. I counted the tin cans again and refigured the two sacks of cornmeal and flour. I tried to make it come out different, but I was right the first time. Four weeks.

A year ago we'd had a tall stack of dollar bills in our savings account at the Interior Ranchers and Merchants Bank. Now, after buying Mabel Walker's land, there must be nothing, not even a copper penny. It gave me a hollowed-out, sick feeling.

Isaac came up behind me, startling me. "I've got good news. Heard it's raining in the Black Hills and it's blowing this way."

"That's real good," I said, but I was checking those supplies again. And even if I hadn't been, I wasn't about to let myself get all stirred up with hope. The Black Hills were some seventy miles west, and rain clouds were prone to drying up between there and the house. I couldn't count the number of times this summer when Isaac had felt rain in the wind, seen it in the clouds, and smelled it in the air.

"Close your eyes," he said.

"What on earth?"

"Just close them."

I did. I heard him pat his clothes.

"Well," he said, "could've sworn I had one more thing." He patted a pocket again. "Well, well. What do you know?"

All at once, a rich, dark smell filled the kitchen, the kind of smell that made me light-headed with pleasure. Keeping my eyes closed, I filled my lungs with it, and just that quick, I was grinding coffee beans in Mrs. DuPree's boardinghouse kitchen. Mrs. DuPree considered coffee one of life's great pleasures. Me too. Every Friday morning, Samuel, the delivery boy from Telly's Market, brought two five-pound sacks of dark beans to the kitchen door. Those beans, Samuel told me once, had traveled all the way from South America. I tried to picture South America from my geography lessons, but I couldn't place it. I'd been out of school too long. So one Saturday afternoon, after I'd finished for the day at

Mrs. DuPree's, I took the streetcar and went to the free library. There, I rounded up my courage and asked the white man behind the counter if he could tell me where South America was. For a minute he looked at me over his eyeglasses like he wasn't sure he had heard right. Likely he wasn't used to twenty-year-old Negro women asking about South America. He tapped his forefinger twice on the counter. Then the library man got up, nodded for me to come, and without a word, he led me past the rows and rows of tall shelves filled with books. He stopped at a table where there was a big globe of the world. He tipped it and gave it a little twist. With a nod, he indicated a continent that was wide in the middle and then thinned down to a narrow point at the bottom. The countries were different colors: brown, and blue, and green, and a few were pink.

"This where coffee comes from?" I whispered.

He moved his finger to one of the countries. Brazil.

I looked closer. "Is Chicago on here?" I said.

The library man tipped the globe and pointed. "Here."

With my eye, I traveled the distance from Brazil to Chicago. After that I took extra pleasure in grinding those Brazil beans, scoops and scoops of them, into coffee as fine as the sand that trickled in the three-minute hourglass I kept by the stove. The smell of those beans, I once told Trudy the housemaid, was even better than the taste of coffee.

Isaac was waiting for me to say something. I opened my eyes. A small burlap bag of coffee beans dangled right before my eyes. As good as it smelled, as good as the memory was, I didn't like it. "What'd it cost?" I said.

"It's a small bag," he said. "It's been weeks." He took my

left hand and when he saw my wrapped finger, the one I'd hurt in the outhouse when Liz was hiding in the dry wash, he raised an eyebrow.

"Caught my nail," I said.

He put the bag of beans in my palm. "There's rain coming. I believe that calls for a cup of coffee."

"But the cost."

"Can't go to town for supplies and not get coffee." Isaac put his hand on the small of my back and pulled me as close to him as my belly allowed. I turned my face away from him, gripping the coffee sack, crushing it, making my torn fingernail throb all the more. He'd bought it to keep people from talking, to keep them from seeing that we were having hard times. He had bought it to remind Mrs. Svenson that he owned the Circle D, a twenty-five-hundred acre spread.

Isaac kneaded his fingers along my backbone, working out the ache, aiming, I knew, to tear down my anger. Stop it, I wanted to say to him. We're broke and pride made you buy coffee.

His fingers rubbed the knobs on my spine. My good sense began to drift. His fingers felt so good working out the aches. I was so tired. My knees began to give way; so did my anger. I leaned my big belly against him, wanting him to take the weight of it, wanting Isaac to make me a young woman again, when everything was good and easy.

He picked up my free hand, and even though Alise and Emma were underfoot, he pressed the palm of my hand to his lips. My fingers curved around his cheek, feeling how he hadn't shaved that morning. It was then that I saw he was tired. The skin around his eyes sagged. The drought was taking its toll, and that made me feel bad for him. I breathed Isaac in, smelling the sweat of hard work. What difference did a small bag of coffee make?

Emma pulled on my skirt. I dropped my hand from his cheek. "Isaac," I whispered, "I've got supper to get on."

He stepped away, shifting the baby's weight back to me. "That's my girl."

And with that, I understood. The coffee wasn't just to buck up his pride. It was meant to make me forget about putting Liz in the well; it was meant to make me think we'd get through the coming winter just fine.

I could have shaken him. The root cellar was empty; the garden had quit on me a month ago. Jerseybell was puny. The scrawny cattle wouldn't be worth a thing come time for market this fall. And what about the cattle we didn't sell? The grass that Isaac had been cutting for feed was little better than straw. The cattle'd starve by Christmas. All those worries but Isaac figured a little bag of coffee would make me forget. Did he think I could be fooled that easy?

But Isaac didn't see any of what I was thinking—he had other things on his mind. "Come on, John," he was saying, "the day's not over yet. Liz, you come help brush down the horses. The dust is this thick." He measured out a couple of inches with his fingers. "You too, Alise. Your mama and Mary have supper to get on."

"But Daddy, I'm hungry," Liz said, looking at the food supplies on the kitchen table.

"You've got chores to do first."

"But I'm hungry now."

"Me too," Alise said, whining.

Irritation crossed his face. He studied Liz and Alise. Their little arms and legs were nothing but knobby sticks. He looked at me, his eyebrows raised as if to say, Can't you give them something? I shook my head, fighting back the urge to snap, *Not if you expect me to make these groceries last.*

"Tell you what, Liz," Isaac said. "Put a pebble under your tongue."

"But that's for when you're thirsty. I'm more hungry than thirsty."

"That's where you've been misled. A pebble's good for both."

"It is?"

He shooed the girls and John out of the kitchen. "Sure is," he said, and then they were through the parlor, out the door, and on their way to the barn. I went to the table and took a tin can of peas from one of the boxes.

"Mama?" Mary said.

Just holding the can made my mouth water. I couldn't remember when we'd last had peas. "What?" I said to Mary.

"Mrs. Svenson—" She stopped.

"She's ignorant," I said, my words snapping. That was what my mother always said about mean-spirited people. "Mrs. Svenson doesn't know better, and we should feel sorry for her. Put your head up and straighten your back when you're around people like her, people what are ignorant. Don't give them cause to think little of you. Show them that you're quality."

Mary cocked her head.

"Your granddaddy was a doctor and your daddy is a

rancher. That's quality. Blood matters. Never forget what you come from."

"We're Negroes."

"And we're proud to be."

"Franklin's proud."

Mrs. Fills the Pipe's visit rushed back at me.

Mary said, "Franklin's granddaddy is an elder. So's his uncle."

Liz and Alise were going to tell Isaac about the Indian boys. They were going to do it before I had the chance.

Mary said, "So that means Franklin's quality too. Like us."

"No," I said. "They're nothing like us. They're Indians, agency Indians. It's not the same. Quality people raise themselves up." I remembered how Inez Fills the Pipe was going east to be a nurse. "You do it by yourself; you don't take handouts. Now let's get these groceries put up." I put the canned peas on the shelf. *Maybe*, I thought, *Liz and Alise won't think to say anything to Isaac.*

"Mama?"

"What is it?"

"Me and Franklin were just taking a walk. I was just being polite. So was he."

"I know it."

"Are you going to tell Daddy?"

"That's between me and him."

"I don't want Daddy to be put out with me."

"I know it." Maybe Liz and Alise had forgotten all about yesterday's visit. Children were like that. Children forgot things in a hurry, especially when there had been a story about a dragon and then chores and supper to think about.

I said, "Let's get supper on. Let's get a loaf of bread going."

"What about Daddy?"

"It'll be all right."

Mary smiled slightly. Could be she believed me.

8

INDIANS

Nothing was said about Indians during supper that night. Nothing was said about Mrs. Svenson, either. The canned meat and the peas and the pears were too good to ruin with such talk. "Slow down," I told the children more than once. "Make it last." But who could when we were so hungry? The only thing missing was milk. Jerseybell was as puny as ever.

Later, me and Isaac did like always. We sat on the porch watching night come to the ranch. Rounder rested near me with his chin on his front paws. To look at us, a stranger would think we didn't have the first worry. Nobody'd know there were only four weeks' worth of supplies in the cupboard or that in two or three days, Liz would have to go back into the well. Nobody'd know my belly was churning with dread. I had to tell Isaac about Mrs. Fills the Pipe, and I had to do it before the girls did.

We rocked back and forth, me waiting for just the right time to tell Isaac. Our chairs bumped unevenly over the wood planks. The wind blew—more than a breeze—but not enough to carry much dust. Isaac took a sip of his coffee and looked off toward Grindstone Butte. For a moment I thought he might say something about Mrs. Svenson. Instead, he held up his blue porcelain teacup. "You don't know what you're missing."

"I've lost my taste for it."

"Must be the baby doing that to you."

"Maybe," I said, thinking that it wasn't the baby even though it was restless. It was the short supplies that Isaac had brought home. It was Mrs. Fills the Pipe's visit. A breeze ruffled his shirt and the hem of my skirt. "Last night in Scenic," Isaac said, "it was hot and still, not a breath of air to be found."

"That so?"

"John and I slept under the wagon behind Fred Schuling's place. Fred offered us the attic, but Alice said no, we'd roast alive up there."

I wondered about that. Isaac and Fred Schuling went back a long way, but that didn't mean Alice Schuling wanted Negroes sleeping in her house. Isaac and Fred had both been posted at Fort Robinson, except that Fred was white and his Eighth Cavalry unit was quartered in a different part of the fort than Isaac's Ninth Cavalry. The thing that made Isaac and Fred friends was baseball. At the fort they pitched for opposing teams, but as peculiar as it seemed to me, that made them friends. Isaac couldn't help but respect a man with an arm like Fred's, and Fred thought Isaac had a good eye for the strike zone. That admiration brought them together.

Isaac was the one what talked Fred into coming to the Badlands once his enlistment was up. Fred didn't want a ranch, though. Instead, he came to Scenic and opened the only tannery in the area. He made a good living but stayed a bachelor until this past Christmas. That was when he surprised everyone by marrying Alice Ludlow, a widow from Interior with grown grandchildren.

"Fred's business is a little slow," Isaac said. "This drought's pinching everybody."

Now, I told myself, *tell him now about Mrs. Fills the Pipe.* I knew what to say. Earlier, when I was getting the little girls ready for bed, I had laid it out in my mind, but before I could get going on the words, Isaac said, "People in town are talking about the war. That and the drought."

I hesitated, then, "What're they saying?"

"That our troops are just now getting over there. Most are landing in France, some in England." Isaac shook his head. "Trenches. That's no way to fight a war. It was different in my day—we didn't have this new kind of war with machines, airplanes, and tanks and such. And this business of mustard gas. God, that's dirty. Our boys'll be all right though. They're fighters; they know what they're about."

"Isaac," I said. "Some Indians came by yesterday."

He tensed. "Was there trouble?"

"No. It was Mrs. Fills the Pipe and her family. You know who she is—she goes back and forth to the Rosebud."

Isaac shrugged his shoulders as if to say that all Indians were alike to him.

I said, "It was real hot yesterday, like you said. She looked washed out; she looked bad."

"So?"

"It worried me. I had Mary bring her up to the porch."

"The porch?"

"Her and her daughter. She looked so puny; it was so hot. Like you said. I gave her a little something—a biscuit—just a half of one. To revive her."

He stood up. Rounder yelped, the back of Isaac's rocker banging against the wall. "You let a squaw on my porch?"

I nodded.

"You fed her?"

I nodded.

"Goddamn it."

I winced.

"I won't have it. You hear me?"

My lips quivered.

"They're nothing but thieves, stealing and begging. I won't have it. I won't have them on my porch. You hear me?"

I tried to swallow.

"Do you?"

"Yes," I whispered. "I'm sorry."

He stepped away then, breathing hard. He went to the edge of the porch, his back to me. Rounder paced between the two of us, panting. Sickened, I sat still, hardly breathing, but my thoughts jumped and jittered. Forgive me, I wanted to say, please forgive me. I pinched back the words, though, keeping my lips pressed as he stood in the shadow. I heard him pulling air in through his nose. I imagined that I felt his anger—it was like a storm wrapped around him. I had let Indians on his porch. His porch. I had disobeyed him. He didn't want to forgive me; he wanted me to suffer over it. And then I was thinking, *Why, Isaac? Why do you hate them so much? The Indians were put down a long time ago. You have your land. They can't take it from you.*

"I'm sorry," I said again.

"You should be. Our children are doing without and you're

feeding Indians." He stepped down from the porch and walked off into the dark.

Sweat broke out on my forehead. Rounder whimpered, nosed my leg. A coyote—not all that far off—started up yipping and yowling. The baby kicked. I jerked and gripped the armrests. One by one, more coyotes joined in, their yammering echoing off the buttes, making it sound like there were hundreds of them.

I swore under my breath. I hated the Badlands. The words hissed through my mind. I hated it all—Indians, the ranch, the drought, what we'd done to Liz. I hated it. I wanted out.

The thought shocked me. *Don't think that way,* I told myself. It wasn't true. I didn't mean it, and then I thought I heard a cry from inside the house. I hurried in, Rounder with me, afraid that the children had heard me and Isaac. I stood listening in the girls' doorway and then in John's. Their breathing was slow and easy. They were asleep; they hadn't heard.

It is the drought, I told myself. It was wearing me down, Isaac too. He was forty-five years old; he wasn't a young man anymore. Five children and one more coming. The worry of caring for us was playing on his nerves. Mine too. No one could be in their right mind with so many worries.

I went to the parlor and lit a lamp, meaning to leave it there for Isaac. Doing that showed that I wanted things to be all right between us. I turned up the light. It caught on the glass doors of the narrow bookcase. I stopped. Inside the bookcase was Isaac's gold army insignia. A wash of sadness came over me. I put the lamp on top of the case.

We had been married a little over a week when Isaac unpinned the insignia from his army hat. It was July, but there was a nip in the air so we had a fair-sized fire going. We had just eaten supper and even though it was cloudy, it was still full light. Days were long in the Badlands, and dark didn't come until late. We sat cross-legged on the ground across from one another, the fire in the middle. We were tired, but in a good way. The two of us had spent the day building the walls of the barn with stacks of sod bricks.

"Don't want to lose it," Isaac said as he held the insignia in the palm of his hand. Ridges of new calluses were forming along the pads below his fingers. He looked at the insignia for a moment before rocking forward onto his knees and reaching around the fire to give it to me.

"It's so handsome," I said. It was two swords that crossed to make an *X*. "Your hat hardly looks right without it. You sure you don't want to wear it?"

"No. Those days are over."

The sadness in his voice surprised me. He looked past me like he was thinking about something from a long time ago. I held the insignia before me, turning it to make it glow in the firelight. Maybe he was sorry he'd quit the army. Maybe he wished he hadn't married me. I said, "What do the swords mean?"

"Means I served with the Ninth Cavalry in the United States Army."

"That's a proud thing."

"That's right."

"It's your favorite thing in the whole world, isn't it? The army."

He got up, took the insignia from me, and put it in one of the knapsacks in the wagon's bed. Then he came back to me and put out his hand. I reached for it and he pulled me to my feet. He ran a finger over my lips. "Right this very minute," he said, "you're my favorite thing."

We'd been married nine days and until then, Isaac hadn't said what he thought of me. I believed that I pleased him when we laid together under the wagon at night. But that didn't mean he'd keep me past a year. It didn't mean I was his favorite thing. I looked up at him, grateful. Then I stood on my toes and boldly slid my hands around the back of his neck. "You are too," I said.

In the parlor, I unlatched the glass door. Beside the insignia was a framed photograph. I couldn't remember when I last took the time to study it. I took it out, and even though I couldn't see it all that sharp, I knew every line and shadow in the picture. It was of Isaac, not yet eighteen, in his work uniform at Fort Robinson. It was the summer of 1890. He was sitting on horseback, his boots pointed up in the stirrups, the reins loose in his right hand, his left hand resting on the saddle horn. His shoulders, not as broad as they got to be, were held back, and he was squinting because the sun caught him full on. There was a half smile on his face like he couldn't keep from grinning even though army men weren't supposed to smile for a camera.

Isaac was thirty-one years old when I married him. He had done a lot of living long before I met him. I understood that Isaac told me only what he wanted me to know about his past. I supposed I did the same. When he talked about his army days, it was always of an adventure. One time, though, I heard something that made my blood run cold. It was the night when Fred Schuling stayed with us. Fred had just gotten out of the army and had been to Interior and Scenic, looking for a good place to start his tannery. It was April. Mary was almost seven months old and the dugout was just two little rooms: the narrow kitchen and our bedroom. We were having a warm spell, so Fred didn't mind sleeping in the barn loft. He had brought a bottle of whiskey, and him and Isaac passed it back and forth—wiping the neck clean each time—a few times during supper. At first, they talked about baseball at Fort Robinson and about the pitcher what took Isaac's place after his discharge. Then they talked about the officers and some of the enlisted men and what had become of them. After a while, Fred said something about the battle at Wounded Knee Creek.

"That ended them," he said. "They were stubborn cusses."

"It was the last of the warriors," Isaac said. "A sorry day." He handed the whiskey bottle back to Fred.

"Always wished I'd been there."

"No. You don't. It was the bloodiest thing I've ever seen." Isaac picked up his fork, put it back down. "The snow. God, I'll never forget that red snow."

The hair stood on my arms. Wounded Knee Creek wasn't all that far off from our homestead. Indians still lived there. I looked over at Mary. She was in her basket nearly asleep; her eyelids drooped. I said, "Did they kill a lot of soldiers?"

"The Ninth lost one good man," Fred said. "But the Seventh got there first. They took it on the chin."

"And the Indians?" I said to him. "Did you get them?"

"The newspapers called it a massacre."

I picked up Mary and held her to me. I never asked again.

I pressed the picture of the young Isaac to me before putting it back in the bookcase. To his way of thinking, it was one thing to let Indians drink from the well behind the barn. It was another thing to allow them on our porch. They were the enemy. I had forgotten that. It was wrong of me to go against Isaac.

I went to our bedroom and undressed. I sat down on our low-slung bed and wiped my feet with a rag, and that was when I remembered.

It was our first summer in the Badlands when the Indian woman showed up. The memory of her came to me as clear as if it had just happened. It was so clear that I recalled the color of her dress, a faded blue. On that day, Isaac was working a shovel up and down, chopping sod that we'd use to build the barn. I was loading the sod in the wagon. The wind was easy, but all of a sudden the hair on my neck stood up. I whipped around and there she was, a few yards off, come from nowhere, her belly filled with a baby. A little boy about four held on to her skirt.

"Isaac!" I said. I'd never seen an Indian before. He whirled around, alarmed by my cry. When he saw the woman, he buckled—he was that startled. "Isaac," I said again, all the more afraid.

He dropped the shovel and nearly ran to the woman. He took her elbow, she flinched, and he pulled her with him, and in doing so, knocked the little boy down. Isaac kept on pulling the woman down to the road, his steps long and angry, the woman barely keeping up, her single thick braid swinging as she tried to yank her arm away from him. I watched; the little boy did too, me and him too stunned to move.

The boy let out a little cry. That was when I took a closer look at him. "Lord," I said out loud. "You're a Negro." It was in his hair and in his lips. I went toward him and the boy drew into himself, scared, and I saw he had Indian in him too. That was in the color of his skin and in the sharpness of his nose. I must have come too close because somehow he got to his feet and took off running down to the Indian woman what was on the road now with Isaac. The two of them were arguing. I couldn't make out their words, but Isaac's back was rigid and once I thought he shook his finger in her face. She stood up to him, though; her back was straight and her head high. Suddenly Isaac gave her a push on the shoulder, and that upset me because she was so big with a baby. She stumbled, off balance. The push seemed to settle things, though. The woman gathered up her boy and helped him climb into her handcart. Then, like a horse, she pulled the cart and they moved slowly up the road.

I ran, my skirt held high, to Isaac, who stood on the road, his arms crossed, watching the woman and the boy as dust rose around them.

"Who is she?" I said, catching my breath.

"Agency squaw."

"What'd she want? And that boy, did you get a good look at him?"

Isaac shook his head and then started up the rise to where we had been cutting sod. I hurried to catch up. I didn't know what to think; I didn't know what to say. All at once, he stopped, and I nearly bumped into him. He looked back toward the woman and her boy as they plodded, the wheels of the cart creaking.

"She's looking for a handout," Isaac said. "Like they all do. Don't ever give them anything, Rachel. That's the first thing you need to know about Indians. They're like stray dogs. Once you give them a scrap, they never leave."

"I won't. But that boy, did you see his face?"

"No."

"He's got Negro in him."

A shadow crossed over his face and for a moment I thought his eyes darkened. I stepped back. My mouth went dry. I was alone in the Badlands with a man what I barely knew.

"I hate them," Isaac said. "I hate what they are, and I won't have them on my property."

I nodded, quick to agree, relieved that it was the squaw what caused the darkness in his eyes and not me. I glanced back at the woman and her boy on the road.

"Forget them," he snapped, heading back to where he'd dropped his shovel. "We have a barn to build."

We didn't say much to each other the rest of that day. Isaac wore a broody look and I did my best to work hard, not wanting to displease him. But from up on the rise while he chopped sod and I loaded it in the wagon, I watched from the corner of my eye as the woman made her way west along the road, one slow step at a time. Sometimes I lost sight of her and the child in those places where the road wound around a butte or dipped low into a depression. But they kept to the road and after a while they'd show up again. When I stopped work to start supper, her campfire didn't look to be more than a few miles off.

It was one night later when Isaac unpinned his army insignia. At the time, one thing didn't seem to have anything to do with the other. Now, though, I saw it different. I had Mrs. Fills the

Pipe's words about buffalo soldiers and Indian women fixed in my mind.

Sitting on the bed, I tucked the dusty rag under the mattress. With my hands, I lifted each leg up onto the mattress. My feet and ankles were swelled up and my skin felt too small to fit. I eased myself back on my elbows and then down onto the mattress and onto my side, the ticking crackling and shifting under me. My spine seemed to sigh with aches.

I ran my hand along the side of the bed where Isaac should be. I thought it likely that he'd rather sleep in the barn than come back to the house. I wondered how it would be between us in the morning, what we'd say to each other, if we'd say anything. Then my thoughts went back to that agency squaw and her half-breed boy. He'd be about eighteen. He was some man's son. Could be that man didn't know. Or if he did, he didn't care.

That was how it'd been in Louisiana. When I was a girl there, living in the quarters with my family at the Stockton sugarcane plantation, Willie Lee Short was a Negro child with light brown hair and skin that turned fair in the winter. He was Mr. Stockton's bastard—everybody knew it. Mr. Stockton couldn't keep from pestering Sally, Willie Lee's mama, and there wasn't a thing she could do about it other than leave and try to make her way somewhere else. Slave days were over, but that didn't mean much to Sally. Where could she go, a young woman alone with a child? Folks in the quarters shook their heads over her. They were sorry for her. They were just as sorry for Willie Lee, what was expected to help his mama in the fields but wasn't allowed to step foot in his daddy's house.

Miss Wilma, the oldest woman in the quarters, once said

that was because Mr. Stockton didn't want the fruit of his sin sitting in his parlor.

Now, the thought stunned me. A sudden stabbing ache pierced my heart and I felt my insides give way. I squeezed my eyes tight. Not Isaac, I told myself. Not Isaac. Not that.

9

IDA B. WELLS-BARNETT

It was the next day when the wind died all at once. The sudden quiet startled me—the hushed stillness was a sound all of its own. Me and Liz had been scraping burned spots from baking pans when it happened. The quiet came on so quickly that my hands kept working even though I leaned toward the kitchen window, unsure what could be big enough to stop the wind.

"Mama," Alise said from under the kitchen table. She and Emma held their rag dolls. "Mama, listen."

There was nothing—no howling, no whistling around the corners of the house, no rattling prairie grasses. We went to the porch. Everywhere, dried bushes of tumbleweed had come to a stop in wide, open places. A turkey vulture, on the ground by the porch, stood stunned as if it had fallen from the sky. The few leaves left on the cottonwood dangled lifeless.

"What is it, Mama?" Liz said.

I went to the edge of the porch. The clouds were flat and stretched out, and along their bottom edges there was a faint orange glow. Isaac had said there was rain in the Black Hills. Maybe he was right; maybe it was coming this way. I shaded my eyes. The sun was as brassy as ever.

"Weather," I said to the girls, fighting down a wave of hope. "'Just weather."

I went to the side porch and stepped down, startling the vulture. It hopped a few steps, its bold black eyes watching me. I hated vultures, and I clapped my hands to get rid of it. Giving me one last hard look, it stretched its wings, stuck out its breast, and beat the still air. It gave a skip and then took off, but only to the barn. It landed on the roof and looked back at me. My skin prickled.

The air was steamy, and my face was damp around the sides of my hair kerchief. Jerseybell, tethered in a patch of shade thrown by the house, moved her head slowly from side to side trying to shake away the flies. Slobber hung in thick strings from her mouth. I looked north. The sky was clear that way.

That was where Isaac was, and I was glad for it. It was better to have him gone than to face the uneasy feeling that stretched between us. We hadn't had much to say to each other. Both of us, I believed, were still smarting from Mrs. Fills the Pipe's visit. When I woke up that morning, Isaac was sitting on his side of the bed, his back to me as he pulled on his boots. I watched him, the ache in my heart coming back fresh. I saw Isaac in a new way. He was a man what hated Indians, and yet I believed he had laid with a squaw. He was a man what had turned his back on a child I believed might be his. There was all this and still he was Isaac DuPree. My husband. I reached out and put my fingertips on his back.

He tensed for a moment and then went back to his boots, grunting some as he worked the left one over his foot. "I'm moving cattle first thing, taking them some feed too," he said. He didn't look at me. "John and Mary'll help. We'll need a packed dinner."

That meant Isaac was taking all four horses and the wagon. It also meant he'd be gone all day.

"All right."

That was all we said.

On the porch, I looked north once again where the White River still had a trickle of water. I scanned the sky. It felt like a storm—the air was thick as if it held rain. I lifted my arms a little, my sides sticky. It might have felt like a storm, but that didn't mean anything. The weather liked to tease. I remembered times when big splinters of lightning split open the sky, making the ground shake and roll from the thunder, sending the children crying to me. Curtains of rain would surround the ranch, and yet not a drop would come our way. Other times it would rain for days on end, making me and Isaac fret about the crops and root rot. Then from out of nowhere, right in the middle of a downpour, the sun would show itself, lifting our spirits, making us think that the crops might just be all right after all. But it would keep on raining, us worrying about rot, the sky bright with a rainbow.

All the same, the orange-tinted clouds off to the west raised my hopes. "Come on," I said to the girls. "Those pans aren't cleaning themselves."

Back in the kitchen, me and Liz finished scraping the bread pans. I put some beans in my small pot to soak in the littlest amount of water possible. From the window, I saw how a shimmering haze had risen up from the earth, reminding me of Louisiana swamplands. I got a pot of mush going, and it didn't take long before the hot cookstove turned the kitchen small and close. My feet swelled up, and I had to use the bootjack to get my boots off. The skin on my swollen toes had a peculiar shine to it, and that unsettled me. Horseflies found their way in through the open front door, and the girls got to crying from the bites that made their skin rise up into welts. I lit three smudge pots, and that helped drive the flies back some.

All that and I couldn't keep from thinking about Isaac. I had aimed for a man with ambition, and I had gotten him. I had been willing to strike a bargain: a hundred and sixty acres for a chance to be his wife for a year. That year slid into fourteen. It happened because I closed my mind to the idea that an ambitious man cared mostly about what he wanted. I helped Isaac get his land, and I helped him keep it. Like putting Liz in the well; I was a part of that too. But Isaac wasn't the only one what wanted something. I did too. Our children. Our wood house. Isaac himself. I had gotten what I had bargained for. It was too late to wish it had come about a different way.

I stirred the mush and poured a few teaspoons of water in it to keep it from sticking. I looked out the window. The clouds still glowed orange, but that wasn't good enough. They needed to be dark. The whole sky needed to be black.

The water that Isaac brought home yesterday from Scenic was getting used up fast. Maybe he'd bring some back from the White River. Or maybe the cattle would drink the river dry, leaving nothing for us. Liz was in the parlor wiping dust from the windowsill. I wondered if she was worrying and hoping for rain the same way I was.

I snapped my dishcloth at the flies crawling over the countertop.

All at once a pushed-away memory rose up in my mind. I stared out the kitchen window as the memory took shape. The squaw and her half-breed boy came back the day after Isaac had sent them away. I had nearly forgotten that. When Isaac saw her coming back on the road, heading our way, he told me to stay by the barn. Cursing to himself, he got something from his knapsack—I couldn't see what—but I saw the tight-pressed look on his face. Without another word, he went to meet her, and that scared me. I gripped the shovel with both hands and watched. Something was said; I couldn't hear what. But not long after, she turned around and walked off, pulling her handcart with the boy sitting in it. I was so relieved that tears came to my eyes. I never saw her again. Or the boy. But six weeks later when Isaac bought his first head of cattle, he brought home only eighteen. That surprised me. On our train trip from Chicago to Interior he had talked about buying twenty, his eyes lit up just from the telling of it. Anything less, he had told me as we sat side by side on our cushioned train seats, would make him look like a greenhorn.

"What happened to the other two?" I had asked Isaac when he brought the herd home.

"Cost more than I figured," he said, not meeting my eyes. I thought he was ashamed. I believed he was worried that I might think less of him, that I'd think he wasn't a real rancher. I looked at my gold wedding band. That was where the money had gone. I took it off. "Here," I said, holding it out.

"No. Put it back on. No wife of mine goes bare handed."

I snapped my kitchen towel again at a cluster of flies, my wedding band flashing.

Isaac had given money to that squaw. That was what was in his knapsack; that was how he got rid of her. At the time I didn't let myself think about it. Now it made me sick.

Under the kitchen table, Alise chattered as she played with her rag doll. Nearby, Emma was on her side, her thumb in her mouth, half asleep but fighting to keep her eyes open so she could watch her sister. Earlier she had been fussy, her gums suddenly sore and bright pink from teething. To ease her hurt, I had given her a teaspoon of children's soothing syrup.

What else could Isaac have done? Take the squaw in? Have her live in the barn? Or take just the boy and expect me to raise him? *Don't think about it,* I told myself. It happened a long time ago, long before Isaac knew me. Think about something else.

I wiped the sweat from my forehead, then sifted flour for soda biscuits. In a few months, I'd be grateful for the oven's heat. A nervous chill swept through me. In a month, there'd be nothing to cook.

Don't think about winter, either. Put your mind on your soda biscuits. Resolving to do that, I measured out the baking soda, the sugar, and the salt with measuring spoons instead of guessing. I spooned the batter onto the baking sheet, paying special mind to make sure that each biscuit would turn out the same size. I spaced them just right. I did all this as if I were new to cooking, as if I had not been cooking since I was six, Liz's age.

How many biscuits, I asked myself, *do you suppose you've made? Hundreds? No, more than that. More like thousands.* I'd probably made that many cookies too. Before the drought set in so hard, every Saturday I made two batches of cookies. I did that to please Isaac. He had a sweet tooth.

He got that from his mother. Mrs. DuPree loved her sweets. And didn't it show, Trudy the housemaid was prone to pointing out. I could fill my kitchen clear to the ceiling with the cookies I used to bake at Mrs. DuPree's boardinghouse. There, I baked cookies with sugary white icing and cookies with big fat raisins. I made molasses cookies, lemon cookies, and oatmeal cookies. Sometimes they were for the boarders, but most times they were for Mrs. DuPree. At Christmas they were for her friends. Cakes too. I baked chocolate cakes with vanilla icing, and pound cakes with just enough brandy to bring out the flavor.

I licked my lips, tasting it all. I put the sheet of soda biscuits in the cookstove and checked the heat. I recalled another hot and sticky day when I had baked two devil's food cakes. I hadn't been working for Mrs. DuPree all that long, maybe four or five months. It was 1896. I had just turned eighteen, and I was talking to myself about how mean Mrs. DuPree was for not letting me open the kitchen window to catch a bit of air.

An open window meant flies, and even with the house closed up, the flies were thick that day. Of course, flies were nothing new in Chicago, especially as close to the slaughterhouse district as we were. But that day the flies were a personal insult to Mrs. DuPree. She was entertaining. Her literary club, the Circle of Eight, was meeting that afternoon in the parlor. This meeting, though, was not the usual book discussion followed by coffee and one of my fancy desserts. Far from it. Mrs. Ida B. Wells-Barnett, writer and owner of Chicago's Negro newspaper, was coming to talk about her recent travels to England.

As soon as the boarders had left that morning for work, I started in on making fresh bread and a spread of olives, nuts, and creamed cheese for tea sandwiches. That finished, I baked the Circle of Eight's favorite: two devil's food cakes, chocolate rich, with sprinkles of coconut on top. I was starting to ice the cakes when I heard Mrs. DuPree in the dining room just outside the kitchen door. She was talking to Trudy.

"Flies," Mrs. DuPree said. "They're the bane of my life. Today of all days. Why me?"

"Flies are the devil himself," Trudy said.

Mrs. DuPree clicked her tongue in a disapproving way. Then, "Of all days. Trudy, I'm warning you. Do not let go of that fan, I don't care how tired your arms get. I don't want the first fly to even think about landing on Mrs. Barnett. Or on her plate. Do you understand me?"

"Yes, ma'am."

"I want it so the ladies see nothing but a wicker leaf fan floating in the air, keeping the flies off, keeping us cool. Do not even let us get close to perspiring."

"Perspiring?" Trudy stumbled over the word.

There was another disapproving click of the tongue. "Sweating."

This was my chance. I went to the kitchen door. "Mrs. Du-Pree, I'll do the fanning. My arms are good and strong."

"Your place is in the kitchen."

I knew that, but that didn't stop the disappointment. There was nothing more in this world that I wanted than to meet Ida B. Wells-Barnett. I admired her; every Negro alive admired her. Her newspaper columns were bold and blunt, and she wasn't scared of anybody. Whenever there was a lynching, even in the Deep South, Mrs. Wells-Barnett was the first one there, searching for the truth with her notebook and pen. That was why she had gone to England. In London she spoke out against lynching—she had said so in her newspaper. She wanted to embarrass the people of

America. She wanted to shame President Cleveland into punishing the killers.

If Mrs. Wells-Barnett could go to England, if she could face Southern white sheriffs, I could stand up to Mrs. DuPree.

"Please," I said. "Could I just say hello to her? Tell her how me and my family read the *Conservator* every Sunday after dinner? Please, ma'am?"

"Most certainly not. Mrs. Barnett has been invited to speak to the Circle of Eight. She does not expect to mingle with the help."

That stung.

Later that day, Rose Douglas, Mrs. DuPree's cousin on her mother's side, arrived first. Rose wasn't a member of the Circle of Eight. Her husband was an uneducated bricklayer. On special occasions, though, Mrs. DuPree invited her to help serve. It was her way, Mrs. DuPree once told me, of allowing Rose to stay in touch with the finer things in life.

"Rose married down, darker too," Mrs. DuPree had told me then. "Jim Douglas was nothing but a field hand fresh off the train from some plantation in South Carolina. He came here looking for a job; he had heard men were needed to build the World's Fair. My aunt nearly died from the shame of it when Rose married him." Mrs. DuPree sniffed. "I don't even want to think how Rose met him." Then she turned her eye on me and I could see what she was thinking. I was from a plantation. I was from the South. Worst of all, I was dark.

She said, "Your father . . . didn't you say he came out of the fields? In Mississippi?"

I wanted to tell her that my mother had once been a housemaid. I wanted to say that my mother could read and write, and that my mother did not think she had married down when she married my father. Instead, I had said, "Louisiana. We're from Louisiana."

The Circle of Eight ladies arrived a few minutes early that day; most of them brought their mothers, aunts, or daughters as invited guests. Mrs. DuPree's friends, members of Chicago's high Negro society, were at least four generations removed from slavery. They were smooth and their voices were like music. Their gloved hands fluttered while they made parlor-room talk. Some of them had gone to what Mrs. DuPree called finishing schools. The ladies were proud of their husbands what were doctors, lawyers, or merchants. They were a cut above the rest of us, and I had overheard enough to know that the ladies didn't approve of Southern Negroes. Southern Negroes' grammar left something to be desired, and they shuffled their feet and bobbed their heads when in the presence of white people. The ladies did not appreciate Southern Negroes coming to Chicago and embarrassing them this way. But since they were there—and the ladies really wished they weren't—it was their responsibility to set an uplifting example.

And that, I couldn't help but think as I trimmed the crusts from the tea sandwiches, was the funny thing about today's guest of honor. Ida B. Wells-Barnett had been born a slave in Mississippi.

I kept the kitchen door half open so I could listen and watch the Circle of Eight. It was a strain; the dining room was between me and the parlor. But if I stood just so, I caught a glance now and then of the ladies in their crisp white blouses with pleated sleeves puffed high at the shoulders and lacy collars that held their necks tall. Wide satin sashes, every color of the rainbow, showed off their waistlines pulled tight by corsets. Their dark skirts flared from their hips. Petticoats rustled when they walked. The ladies wore brooches pinned to their collars. Earrings of colored crystal beads dangled from their ears. Their broad-brimmed hats dipped, throwing shadows on their faces. Their maids, I knew, had worked hard to make the ladies look that good.

I couldn't imagine wearing fancy clothes on a Tuesday afternoon. I didn't even have anything half as fine for Sundays. I put a hand on my collar. No brooch for me. Instead I had on the black dress with the starched white apron that Mrs. DuPree made me wear when special guests came. Trudy liked wearing hers. She was proud of it and especially liked how the apron strings made a crisp bow in the back. But I thought it was the kind of dress you'd expect to wear if you worked for a white woman.

In the parlor the ladies talked, their voices high with excitement. I tiptoed into the dining room, stood close to a side wall, and peeked out. There was Trudy, standing to the side of the sofa, waving the fan, her face wet with sweat. Some of the younger women circled around the room looking out the windows, unable to sit still for more than a minute. They were as excited as I was about Ida B. Wells-Barnett.

"I just don't know what to call her," Mrs. Fradin said. Her husband was a lawyer and had an office on the edge of downtown. Mrs. Fradin snapped open a fan. On it a picture of a pasty white woman with slanted eyes dressed in a long black narrow dress flashed before Mrs. Fradin's coppery round face. "Should we call her Miss Wells, or is it Mrs. Wells-Barnett? Or Mrs. Barnett? I've heard it all three ways."

"She's a married woman with two babies," Mrs. DuPree said. "I'm calling her Mrs. Barnett."

"Yes, but her columns say Ida B. Wells. They wouldn't say that, would they, if she didn't approve? She's the owner, after all, she and her husband." Mrs. Fradin's free hand played with her earring. "I wonder what he thinks about this business with her name?"

"When I sent her my invitation," Mrs. DuPree said, "I addressed her as Mrs. Barnett. She's a married woman and that's her name."

Rebecca Hall said, "I do believe that she prefers Mrs. Wells-Barnett. With a hyphen." She leaned back in the black love seat. "Wells-Barnett is so modern. Don't you agree, Mother?"

Eve Hall raised her eyebrows. "I most certainly do not. I'm proud to be Mrs. Wilbur Hall, and someday, young lady, you'll be proud to take your husband's name."

I saw Mrs. DuPree frowning at me. I went back into the kitchen. Seemed to me that being modern didn't have a thing to do with it. Ida B. Wells-Barnett had to keep her maiden name when she got married three years ago. If she had changed it, folks would feel like they didn't know her. They'd worry that she wouldn't speak her mind anymore. They'd say that marriage and motherhood had turned her soft.

A little past three she arrived, and then I was tearing around the kitchen pouring coffee into the polished silver urn and arranging tea sandwiches on Mrs. DuPree's white scallop-edged platter. Rose Douglas hurried into the kitchen and hurried back out with the coffee urn. A minute later she was back for the tea sandwiches.

"Mrs. Douglas, let me carry that for you," I said. "You're wearing yourself out."

Sweat beaded Rose Douglas's forehead, dampening a row of pressed curls. I gave her a handkerchief; she dabbed at her neck and face.

"I don't know," she said. "Elizabeth said you weren't to—"

But I was already past Rose Douglas, the platter held high. I didn't care if Mrs. DuPree fired me. I was not going to miss the chance to see the world-famous Ida B. Wells-Barnett.

I put the platter on the dining-room table. The ladies were talking, but I couldn't make out any words, my ears were ringing so loud. I took a deep breath and went into the parlor. The ladies were a blur of hats and white blouses.

I swallowed. Then I saw her.

Mrs. Wells-Barnett was plainer than the Circle of Eight ladies. Her navy skirt wasn't as full as the other ladies'. Her cream blouse was simple, with few lacy frills, and she didn't wear a brooch. Her brimless hat had only one feather. She was round, and her skin was as black as mine.

My heart pounding, I looked right at Mrs. Wells-Barnett and curtsied. "Refreshments are served," I said in my best voice.

From the corner of my eye I saw Mrs. DuPree. She was reared back in her chair, glaring and warning me off with several quick shakes of her head. I ignored her.

"Why, honey, thank you," Mrs. Wells-Barnett said to me. She talked Southern, like my parents. "That is so good of you. And here we are, enjoying ourselves while you," she turned toward Trudy, "while you both are working so hard."

I curtsied again, and Trudy bobbed, her fan dipping with her.

"No need to curtsy me," Mrs. Wells-Barnett said. "I'm not royalty—wouldn't want to be." She held up her teacup. "There's more African blood than white in my veins." She paused. "Obviously."

I drew in my breath. Somebody made a sharp, gasping sound. Mrs. Wells-Barnett's eyes smiled at me as she drank some tea. I raised my chin, a chill running along my spine. For the first time I was proud of my black skin.

"Rachel," Mrs. DuPree said, her voice hard. I flinched and then hurried back into the kitchen, the door closing behind me. There, I did a little two-step dance. Nothing Mrs. DuPree said or did was going to ruin what had just happened. Ida B. Wells-Barnett had looked me right in the eye and thanked me like I was somebody important.

I heard what Mrs. Wells-Barnett really said behind her words: I know what it's like to be a maid. That's what she meant when she told me not to curtsy. I know how it feels when other people think you don't count for much. Put your chin up, Rachel Reeves. Change their minds. Show them what you're made of.

"I will," I said out loud in the empty kitchen. "I'll make you proud. You'll see."

Not that it'd be easy. Changing people's minds never was. Especially people like Mrs. DuPree and the Circle of Eight ladies. But it could not have been easy for Mrs. Wells-Barnett. Her parents had died when she was sixteen, leaving her with five little brothers and sisters to rear. But she did all that and got an education too, good enough to be a newspaper lady. Mrs. DuPree was always saying education was the key to advancement for the Negro race. Maybe she was right, even if I didn't care to admit that anything Mrs. DuPree said might be true. Ida B. Wells-Barnett was a living example of what a woman—a Negro woman—could be.

Then and there, I vowed to do better. It was too late to go back to school; I had quit five years ago. But I could still improve my mind. That very night, I decided, as soon as the supper dishes were washed up, I'd ask Mrs. DuPree if I could borrow one of the books she kept locked in the parlor bookcase. That was, if she didn't fire me. But if she said yes, I'd read two pages—no, five pages—every night, no matter how tired I was. And I wouldn't quit just because I didn't know all the words. I'd ask my mother and Sue to help me. If they didn't know the words, I'd just have to ask Mrs. DuPree.

I'd start saving my money too. After all, everyone knew a person couldn't get ahead without a little savings. That'd mean no more Saturday evenings at the Peppermint Parlor. My spirits drooped. The Peppermint Parlor was something to look forward to every week, that and church on Sunday mornings. Thinking about the Peppermint Parlor made getting out of bed on Monday mornings easier. It was where I went with friends for ice cream; it was where men courted young women.

I could still go, I decided, if I settled for an iced drink instead of an ice cream soda. That saved money. Of course, I gave half of my wages to Dad—that was only fair. And some went in the church collection basket. But I didn't have to have fancy buttons for my dresses, and I didn't have to have a new pair of gloves every winter. I'd save for my future instead. Like Ida B. Wells-Barnett must have.

And men? Mrs. Wells-Barnett was over thirty when she got married. She might have been born a slave, but that didn't mean she kept her sights low. She married a newspaperman. She waited for a man of proven ambition. I didn't know where I'd meet such a man, but if Mrs. Wells-Barnett managed to do it, so could I.

The clock in the parlor chimed four times. Time to start supper.

I was cutting up chicken parts to fry when the ladies applauded. Rose Douglas banged into the kitchen door with the empty urn. "More coffee," she said. "And it's time to serve the cake."

"Isn't she something?" I said, wiping my hands on a damp washrag.

"I'll say. She's certainly no lady."

I stared.

"Embarrassed Elizabeth something awful. Told her her name is Mrs. Wells-Barnett. Of all the gall, treating her hostess like that."

I turned away to hide my smile.

"That was just the beginning. She'd hardly sat down when she saw Mr. Booker T. Washington's photograph on the mantel. She looked right at Elizabeth and said, 'That man has sold out the black race, bowing and scraping to the white man.' I thought Elizabeth was going to strangle her. And she didn't say anything about sightseeing in England, not even when we asked her about Buckingham Palace and Westminster Abbey. All she talked about were lynchings, how we need to organize protest rallies, stop being so mealy-mouthed like Booker T. Washington. Then she passed around a picture of this colored boy hanging from a tree, his neck all twisted. It turned my stomach. He'd been set on fire."

Rose Douglas picked up the coffee urn. "Hurry up with that cake. The sooner we eat, the sooner we can get that woman out of here." She backed out of the kitchen with the urn.

Her standing up to the Circle of Eight made me admire Mrs. Wells-Barnett all the more. It pleased me that she had shocked them. They should have known better. If they'd been reading her columns, they would have known what kind of woman she was.

I scooted the chicken fryers to the side, waved off a scattering of flies, and wiped my hands again. I sliced the cakes, making sure that the servings were the same size. I arranged each slice just so on the china dessert plates, knowing Mrs. DuPree would notice if I got it wrong. From the icebox I got out the wooden container of vanilla ice cream and scooped one dip for each slice of cake. Rose Douglas hurried in and out of the kitchen with the tray, doing her best to serve the desserts before the ice cream melted.

I wiped my neck and face with a dish towel, then flapped it at the flies crawling on the bloody chicken parts. What I would give to see Mrs. Wells-Barnett one more time.

I looked out the back window, wishing I was in the parlor sitting right next to her. Outside, Peaches Orwell from two doors down was walking her baby in the alley, carrying her on her hip, trying to get her to stop fussing. Peaches had a tight look on her face, and I didn't blame her. Lily cried all the time. Ignoring her didn't stop her, and giving her attention just gave her more reason to cry. Lily was a baby born to scream.

A train on the elevated tracks a few blocks over thundered past, rattling the kitchen walls and blocking out the baby's cries.

Mrs. Wells-Barnett had sure cooked her goose. She wouldn't be getting any more invitations from Mrs. DuPree, not if she didn't see eye to eye with her over Booker T. Washington. Mrs. DuPree thought he was a living example of a self-made man what had overcome the shameful obstacle of being the son of common slaves. He was a college president, and for Mrs. DuPree that was almost as good as being a man of medicine. Then too, she approved of his views. She liked how he encouraged Negroes to be clean, go to school, and learn a trade like bricklaying or carpentry.

"You'd do well to remember that," Mrs. DuPree had told the boarders more than once.

Baby Lily shrieked right in my ear. I jumped, nearly dropping a bread pan. It wasn't Baby Lily, and I wasn't in Chicago. It was my two-year-old Emma screaming, sitting next to the cookstove, her legs ramrod stiff out before her, her face balled up tight with pain.

I tried to reach for her but my big belly was in the way. I dropped to my knees, ignoring the pain that shot through me. I grabbed Emma's arms to pull her to me. She jerked away and screamed louder, flapping her right hand high in the air. I caught her arm; her palm was slashed with red streaks. White blisters bubbled to the surface on her fingers.

The cast-iron cookstove. Emma had put her hand on it.

I got myself up. I dipped a rag in the water bucket and got back down on the floor. Emma arched her back, screaming, and kicked at me. I heard a funny yelp. Alise sat wide-eyed under the table, staring in horror. I pinned Emma to the floor, half lying on her. I wrapped the wet rag around her burned hand. She screamed louder, flinging the rag.

"Liz!" I hollered. "The blue compound." I looked over my shoulder. Liz stood frozen by the table. Emma bucked and shrieked with pain.

"The blue compound," I hollered again at Liz, jerking my head at the cupboard.

Liz's hands fluttered but she couldn't get her feet moving, and it wouldn't have mattered if she had. The compound was on the top shelf. I got to my feet, Emma's screams tearing at my nerves.

By now all three girls were crying. "Stop it," I snapped at Liz and Alise. "Right now!" I got the compound and the soothing syrup. I got myself back down on the floor, held up Emma's head, and between screams, poured syrup in her open mouth. She sputtered and spit.

She buckled then and fell back, her head thumping on the floor. Pinning her down, I grasped her wrist. I dabbed ointment on her blistering palm.

Emma screamed again; I got a little more syrup down her. Then, because it looked like Liz and Alise were working up to having another good cry, I gave them each a sip of the syrup. Waiting for the compound to deaden the pain, we sat on the floor, me rocking Emma while she cried, her hand curled up close to her chest. Liz and Alise huddled against my back. Sniffling, they wrapped their arms around my neck and shoulders.

"My handkerchief," I said to Liz. Just as she was reaching to pull it from my sleeve, a bitter stink filled the kitchen.

I slid Emma off my lap and onto the floor. She let out a wail. I got up, tears now running down my face. Grabbing the potholders, I pushed the pot of mush off the cookstove's burner.

Too late. The mush was burned and stuck to the bottom of the pot. Supper was ruined.

I stood over that pot and let myself cry. There were supplies for four weeks, and I had let some of it burn. I had let Emma burn her hand. I hadn't been watching; my mind had been wandering. Now the pan needed a hard scrubbing, Mary wasn't home to help, and I had to start over on supper. I cried all the harder. Liz and Alise had their arms around Emma, all of them making whimpering sounds, watching me. They weren't used to seeing me cry.

I wiped my face with a rag, ashamed of myself, a grown woman bawling like a baby. I said, "It's all right, girls, it's all right." They blinked back their tears, even Emma with her hurt hand tucked close to her. I wiped their faces. I got a fresh rag, wet it, and this time Emma let me wrap it around her hand.

"You're my good girl," I said. "Mama's brave girl."

Liz picked up the compound jar and the bottle of soothing syrup for me. It was a wonder, I thought, that the bottle hadn't overturned. I held it up. It was two-thirds full. Emma, I knew, was going to need more in a little while and again at bedtime.

"Come on out on the porch," I said to the girls. "It stinks in here, hot too. Can't hardly breathe. You can have your naps out there."

"I'm too big," Liz said.

I gave her a warning look. "Get the red blanket," I said.

I put the compound and the syrup on the shelf. On the label of the syrup bottle was a picture of a smiling white woman. Her lips were red and she wore a frilly blouse, just like Mrs. DuPree and the Circle of Eight ladies. The white woman's yellow hair was piled high and there wasn't a strand out of place. She has a maid, I thought. In one hand she held a bottle and in the other she had a big spoon filled with what I took to be the soothing syrup. She leaned toward her little boy. He had yellow curls like hers. He sat up against crisp, clean pillows. His round white arms rested on a turned-down blanket. He smiled up at his mother. He didn't look the least bit sick.

I looked over my shoulder. Alise and Emma weren't looking; they were studying Emma's wrapped hand. The white woman on the bottle didn't have the first worry. I picked it up and unscrewed the cap. I heard Liz coming down the hall with the blanket. I took a quick swallow. Then I took another. Just the taste of it on my tongue made me feel better. I'd get to the burned pot in a few minutes; supper wouldn't be all that late. I put the cap back on the bottle.

I gathered the girls, and we went outside to let our nerves settle.

10

JERSEYBELL

I sat in my porch rocker with Emma on my lap. It was hot, but I wanted her close. It was going to take a long time for her hand to heal, and even when it did, she'd likely have scars. *What kinds of stories,* I wondered, *will Emma tell about them.*

I rubbed her back, making big circles. She looked up at me and then put her head on my big belly, stuck her good thumb in her mouth, and held her burned hand close to her chest. Liz and Alise, on the red blanket, laid on their bellies with their heads propped up in their hands.

An easy breeze had come up. The high clouds overhead had a pink cast along the bottom, and off to the far west, they were dark. I couldn't let myself hope, though. The sun was as bright as ever, and to the north, there wasn't the first cloud.

"Which way's Daddy and the others?" Liz said.

I pointed northeast toward Vulture's Pinnacle. Liz and Alise strained their eyes. "Can't see them," Liz said.

"Maybe they're behind a table somewhere," I said.

Tall squares of flat-topped grass rose up everywhere in the Badlands. They put me in mind of sheet cake sliced perfect on all four sides. Isaac had laughed the first time I told him that. "I guess you could say that," he had said. "But out here we call them tables."

"How'd they come to be?" I said.

"Erosion."

I wasn't all that sure what the word meant, but it made me think about how the land in Louisiana ran in dark streams after a storm. I said, "It rains that hard?"

"Sometimes. But mostly it's the wind."

Rocking back and forth, I patted Emma's back. I lifted my chin, letting the breeze dry the sweat on my face.

"Tell us a story, Mama," Alise said, now lying flat on her back.

I didn't feel like telling a story. I just wanted to sit; I just wanted to be quiet with my girls close to me. The soothing syrup made me feel slow, and I didn't have it in me to think up a story. "No," I said. Then I thought about Mrs. Wells-Barnett. She would expect me to do better.

I said, "Liz, get the Longfellow book."

She acted as if she hadn't heard me. "Liz," I said, and this time she got up and went into the house to get the book.

The Longfellow book of poems had been Mrs. DuPree's gift when Mary was born. It was the first piece of mail we'd gotten from her even though Isaac wrote her a letter the third Sunday of every month. When the book came, surprising us both, Isaac said it was a peace offering. I didn't see it that way. The book was empty—no letter or signature on the title page. That was how all Mrs. DuPree's books came. They were just empty recognitions of the birth of each of our children.

It was me what wrote the child's name in each book. It was me, using my best Palmer penmanship, what wrote, *From your loving grandmother, Elizabeth DuPree.* If Isaac ever noticed that it wasn't his mother's hand, he never said the first word. Neither did I.

Liz brought the book to me and got back on the blanket. I opened it to "Hiawatha." It was a restful poem, not like "Paul Revere's Ride," that dashed with excitement all over the countryside. "Hiawatha" was a poem about a lake and forests of pine trees, a place different—better—than the Badlands. Then, too, it made me think about when I was a schoolgirl. I had recited the first part of "Hiawatha" at my eighth-grade commencement.

I began to read to the girls, one arm around Emma.

By the shores of Gitche Gumee,
By the shining Big-Sea-Water,
Stood the wigwam of Nokomis,
Daughter of the Moon, Nokomis.

Indians. I had picked a poem about Indians. I stopped. The girls looked at me, waiting. I read on.

Dark behind it rose the forest,
Rose the black and gloomy pine-trees,
Rose the firs with cones upon them;
Bright before it beat the water,
Beat the clear and sunny water,
Beat the shining Big-Sea-Water.

The sound of the words lulled me. The soothing syrup did too. Emma burning her hand, I told myself as I read the familiar words, was an accident. Accidents happened to children.

An accident was how our Isaac Two died. He had just turned five; it was February 27, 1911. On that particular day, spring came for the afternoon, melting the icicles that hung from the dugout's roof and turning the skin of snow on the ground to a slippery slush. Isaac had ridden off to the south pasture to check on the cows expected to calve come April. I was slow and headachy, but I wanted to hang the laundry outside. Mary, Isaac Two, and John played soldiers and Indians on a small outcrop of low rocks. They hid and ducked as they pointed their forefingers, pretending to shoot each other and making soft popping noises with their lips.

I had been watching; I always did. But it didn't matter. Isaac Two slipped and fell. A sharp point on a rock pierced his right temple, and he was dead before I could spit the clothespins from my mouth.

Three days later, Liz was born.

On their blanket, Liz and Alise looked more asleep than awake. Emma's eyes were closed. The wind had picked up, making the grasses ripple.

> At the door on summer evenings,
> Sat the little Hiawatha;
> Heard the whispering of the pine-trees,
> Heard the lapping of the waters,
> Sounds of music, words of wonder.

Accidents happened everywhere; I knew that. It wasn't just the Badlands, but it seemed to me that accidents and death were harder to bear here. When you lost a child, you wanted your family. In the Badlands, though, neighbors had to stand in. When

Isaac Two died, Isaac got the preacher from Interior, a white man not much over twenty. He didn't know what to do for me, so he read from the Bible, standing over me as I sat blank-eyed in my rocker. It was the neighbor women, Mindy McKee and Mabel Walker, what washed my face, fixed my hair, and dressed me. They did the same for Isaac Two. During the burial, they held on to my arms, keeping me on my feet. It was Mindy, with her red hair that always flashed in the sunlight, what saw I was in labor and stayed on to help with the birthing. It was Mabel, whose mouth was usually set in a frown, what came back after Liz was born and told me the new baby needed me more than the memory of Isaac Two did.

I was grateful to Mindy and Mabel; I'd always be. But when accidents happened, it was my mother what I most wanted.

The girls were asleep. I stopped reading. Off to the west, the darkening clouds rolled on top of each other like they were being chased by something bigger. The wind picked up. The sky glowed silver, and clouds were piling up in the north. A scattered flock of magpies blew past, pitching wildly, their hard-beating black wings sparkling in that sky's funny color.

The air smelled of dusty rain. Tumbleweed skittled past. The buttes shined pink. My heart began to beat fast with hope, the sluggishness in my arms and legs brought on by the soothing syrup suddenly gone.

I sat there watching the sky, waiting, the Longfellow book in one hand, my other arm around Emma. I knew that Isaac would be watching too. I hoped that he, Mary, John, and Rounder were heading home, doing their best to beat the storm that was surely going to break loose any time. I shook my head. *Don't get your hopes up,* I told myself. *Don't.* These clouds could pass, turn into nothing.

I rocked back and forth, the girls asleep, my eyes fixed on the clouds as the day's light turned dark.

If it rained, things would work out. If it rained, I'd put the Indian woman and the half-breed boy behind me. If it rained, things between me and Isaac would be like before. That was what I told myself.

The wind gusted. There was a chill in it. All at once, snakes of lightning etched the sky everywhere. I braced for the thunder. When it came, it started with a moaning rumble and then gathered itself, rumbling louder and louder until it cracked into a boom. The girls, startled awake, started to cry. I drew them to me.

"A storm," I said to them, my heart skipping. "A storm."

Raindrops, one at a time, hit the tin roof. Single drops pocked the white grit on the ground, making little craters. I lifted my face, closed my eyes, and waited, scared I'd run the rain off if I wanted it too much. A raindrop splashed on my cheek.

"Mama!" The wind had taken the red blanket, and it tumbled down toward the cottonwood. "Let it go," I said, and then I smiled.

Lightning darted across the sky and this time the crack of thunder made me jump. The girls yelped and then cried all the louder.

"Lord," I said, thinking how this was just like the Badlands to hit us hard when it finally rained. The rain began to come in earnest. "Lord," I said again, and this time it was praise. I slid Emma to her feet. "Come on," I said, all at once in a hurry. We went inside, the Longfellow book in my hand.

We gathered up all the washbasins, every pot and pan, anything I had that could hold water. I lined them up on the edge of the porch, the plinking of raindrops in them filling my heart with joy. Back inside, I wanted to sit at the parlor window and watch the prairie grasses come alive. I wanted to see the rain barrels overflow, and I wanted to see the wells fill up. I wished for Isaac so we could see it together. The Indian squaw and her boy, Isaac's anger about Mrs. Fills the Pipe, my hard feelings against the Badlands, Liz in the well, all of that was gone. The rain changed everything.

Lightning flashed. "Mama!" Hands pulled at me. "It's all right," I said. I looked out the kitchen window and my heart dropped. Jerseybell. She was staked to a wooden post on the side of the house, scared silly. Her neck was stretched as she pulled against her rope, wanting to break free. If there was any chance for milk, being out in this storm would put Jerseybell off for good. I had to get her in; I should have done it at the first sign of the storm. At least there weren't the horses to worry over. Isaac had taken all four.

The rain was harder. Thunder surrounded us with its crashes; lightning lit up the room and just as quick, left us in the gloom. "Just a storm," I told the crying girls. "We're all right, just a little thunder."

They held fast to my skirt. "Come on," I said, and I shuffled them to their bedroom. "Get under the bed."

"Why?" Alise said.

I gave them a little push. "Because I said so." They scurried under, Liz helping Emma, who kept her burned hand tucked against her chest. On their bellies, they peeked out at me, not blinking. "Don't move till I get back," I said.

More lightning flashed. "Mama!" they screamed.

"None of that. Liz, look after your sisters." I turned my back on them and left them under the bed crying. I had to. Jerseybell was our milk cow.

I put on my boots, my duster, and Isaac's broad-brimmed hat, the one he waxed with paraffin to keep out the rain. I tightened the stampede strings. Outside, the rain was cold and coming down hard. I couldn't button the coat over my belly, and it flapped wildly in the wind. Going out in this weather was foolish; I knew that. But nothing was going to stop me from getting Jerseybell to the barn.

The ground that had been so hard packed was already turning to mud. It pulled at my boots as I slogged my way to Jerseybell. Pain shot through my back, making me walk hunched over like an old woman. Jerseybell strained against her rope, twisting her head from side to side, her chin low to the ground. My wet hands slipped as I tried to untie the taut rope from the wooden stake. Poked-out nails ringed the top of the stake to keep Jerseybell from sliding the rope up and off. They stopped me from doing the same. I worked at the knot, sharp pain piercing my torn fingernail. The sky lit up with lightning. I could get struck dead. My girls would be left all alone under the bed until Isaac got home and found them. I worked harder at the knot, my nail bleeding, the rain in my eyes. The knot gave. I grabbed the rope and as I did, Jerseybell dragged me a few yards. I dug in my heels.

I tried to turn her toward the barn. Thunder rolled, shaking the ground. Wild-eyed, Jerseybell worked against me. She dragged me a few more feet.

"Jerseybell," I screamed above the storm. "This way, this way."

Streaks of lightning darted across the western sky. I flinched. Jerseybell bolted; the rope jerked from my hand. I reached to catch it. I slipped and fell on my swelled-up belly, the air whooshing out of me.

When I came to, I was on my side, the rain bearing down. I waited for my belly to seize up. It didn't. I pulled in some air, blew it back out. Still nothing. From somewhere far off, Jerseybell bellowed. I got myself up on my elbow. *It was just a little fall,* I told myself. *It didn't hurt the baby, it didn't hurt you. Now get up.* I stumbled from the weight of the wet duster, nearly falling again. Through the rain I saw Jerseybell dart, stop, and start, jerky, as she headed toward the cottonwood. *Get her,* I told myself. *Don't let her fall in the wash and break her neck.* We needed her milk. I began to move, the mud sucking at my boots.

Halfway to the cottonwood, Jerseybell stopped and bellowed. She turned around in a circle, her front feet churning in the mud. Lightning streaked the dark sky. She bolted again, this time to the barn. I hurried. It hurt to breathe, there was a stitch in my side. My coat flapped in the wind, the baby heavy in my belly.

Jerseybell rammed into the barn wall. She shuddered, and then stood still as if stunned, her sides heaving. I hurried, scared of falling again, the mud slowing me down.

She was still standing there when I got to her. I picked up her rope, heavy with mud. She let me lead her to the barn door. I opened it and took her to her stall. Shaking, I leaned against the stall railing. I wiped the rain from my eyes. I dripped mud. My knees throbbed. My back ached. I had fallen hard; I was fooling myself to say different. It didn't have to mean trouble, though, not bad trouble. I had fallen once with John, and nothing happened to him. But I hadn't been nearly as far along.

My legs wobbled. Jerseybell's breathing was labored, and she was hot to the touch. I was the same way. I wanted to sit and rest but couldn't, not with the little girls waiting for me. Bracing myself, I went back out into the storm.

I made my way up the rise in the heavy rain to the house. The mud was turning into a mush that oozed like quicksand. I slipped twice, landing on my knees, but the falls were slow and didn't hurt all that much. I told myself that I had done what needed doing. I had gotten Jerseybell in.

On the open porch, my arms almost too tired to do it, I took off my wet, mud-covered coat and hat and hung them on a wall nail. Before I had both boots off, my dress was soaked. The girls, I knew, were scared stiff. It was cold and my teeth chattered, but I stayed in the rain anyway. I took off my dress and let it fall on the porch floor in a muddy heap.

I stood on the porch in my underdress. I let the rain wash the mud from my legs and feet. I closed my eyes against the lightning. I raised my face. Rain. Sweet, sweet rain. The baby was all right; it had to be. I couldn't take it any other way. Mud ran from my hair. Rain, sweet rain. I began to cry. No more putting Liz in the well. No more going without water. We were saved.

I drank in more rain. Grit crunched in my teeth. The wind gusted. I shivered with a chill. Winter. Winter was coming. Don't think about it. God sent this rain to ease your worries. Now stand up and make the best of it. That was what my mother used to say.

The words gave me courage. I drew a ragged breath. I went inside then and saw to the girls.

The worst of the storm passed while I scrubbed the burned pot. The rain didn't stop though. It rained while I got a fresh pot of mush going and it rained when me and the girls sat down to eat. After supper, I got some water from one of the rain barrels, heated it on the cookstove, and put the girls in the washtub. I scrubbed their hair. I dug the dirt out from between their toes, and I got it out from under their fingernails. I washed their elbows and their ears. I scrubbed and scrubbed and they let me. The girls played— Liz too—laughing as their small hands patted the water. When I finished, I got some more fresh water and washed Emma's burned hand, even though this made her cry. Everybody sparkling clean, I put them to bed and read them a story. Then I went to the parlor and put a lantern in each of the two windows. There, sitting in one of the red upholstered chairs, I waited for the baby to kick, a sign that it was all right.

A watched pot never boils; that was something my mother always said. And the baby wasn't going to kick if that was all I thought about. I got up and started a fire in the potbelly stove to get the wet chill out of the house. The rain beat down on the tin roof, and that was a pleasing sound, but the ground had turned into a boggy gray sand. When it got that way a person could sink up to his ankles in it. I didn't see how Isaac could get everybody home. The horses couldn't make it. Neither could Mary and John; it'd wear them thin.

It worried me. There weren't any stars to guide them home. I hoped they had taken shelter in a calving pen. Or maybe, if they were lucky, the three of them had made it to the empty Walker house.

It was easy to get turned around in the Badlands. From time to time we heard stories about someone getting lost and wandering miles off track. Or worse. Last fall, Ralph Nelson, an old-timer who had lived in the Badlands for over thirty years, disappeared. He'd been searching for a handful of stray cattle. When he'd been gone over a week, his sons got worried. They put together a search party, and all of the men—Isaac too—had helped out. After three days of looking, they lost Ralph Nelson's track and gave up. They figured he was dead in the bottom of a canyon, his neck broken, his body picked over by vultures. They figured the same for his horse.

I told myself Isaac wouldn't take the chance, not with Mary and John. All the same, I had those lanterns burning in two windows.

The fire in the potbelly stove popped. My thoughts shifted to my parlor. It was my pride. I dusted it most every day and swept the scrap-rag carpet every Tuesday. The children knew better than to sit on the red upholstered chairs or to touch the bookcase, the writing table, or the clock. When I had company—Mindy McKee or Mabel Walker before she sold out and moved back home—I always invited them to the parlor for our visit. The parlor made me feel like a lady.

Most everything in it came from the ranches we had bought over the years. But the framed picture of President Lincoln that hung over the writing table had been Isaac's since he was a boy.

He admired the president. Mr. Lincoln not only set the slaves free but he also promised every freed man forty acres of farmland once the war was over. The president, Isaac believed, understood what land could do for the Negro race. He understood that land was an opportunity, that it made a man proud. Things would have been different, Isaac said, if Mr. Lincoln hadn't been shot dead.

Tacked beside the president's picture was a small yellowed drawing of Ida B. Wells-Barnett cut from a newspaper years ago. That was mine. Through the years I liked to think that she was proud of me for marrying a man with ambition. I liked to think that she was as proud of my wood house as I was. That night, though, as I sat alone in the parlor, it struck me that Ida B. Wells-Barnett might pity me. I lived in the Badlands, a country so backward and harsh that even Indians didn't want it.

All at once, my cheeks burned with shame. Three days ago I used my hand-painted rose platter to serve broken-up biscuits to Mrs. Fills the Pipe and her family. I gave her and Inez the last of the chokeberry tea. But none of that mattered. Mrs. Wells-Barnett would have served tea to Mrs. Fills the Pipe in the parlor, not on the porch.

She wouldn't have cared if doing that made her husband angry. She would have done it anyway. Mrs. Wells-Barnett would have asked Mrs. Fills the Pipe about those Indian women what had been used by the army men. She would have asked where those women were now, and she would have asked after the children.

It never entered my mind. Fourteen years ago it hadn't entered my mind either to worry about the Indian woman what had showed up with her half-breed boy. Or the child she was carrying. Instead, I put them out of my mind. Nothing was getting in the way of me making a home with Isaac.

Mrs. Wells-Barnett would say I'd been wrong.

A restlessness came over me and my teeth took to chattering. *Too late,* I thought, *to worry about what Mrs. Wells-Barnett would say. All that happened a long time ago. Put it out of your mind.* I got up to put a few more cow chips in the stove. The stove door stuck, and I had to pull on it a few times before it gave.

I sat back down, wishing the baby would kick. Even a little tap would be enough. I shifted a few times to find a way to take the ache from my back. I sat up straighter and told myself that helped.

I was proud of the parlor stove. It had four skinny curved legs and a long stovepipe that disappeared into the parlor ceiling. Every summer I took the pipe down and flushed it clear of ashes. I polished the stove to keep it a shiny black. It was mid-October of 1903 when the potbelly stove showed up at our door. That made it, I recalled, about three months after the Indian woman and her half-breed boy had walked up the rise. Me and Isaac had finished building the barn and the two-room dugout. The fireplace in the dugout's bedroom was small, and I was still cooking outside over an open fire. Mornings were so cold, and evenings too, that I had to wear gloves. That kind of cooking tested my patience, and it shamed me to serve my new husband biscuits that were burned on the bottom and mushy in the middle. The coffee didn't do right, either. It was either scorched or lukewarm; there was no in between. Isaac never complained. He thought it was good; he was used to army food. I told myself that it didn't matter. A cookstove could wait. We had spent all our money, I believed, on the cattle, horses, and a plow. So it took me aback when on a cool October day a wagon with two big crates in the bed came up the road. I was alone—Isaac was out in one of the pastures seeing to the cattle. I kept my eye on the wagon for a while, and then when I saw there were three white men sitting on the buckboard, I went inside the dugout. I watched the wagon from the one window in the front.

I didn't know what to do when the driver turned the two oxen from the road and brought the wagon up the rise to the dugout. After the wagon stopped, one of the men let out a shrill whistle. Behind the latched door, I held my breath. Three white men and one Negro woman.

"Anybody at home?" somebody called out.

Go away, I thought.

The man called again, this time louder. Isaac would expect me to see what these men wanted. He'd expect me to be able to take care of myself. I got a kitchen knife and put it in my apron pocket. I unlatched the door and stepped outside.

The men started when they saw me. They looked at each other, their eyebrows raised. "Well, well," the driver said.

I fingered the knife in my pocket. "What can I do for you?"

The driver gave a little snort. His face was lined, and the hair that stuck out from under his slouch hat was gray. His neck was thick, and I figured his arms were too, from the way his coat strained. One of his cheeks bulged. The two other men with him were younger and rail thin, their Adam's apples bobbing. The driver's sons, I figured. Their noses all sloped the same way.

The driver narrowed his eyes. "Heard there were Negroes

out here." He worked his mouth, leaned over the side toward me, and spat out some brown juice. It landed a few feet from me. It took everything I had to not run back into the dugout. He said, "Didn't expect to run across any today."

"Ain't that just like Anderson," one of the other men said, "not to tell us?"

"Yeah, that's Anderson for you," the driver said, not taking his eyes off of me. I lowered mine. He said, "You any relations to those other Negroes north of the Black Hills?"

I shook my head.

The wagon groaned as the driver shifted his weight. "My father served with the First Minnesota. At Gettysburg. Had his feet blown off."

I nodded, my mouth dry.

He waited, and I realized that he expected me to say something. I said to his chin, "I'm sorry."

He made a grunting sound, and I understood that he expected more from me. I swallowed. "I'm obliged to your father for his sacrifice. And to your mama." I paused and then looked right at him to show that I meant it. "And to you. I'm much obliged."

I lowered my eyes again, sweat running down my sides. I gripped the knife in my apron pocket. The buckboard creaked and somebody tapped his foot. At last the driver said, "I'm looking for someone by the name of Isaac DuPree. You know him?"

I nodded. "My husband."

"He a Negro too?"

What else would he be? "Yes."

"How'd a Negro come by this kind of money?"

I didn't know what he meant. A thick silence hung in the air.

Then the driver spat again, his spit landing farther away from my feet this time. "Come on, boys," he said. The men jumped down from the buckboard. I backed away, my hand searching for the dugout door, but they'd lost all interest in me. They sprang open the wagon's tailgate and, using rope and muscles, they hauled two crates to the ground. Sweating, they took off their coats and tossed them onto the buckboard. The younger men got crowbars from the wagon bed, and then they all set upon one of the crates, the boards cracking and screeching as they pried it open.

"Lord," I said, nearly forgetting how scared I was.

It was a cookstove, shining in the Dakota autumn sun. Not just any cookstove—it was a four-burner cookstove with a halo of raised ivy ringing the oven door.

The men tore open the other crate. Inside was a potbelly stove.

The driver said, "Where you want these?" I pointed to the dugout, and when I realized that he wanted to know exactly where, I hurried in and showed him the longest wall in the kitchen. "The cookstove goes right here," I said. Then I pointed to the bedroom, not wanting to go in there with the white men. "And the potbelly," I said. "It goes along the back wall in there."

I waited outside in the sun as the men worked the cookstove and then the potbelly through the door. *Isaac*, I thought. He didn't tell me; he kept this a secret. He wanted to surprise me. I wondered how he managed it. I always went to town with him on Saturdays. He must have placed the order at Len Anderson's store when I was in the back admiring all the bolts of fabric.

"You there," the driver called out to me. I went to the open doorway, my hand on the knife, scared all over again. He was rubbing the top of the cookstove with a clean rag. The other men stood off to the side. "Come here," the driver said to me. I took one step into the dugout. Without looking at me, he got down on his knees, opened and closed the door. He nodded, looking satisfied. "It's a Moore, same as the potbelly. Ain't cheap but none better. A man does right when he buys the best." He glanced over at the other two men. "Their mother's got one of these. It'll last you a lifetime. Probably your granddaughter'll be browning her biscuits in it someday."

He got up using the stove to help him. He turned to me. "You know anything about breaking in a new cookstove?"

I wanted to say that I did, just to keep from showing my ignorance. But I wanted the cookstove to work right. I wanted it to last for the granddaughter this man made mention of. I said, "No."

"Didn't think so." He worked his mouth. The bulge that had been in one cheek disappeared and then showed up in the other cheek. He said, "Keep a low fire going a couple days before cooking. Burn the rawness out. Same with the potbelly. Before it gets any colder, make yourself a few easy fires, not too hot, mind you."

"Yes," I said. "All right."

One of the sons along the wall crossed his arms. "Ma likes her stove as much as she likes us," he said.

"More," the other boy said, and they all three laughed loud and long like they had just told a joke. I smiled as if I understood, and then to my surprise, I found myself wanting to do something for these men what all at once looked to be better people than I first supposed. Without thinking I said, "You're welcome to stay for noon dinner. I've got some stew going outside. My husband'll be along any time."

The men suddenly tensed. Their eyes darted to one another. Without a word they tossed around the idea of sitting down to dinner with Negroes. My mouth went dry. I wanted to take back the offer. I had never fed white men before; I didn't know anything about how to do that. The driver shook his head slightly. The sons blew out some air. "Can't," the driver said. "Got to get over to Rapid by morning."

"Well, then, help yourself to the well by the barn," I said, much relieved. "There's a trough for the oxen."

"Appreciate that." The driver gave the stove one last wipe and stuffed the rag in his back pocket. Then he looked at me and put his hand to the narrow brim of his slouch hat. He tugged it into place and as he did, I imagined that he tipped his head to me.

As I remembered that day, sitting in my parlor, a strange thought from out of the blue came to me. That driver had it wrong. It wouldn't be my granddaughter baking biscuits in the cookstove. It'd be some white woman, somebody I didn't know. I saw it as clear as day: a white woman and her husband in my house picking over our belongings. At first these people would claim they'd come for curiosity's sake. They'd never want anything that once belonged to Negroes, especially the DuPrees, the Negroes what held themselves out as equal to whites. But after a while the man would note the sturdiness of our bed's headboard, and his wife would take a notion to run her finger around the circle of ivy on the cookstove's door. They'd see the potbelly stove; they'd admire its high shine. "It'd be a shame to let such things go

to waste," the woman would say to her husband, just like I had
when Isaac bought somebody's ranch.

Upset by the thought, I got up, opened the door to the porch,
and breathed in the cool air to clear my head. It was still raining.
Isaac, Mary, and John were out in this weather, cold, wet, and
hungry.

Isaac would never let strangers have our ranch. Not unless
he was dead. I closed the door, slamming it too hard.

Earlier I'd told myself that if it rained, everything would be
all right. I'd said I'd forget about buffalo soldiers and Indian
women. Now that it was raining, things would be better between
me and Isaac. We'd pull together; we'd get through the coming
winter. Supplies might be short, but I'd make them stretch. I'd
feed our children. I'd stand up and make the best of things. Like I
always had. Like Isaac expected.

I left one lantern burning in the parlor window. Taking the
other one, I went into the bedroom.

It was raining too hard to use the outhouse, so I used the
chamber pot. That was when I saw the blood. Not much, but
enough to scare me. I stuffed a rag in my drawers. The baby, I
realized with a shock, hadn't kicked all evening.

11

AL AND MINDY MCKEE

It was still raining the next day, and Isaac, Mary, and John weren't home. I thought the worst—they were lost, lightning had struck them dead, they had fallen in a wash and drowned in a fast-moving current. As the day wore on, I knew I had to go to Al McKee's to get help, but I kept putting it off. The McKees were about three miles away, and by horse it didn't take all that long. But Isaac had the horses and that meant walking. The girls couldn't do it. The slimy mud pulled like quicksand; they'd never stay upright. I'd have to leave them home, and that wasn't something I cared to think about.

I told myself that if Isaac and the older children weren't home by the time I finished scrubbing the laundry, I'd go then. Once that was all done, I decided to wait until after I had the laundry hung to dry in the kitchen. When that was all done, I said I'd wait until after Emma's afternoon nap.

She was still napping when Rounder, looking like someone else's dog, showed up. His black and white coat dripped with mud the color of long-dead fallen leaves and his fur was so slicked down that his legs looked like knobby sticks. His muzzle was as pointed as a fox's. Walking up the road were Isaac, Mary, and John. I nearly collapsed with relief.

If they hadn't been wet clear through and coated from top to bottom with mud, I would have thrown my arms around the three of them. I met them on the porch with towels and slices of soap. "Lord," I said, "look at you all."

"We're a sight, aren't we?" Isaac said.

"For sore eyes."

He had wiped the mud away from around his eyes. His skin there was drawn and bruised looking. Likely Isaac had half carried Mary and John home. All the same, he was smiling. The drought was over. He had been right all along. Things would work out.

"You two go wait in the dugout," I said to Isaac and John. "I'll heat up some water and Mary can wash up on the porch. Then it'll be your turn. I've got fresh clothes for you."

"Where're the horses, Daddy?" Alise said. "And the wagon?"

"At the McKees'."

The McKees'? At best, I had placed Isaac and the children at the deserted Walker place. "Go on, now," I said, and they did.

A little later the three of them were as fresh scrubbed and as close to dry as a person could be when it was still raining. Everything had a damp feeling. Even the inside of the house was soggy, with the two rows of wet laundry that hung along the back wall of the kitchen.

John plunked down at the kitchen table. "I'm hungry, Mama." Isaac and Mary sat down with him. So did Liz and Alise. Emma, just waking up from her nap, wandered out from the bedroom. Isaac patted his leg and then pulled her up. "What's this?" he said, looking at her wrapped hand.

Emma held it up. "Burned it, Daddy. See."

Isaac looked at me. "What happened?"

"It was an accident," I said. "She touched the cookstove. She's all right."

What else could I say? That my mind had been on the past? That I'd been thinking about Ida B. Wells-Barnett so I wouldn't have to think about the Indian woman and her half-breed boy?

"It was an accident," I said again. I spooned out pinto beans onto three plates.

Isaac picked up Emma's bandaged hand and studied it. "Well. That'll teach you to stay away from hot stoves."

I heard the blame in Isaac's voice. I should have been minding Emma. I was always to blame when something bad happened to the children. Six and a half years ago, I was the reason Isaac Two slipped on the rocks. I should have been watching. Eight years ago, I was the reason Baby Henry lived only an hour. Baby Henry was born too soon, and even though Isaac never said it, I could tell what he thought by the way he looked at me when we buried our baby boy. He thought there was something I could've done to stop the bleeding that had started the week before Baby Henry's birth. Maybe there was some kind of tea I could have drunk, or maybe I should've taken to my bed. But if there was such a tea, I didn't know about it. And a woman didn't rest for hours on end when she had three little children and no one else to mind them.

Like now. I was bleeding some—not nearly as much as with Baby Henry—but I couldn't just take to my bed, not even with Mary to help out. That was why I'd decided to keep still about Jerseybell and how I'd fallen and landed on my belly. Isaac didn't need to know.

I said, "You rode out the storm at the McKees' place?"

Isaac had a bite of beans, smiled his appreciation, and just like that, I knew he had forgiven me for Emma's hand. That was Isaac for you. He could, when it suited him, let go of something before it had a chance to turn into a hard grudge. Nothing, I understood, was going to get in the way of him being happy about the rain. I'd do the same. I smiled back at him.

He said, "It was Rounder that warned us early about the storm. He got skittish long before the wind picked up. Got to barking; he was nervous about getting home. Should have listened, but we still had some cows to move. By the time the clouds rolled in, it was too late. We were halfway between the McKees' and the Walkers' so we took a vote. The McKees won fair and square."

Mary said, "We got the horses in their barn just when it started to pour."

"I thought maybe you were out in that storm."

"You weren't worried, were you?" Isaac said.

I sat down at the table. "No."

"It got real dark, Mama," John said. "There was lightning everywhere. And thunder. Rained cats and dogs—that's what Mr. McKee called it."

Isaac said, "John and I expected to sleep out in their barn; their house is only the three rooms. But you know how Mindy is. There's plenty of room, she said, though I didn't see where. That is the most crowded house I've ever been in."

"There's a piano in the kitchen," John said. "They just got it."

"A piano?"

"Al won it in a poker game over in Deadwood," Isaac said.

"Mindy cleared a spot the width of a toothpick in front of the stove. That's where she put me. Mary slept under the kitchen table, Rounder on one side of her, Al's hound dog on the other. John bunked with their oldest boy."

"He's just a half-pint," John said, "but at least he's a boy."

"Nothing but boys at that place," Isaac said. "Good God, they're a tumble."

Mary rolled her eyes in agreement.

"Yeah," John said. "And right before bedtime, there was a bunch of loud thunder, and we were all sitting in the kitchen when this ball of fire came down the stovepipe. It was this big." His cupped hands showed the size of a popcorn ball. "It was shooting sparks clear across the room. You should've seen it. It went round and round the cookstove, sizzling and cracking just like this." He filled up his cheeks and made exploding sounds.

"Lord, John," I said.

"He's telling the honest truth," Mary said.

"You should have heard Rounder and Big Blue howl," John said. "The fireball went back up the pipe, sizzling and popping, sparks flying everywhere, and then it was gone."

"Gone?" Liz said.

"Gone."

Pleased with his story, John sopped up the last of his beans with a piece of bread.

Isaac said, "When I was in the army I heard about those fireballs. It's a bolt of lightning that runs down a piece of metal. I'll tell you what, it took awhile getting the children settled down after that. It was something else." He ran his fingers up and down one of Emma's short braids. "Al, Mindy, and I sat up through the biggest part of the storm. Been so long since it's rained, none of us wanted to miss it. It was a beaut of a storm."

"Yes," I said. I had nearly lost Jerseybell. I was bleeding. I had been worried sick about him and the children. But Isaac was right. The storm was a beaut.

"Daddy," Mary said, "you haven't forgotten, have you? About the letter?"

A shadow crossed Isaac's face and suddenly he looked tired again. He scraped his fork over his empty plate like he expected to find something more. He lowered his voice a notch. "There's a letter for you." My throat tightened. He said, "Al was in Interior; he picked it up for you. It's in my knapsack on the porch. John, go get it for your mother."

I swallowed past the lump forming in my throat. "Who's it from?"

"Looks like your sister's hand."

"Aunt Sue?" Liz said. "But it's not Christmas."

Mama, I thought. *Something has happened to Mama.* I got up and took Isaac's and John's empty dishes. Mary got up too. An unexpected letter, I believed, most likely carried sorrowful news. I put the dishes in a shallow pan of water. When John brought the letter to me, I didn't look at it. I put it in my apron pocket, ignoring the disappointed looks the children gave me. Isaac and I always read our letters when we were alone. That way we had time to mull over the news. That way we had time to decide what parts to read to the children and what wasn't meant for their ears.

Isaac said, "As soon as things dry out, I'll go back to the Mc-Kees' and bring home the wagon. Any sooner in this mud and the horses'll sink to their knees. I'll get your patch tilled and you can put in your fall garden." He tightened his arms around Emma for a moment and then put her down on the floor. He got up. There was work to do.

Isaac stepped close and put his hand on my arm. He whispered, "You all right? You don't look yourself."

My hand went to the letter in my pocket. "I don't know."

"I'll be in the barn," he said.

I nodded.

The rest of the day I found myself fiddling with the letter in my pocket. It was thick; more than a page or two. From time to time when nobody was looking, I studied the envelope. The handwriting was runny like it had gotten wet, but Isaac was right. It was from Sue.

That evening it stopped raining long enough for me and Isaac to sit on the porch. It was cool, and I had on my blue shawl. It had gotten dark early, and I couldn't do my mending. I didn't mind, though. It felt good to give my eyes a rest.

Isaac said, "Read Sue's letter yet?"

"Haven't had time."

"Maybe it's good news."

"Maybe."

"Want me to read it first?"

"No." I wasn't ready to know what was in it. I couldn't bear any hard news from home. To stop thinking about the letter, I said, "How are the McKees holding up with this drought?"

"About like us."

"You didn't tell them about Liz, did you?"

Isaac looked at me.

"About the well?"

"No." Isaac leaned forward and put his elbows on his knees. "I've got some news." He paused. "Al's joining the army."

"What?"

"That's right. Can hardly wait to get to the front lines. Figures he'll show the Germans what Americans are made of."

"But why?"

"He wants to do his part."

"But what about those three little boys of his?" I said. "And Mindy? He can't take off like that; he could be gone most of the winter."

"They'll be all right. She and the boys are going to her folks in Des Moines."

I sucked in some air. First Mabel Walker and now Mindy. Until she came back, that left me the only woman out here. I'd have to go five miles to Interior just to see another woman, and I didn't have anyone there that called me her friend. That left me with nothing but the Indian women what passed by on the road.

"Surprised me too," Isaac said. "Told Al I'd see to his cattle until he gets back from France. But he says that after the war he wants to give the Colorado Rockies a try. He's had it with the Badlands. This drought's made the decision easy for him." Isaac shook his head. "Hate to see them go. I'll miss them."

I slumped back in my chair. I hardly knew what to think. I couldn't imagine the Badlands without Mindy. She was my friend; I didn't know what I'd do without her. She had stood by me when Isaac Two died, and she had been with me when Alise was born.

I had done as much for her. I'd helped her when her boys were born. Once, when her middle boy, Will, had a fever so high that Mindy was sure he'd die, I sat up with her all through that long night. Together we kept cool, wet rags on Will until his fever broke and the glaze left his eyes. Usually every winter, about February, when Mindy didn't think she could stand her house a minute longer, Al brought her and the boys over for a visit. Me and her'd quilt for the day, the children playing around our feet. Every Independence Day in July we went to their place for a picnic. The Walkers came too. Me, Mindy, and Mabel put food out on a table while the men and the older children played baseball. When it got dark and everybody was filled up with potato salad and roasted chicken and German chocolate cake, the men built a big fire and we'd sit around it, our way of saluting the country's birth.

Mindy hadn't always been in the Badlands. Al had staked his claim during our second summer there. He was a boy then, just turned eighteen, but he was broad shouldered and his beard was thick. With a wink and an extra five dollars, he convinced the man at the land office that he was twenty-one. Isaac helped him build his dugout and then, three years later, his wood house. That was just before Al went home to Des Moines to visit his folks. When he came back to the Badlands in the spring, he brought his redheaded bride, the seventeen-year-old Mindy.

I took to her right off. I liked the way her green eyes came close to disappearing whenever she smiled, and I liked how she laughed over the least little thing. She didn't seem to care that me and Isaac were Negroes. The first time I met her she said how grateful she was that Isaac had helped Al build his house. She was happy to have me for her neighbor. Knowing I was nearby, she'd said, was a comfort. Al liked to roam, she said, and that was true. He had a tendency to disappear in the Black Hills for a few weeks at a time, sometimes longer. Al was living the wrong life, Mindy once told me when we were quilting. She laughed over it. He should have been a mountain man, not a rancher.

Now he wasn't either. He was going to be an army man. And I'd never see Mindy again.

"When?" I said to Isaac. "When are they leaving?"

"Mindy's going by the end of the week, Al a few days later."

So soon. I said, "They're coming by so I can say good-bye, aren't they?"

"Don't think so. I asked her to, but Mindy said she's not good with that kind of thing. Said she'll write as soon as they're settled in Iowa."

It was all I could do to keep from breaking down and crying. There was going to be nothing around me but falling-down ranch houses and miles of empty country. Not that I blamed Mindy; I'd do the same. I pictured how it'd go for her. On her last morning, ready to go, there wouldn't be anything left to do other than wash and pack the breakfast dishes. That done, she'd close the front door behind her and climb up on the wagon, where Al and the boys waited for her. They'd pull away from the house and Mindy wouldn't look back; that wasn't her way. At the depot in Interior, Mindy would kiss Al good-bye and tell him to give those Germans a piece of her mind. She'd board the train on the second call. She and the boys would wave good-bye to Al, their faces pressed flat against the window. After a while, when the boys got to fussing, Mindy would open her hamper and give them slices of buttered bread to quiet them down. They'd watch the countryside smooth out and turn green. Ranches would give way to farms until at last, the conductor would call out "Des Moines," and Mindy would cry from the gladness of being home again with family.

Isaac said, "Any other time, I'd buy his ranch outright. But until I can, and Al's agreed, I'm leasing grazing rights from him."

I didn't understand. We didn't have a red cent to our name. The short supplies Isaac brought home a few days ago showed that. My hands began to pat my swelled-up belly.

"When I go back for the horses," he said, "I'm going through the rest of Al's herd, see what I want before he takes them to market."

I was too stunned to say anything.

"It'll be tight," Isaac said, "but Al's got some good rangeland. And this is a chance to replace the cattle we've lost this summer. It'll get us back to where we were. I'm taking Al's bull. That animal's top-notch . . . smooth back, good-angled legs, easy disposition. I'll lease him out; he'll pay for himself in no time flat. Like he did for Al." He paused. "With a lot of hard work and a little luck, it'll be like this drought never happened."

I couldn't get any air. Isaac said, "The rain's turned our luck. You can put in your garden. I'll get the winter wheat planted. And here's something else. Al wants us to have that Deadwood piano. Maybe one of the children has your brother's knack for music."

There was less than four weeks' worth of supplies in the kitchen. The root cellar was bare. Winter was coming. I said, "How many cows are you buying? Along with this bull?"

Isaac rubbed his thumb across the tips of his fingers like he was counting, like he hadn't already thought it out. "A hundred or so. About half of them are settled. That'll be close to a hundred and fifty after calving season."

"A hundred? I thought we were nearly broke. I thought most of it went for Mabel Walker's place."

"I've got it all worked out."

"How?"

The air tensed. Since the day I'd married Isaac, I had never questioned his judgment. He always knew what to do; I even let him put Liz in the well. But not now. If there was money, it had to be for supplies, not grazing rights and more cattle.

"Please, Isaac," I said. "Tell me how you're going to pay for all this."

He didn't say anything; he just stared off toward Grindstone Butte. Finally he said, "Al's agreed to let me pay him next spring."

"Spring? Where's the money going to come from? And what about supplies?"

"What about them?"

"You only brought home four weeks' worth."

"We'll manage."

"I don't see how. Can't even count on having any cabbage and squash, not when we haven't planted yet."

"We'll be all right. I told you I've got it all worked out. The war, it's going to save us."

"The war?"

"Cattle prices are sure to shoot up. Even stringy beef will get a decent price."

"But what if it doesn't?"

"It will. It's driving up the price of gold too. Al McKee told me, and Fred Schuling's heard the same thing, that they need more men at the Homestake Mine, over in the Black Hills. I'm going to see about hiring on for the winter."

My hand found the letter in my pocket. I gripped it like it was Sue's hand I was holding.

"I'll leave mid-November. I'll be back before calving season. Fred said he'll come by whenever he can."

The porch floor tilted; I was dizzy with disbelief. "I don't understand. You're leaving us?"

"Wages are good at the gold mine."

"You're going to be gone? During the winter?"

"Fred'll come by. I'll send him my pay; he'll bring supplies."

"We'll be here by ourselves? Is that what you're saying? Me and the children?"

"You'll be all right."

"No. No."

"Rachel."

"Don't leave us."

"I have to."

"Then send us to my mother's, like Al's doing for Mindy."

"I need you here, to look after the livestock."

"But I can't. I can't make paths to the barn, not when the snow's up to my waist. I can't get hay out to the cattle. I can't chop ice when the stock tanks are froze up. Not with a baby."

"You've got Mary and John."

"They can't take your place."

"They'll come close."

"What about your mother? Ask her—she has money. Then you won't have to work the mine."

"No."

"We'll pay her back."

"It's a handout."

"It's your mother."

"I said no."

I turned my head like I'd been slapped. Far off, coyotes yipped and howled. My skin crawled. Isaac was going to the gold mine. He didn't care what I thought. His mind was made up. He was going, and he expected me to run the ranch.

The coyotes' howling sounded like demons, circling, coming closer. I pinched the corners of my eyes to stop the tears.

"Rachel, look." Isaac was calmer now. I pinched harder at my eyes; I knew what was coming. He was going to talk me into liking the idea. But not this time. This time he was asking too much. I steeled myself.

He said, "Look, I know this comes as a surprise, and I don't like it either. But it's a chance; it's an opportunity to pull us out of this hard time. I have to do it. They—" He stopped himself, and in that moment I believed I heard what he was thinking but couldn't say. *People expect me to give up; they think I've bit off more than I can chew. No Negro, not even Isaac DuPree, is smart enough— tough enough—not when times get hard. But I am, and I'm going to show every last one of them.*

"Don't do this thing," I said. "Please."

"I have to. There's no other way around it. I'm not saying it'll be easy; it won't be. But you can do this, Rachel, I know you can. You've chopped sod, you've strung fences, you've driven the horses during planting season. Usually you've had a baby in your belly or one on your hip. You've done without. You lived in that sod dugout over there longer than most would've. You've built this place, same as me. Twenty-five hundred acres, Rachel. You and me. Nothing's too big for you."

I stared at him.

"Not many men can say that about their women. But I can."

Nothing's too big for you. Isaac DuPree admired me. It was in his words and in his voice. It bucked me up. In the dark I felt him looking at me. I imagined a shine in his eyes. Heat rose from my chest, ran up my neck, and made my cheeks burn.

It all came down to this: I still wanted to make Isaac glad that he had married me. I wanted to live up to his admiration. I wanted to hear it again in his voice.

He found my hands. "Come on," he said, "let's get some sleep." I let him pull me to my feet. My hands in his, he rubbed his thumbs along my fingers. *Maybe I can do it,* I told myself. Isaac had a way of making things work out. It might be a mild winter. Fred Schuling could bring supplies. The shame of giving up would be a burden too heavy to carry. Better to try than to quit.

"All right," I said.

"You're made of grit," Isaac said. He put an arm around my shoulders and steered me to the door. The letter in my apron pocket crackled. I put my hand to it.

"Not now," Isaac said. "It's late."

I nodded. Whatever Sue had to say could wait.

12

JOHNNY

Nothing's too big for you. Those were the words I heard in my mind the next day. I heard them when the rain started back up again, beating the tin roof. I heard them as water ran into the downspouts and gushed into the rain barrels. Rain pinged in the basins that lined the edge of the porch, and the words tapped in my mind. Three days of rain and everything was better. Three days of rain and a fast-moving stream coursed through the wash by the cottonwood.

It was a day for inside work. Isaac and John were in the barn going over equipment, seeing what needed cleaning and oiling and what needed fixing. Me and Mary worked in the kitchen and the little girls played under the table with their rag dolls. Mary stirred the big pot on the cookstove; she was boiling pillowcases. I folded one that she'd finished and cranked it through the wringer. A basin caught the squeezed-out water. I'd use it again. I wasn't about to waste a drop.

A cool breeze came through the kitchen window. *Fall,* I thought. *It's come.* The baby still hadn't kicked, but the bleeding had slowed down. Emma's burned hand was some better. The drought was broken; determination had taken hold of my mind. I believed myself able to face all things, even Isaac's faults. I was determined to live up to his admiration. Me and the children would stand the winter without him.

I hung the pillowcase on the clothesline we'd put up earlier in the kitchen. It'd be a few minutes before there'd be another one to wring. I put my hand in my apron pocket and felt the unopened letter from Sue. "Mind the girls," I said to Mary.

I went to my bedroom, closed the door, and got out Isaac's magnifying glass. I eased into my rocker; it was good to get off of my legs. I slipped my thumbnail along the flap of the envelope and pulled out the folded pages.

My nerves balling up on me, I held the pages to my nose and breathed them in. I could almost smell the black ink. The letter came from a home that had electric lights, a kitchen sink with running water, and an icebox packed with cuts of meat. It came from a city where people went to movie houses, listened to music on phonographs, and drove Model Ts on paved roads. Telephones rang, and in narrow apartment hallways, neighbors spoke to one another.

I smelled the pages again like I could bring that kind of life to the Badlands. Then I told myself it was time. I held the letter to the light that came through the small window over the bed. I put the magnifying glass to Sue's words. They rose up big before me.

August 10, 1917

Dear Sister,

The Kids are asleep and Paul left just now for his shift at the hotel. At last I have a few minutes to finally write this Letter. I have put it off long enough. Mama tried but couldn't bring herself to. I my-

*self am real tired and my hands ache bad so I will keep this
short.*

*I do not know what you hear way out there. Probably not
much but surely you heard about the troubles in East St Louis and
are worried sick about our Brother. You are right to be worried. I
do not know how to put this other than Johnny is dead.*

The pages dropped to my lap. I felt like crying and laughing
all at the same time. I thought it would be my mother. Johnny
never crossed my mind. I read part of the last sentence again.
Johnny is dead.

*Me and Mama were in the Laundry Room when we heard about
the Race Riot down there. That is what the newspapers called it. A
Race Riot. When we heard about it Mama got a real bad feeling.
She ran out the Hotel and went to the Telegraph Office and sent a
Telegram to Johnny. We waited two days to hear from him. It was
hard. Mama finally asked Mrs Fuller if she could use one of the
Hotel Telephones to call Johnnys Boarding House. She said yes but
she would take it out of Mamas pay. I would say that woman does
not have a heart but she helped Mama make the Telephone Call
which is not so easy it being Long Distance.*

*Pearl came on the Telephone Line and she did not know
where he was, she said that mobs of White Men were hanging Negroes and she was packing their things cause it was not safe. White
Men were kicking down doors telling people to get out of town and
then setting fire to their houses. She was crying and Mama could
not make out half of what she said. Mama asked her where was
Johnny and she said she did not know. Johnny had not been home*

in two days and she was too scared to go look for him. Mama told
her that when Johnny comes home tell him to send his Mother a
Telegram right away she was worried sick.

Rachel my hands hurt bad I have to quit.

August 11

I told the kids to be quiet I have to finish my letter to you.

After Mama talked to Pearl a whole week went by. Then
Mama got a Letter instead of a Telegram and it was not from
Johnny but from some man by the name of Quince Armstrong. A
Friend of Johnnys. He said in his Letter that a mob of White Men
busted into Connies. That is the place where Johnny was playing.
These White Men were swinging baseball bats and Johnny got hit
real bad on the head. He held on for a few days but never said
nothing. Then he passed away. July 6. He is buried down there and
Mamas heart is broke cause he is so far away from home in some
Potters Field with no marker. She wants to have him dug up so she
can bring him home but she does not have the money. Paul says
we do not have it either.

And we want to know what happened to Pearl and the ba-
bies. We want to bring them home. Mama wants them here. But
we do not know where they are. This has taken the Life right out of
Mama. I am worried about her.

August 16

This Letter is worrying me. I promise you I will finish it tonight.

Sister every body is nervous here. We are careful to stay on our side of town. So many Southern Negroes have moved to Chicago to work in the factories for the War Effort that the White People and some Negroes too are saying there are too many. That is what they said in East St Louis and look what happened to Johnny. Johnny never hurt a fly. You are lucky to be where you are. Nobody can say The Badlands is crowded with too many Negroes.

This is Sad News. I am sorry to be the one to tell you.

Your loving sister,
Sue

P.S. Quince Armstrong sent some of Johnnys music. He said that Johnny wrote them. Having them is a comfort to Mama.

I folded the pages, careful to keep the same creases. I put the letter in the envelope. Johnny had been dead almost ten weeks, and I never even had a feeling about it. When we were children, I always knew when something was wrong with him. I could read his face; I could tell what he was thinking. He could do the same with me. When Mama scolded one of us, it hurt both of our feelings. If one of us did good on a school examination, we were both happy. That was, I always believed, because Mama raised us as twins. Johnny was just eleven months and three days older than me.

We weren't twins, though. I was everyday plain, but not Johnny. He was the one with a God-given gift. He played the piano. He played so well that his music glided in the air like loose strands of light blue silk long after he bowed his head and his fingers left the keyboard.

Pain squeezed my chest. Johnny couldn't be dead. But the words were on paper, and those papers were in my hands, and that made it true.

I put the letter back in my apron pocket. I got my shawl. I walked through the kitchen. "Mind the girls," I said to Mary.

"Mama?" she said.

"Mind the girls."

I put the shawl over my head. I went out into the rain and stepped off of the porch into the mud. I sank up to my ankles. I lifted each foot, one at a time, the mud sucking at my boots. It coated the hem of my dress. I made my way down the rise to the barn, seeing nothing but Johnny's face. From the time he turned fourteen, his brown eyes carried a nervous look. That was about the time when Dad started talking about Johnny being old enough to work in the slaughterhouses.

"My hands," he would tell me when no one else was around. "Butchering will kill my hands."

"You don't have to," I always said. "Not you. You're meant for more."

I pictured him bent over a piano, his long fingers barely touching the keys. I saw a swinging baseball bat smack the back of Johnny's head, knocking him into the front of a brown upright piano, its wood scarred with cigarette burns. Sheets of music scattered as the last notes that Johnny ever played crashed under his collapsed weight.

"Isaac," I said when I got to the barn door.

"In here," he called.

I stepped into the barn and wiped the rain from my face. It

took my eyes a moment to adjust to the gloom. Isaac was with Jerseybell in her stall. The rotten stink coming from her was so strong that I put my hand to my nose like that would make a difference. I went to her stall. Long, ropy strings of dark drool hung from her open mouth.

"I was just coming to get Mary," Isaac said when he saw me. "I need a hand. Had to send John out to upright a few fence posts. A little rain's nothing to him."

"Isaac," I said, but that was as far as I got. My mouth wasn't working right, and my face was numb.

"She's in a bad way," Isaac said, and he could have been talking about me. He ran a hand along Jerseybell's back. "Poor girl. She's served us well, hasn't she?"

"Yes." My eyes began to water.

He said, "I've got one last thing to try. If that doesn't work, I'll have to put her down." He picked up a long, black rubber tube. "It'll go hard on Mary. If it comes to that."

Isaac had Jerseybell on a short rope tied to the railing. "Hold the lantern for me, will you?" he said. "Hold it high." He pried open Jerseybell's teeth and looked into her mouth. Her startled eyes rolled, but she didn't make any effort to pull away. "Stinks," Isaac said, shaking his head. He glanced at me. "This making you queasy?"

"No."

Isaac looked again at me. "You look queasy. You all right?"

"I'm all right."

He took me at my word. He cleaned the snot from her nose with a rag. I looked away; cow snot was the one thing I couldn't take. Then, with one arm tight around Jerseybell's neck to hold her still, Isaac snaked the tube through one nostril. When the tube was in her front stomach, Isaac said, "Get the castor oil going." He kept one hand on the tube at Jerseybell's nose.

I hung the lantern up, took off my shawl, and put it on a railing. I found the funnel and began pouring the oil into the tube.

Jerseybell didn't bother to jerk her head away from Isaac's tight hold. She watched me, her eyes rolling like she was pleading for me to stop this, like she wanted to be left alone so she could die in peace. "Don't blame you," I said to her.

"What?" Isaac said.

I cleared my throat. "I'm going to need milk in about a week's time."

Holding the tube in place, Isaac glanced at me, his eyes going to my bosom. I shook my head and said, "Something's not right."

"What do you mean?"

"I'm not sure. I'd just feel better if we had a milk cow."

"Why didn't you tell me?"

"Didn't want to burden you."

Jerseybell began to wheeze. Isaac used his fingers to clear the snot from her nose. My belly rolled; he wiped his hand on the rag that hung from his back pocket.

Isaac said, "Al's got a milk cow he won't be needing."

"What's he asking for her?"

"He'll be fair."

I didn't have it in me to worry all that much about the money. I put my mind to pouring the oil down the tube. I measured it out slow; I didn't want to drown Jerseybell. I did all this, but it was like I had stepped outside of myself and was watching from a distance. And yet everything was clear and sharp: the pain in Jerseybell's eyes, the white in Isaac's sideburns, the dirt under his fingernails.

When I started pouring the second bottle of oil, Isaac said, "I'll get you a hired hand for the winter."

"And have a man here with you gone?"

"It'd have to be a boy." Isaac gave the tube a little twist. The oil gurgled. "Can't pay for a man. A boy might be willing to work for food and board."

Another mouth to feed. I said, "A white boy?"

"Most likely."

"One what's willing to mind a Negro woman?"

"He will if he's hungry enough."

"Mary," I said. "There's Mary to think about."

Isaac shot me a quick look.

"A boy might—"

"She's just twelve."

The memory of Mary walking with Mrs. Fills the Pipe's nephew came to mind. They had walked close with their shoulders nearly touching. Franklin had held Emma. He had put his hand on Mary's arm when he passed Emma to her.

"She'll be thirteen in a few weeks," I said.

"Then you're turning down a hand?"

"No," I said. "I'll need the help."

"All right then."

I put the empty bottle and the funnel down. I'd think about this white boy when he showed up on our doorstep. Maybe he'd be the shy, quiet kind that wouldn't be any trouble. Maybe he'd be too young to care about girls.

Isaac began pulling the slippery tube out of Jerseybell. When there was just a few inches of it still in her nose, Isaac stepped to her side. He gave me a warning look. I left the stall and turned my back, my hand to my mouth. I heard Isaac pull the tube out and Jerseybell snorted, blowing snot everywhere.

When my stomach settled, I went back to the stall. Isaac was on his knees rubbing Jerseybell's underbelly, trying to work the bloat out. I put my hand on the letter in my pocket and looked around the barn, taking in the rafters and then the four horse stalls across from Jerseybell's. The horses were at the McKees' place and that made the barn big and lonesome. When Isaac and I built the barn during the summer of 1903, stacking rows of cut sod, we imagined a barn full of horses and milk cows. It ended up bigger than the dugout by a good forty paces.

I said, "My mother needs me."

On his knees by Jerseybell, Isaac cocked his head and gave me a funny look. Then all at once a knowing look came into his eyes. "Sue's letter," he said.

"It's not Mama. That's who I thought it would be. But it's not, it's Johnny. Sue says he's dead. Says somebody killed him."

Isaac stared at me.

"I want to go home," I told him. "My mother needs me."

"Somebody killed Johnny?" Isaac said.

"Yes." I got the letter and magnifying glass from my pocket and put them on top of the railing. I put my shawl back over my head. "I've got supper to get on," I said and left the barn.

After the supper dishes were put away, I didn't sit in the parlor with Isaac to listen to the rain. Instead, I went to bed. It wasn't close to dark but Isaac thought it best; he thought I looked peaked. Mary got a spring quilt to keep me from getting a chill and helped me get into bed. I didn't like that she had to take care of the little girls by herself, and I was sorry that Isaac was left to be the one to tell the children about Johnny. I didn't know how he'd explain such a thing. I let him, though. I was worn out clear to my bones, sick with sorrow.

I rested on my side, listening to the rain tap on the tin roof. It was a peculiar thing being in bed before full dark. It was even more peculiar to be sad about Johnny while at the same time taking pleasure in being left alone with nobody wanting anything from me.

The house was quiet when Isaac came into the bedroom. "You awake?" he said.

"I'm awake."

He set the lamp on the high dresser and sat down in my rocker. His shadow stretched to the side of him. It flickered on the wall as he rocked back and forth. Isaac said, "This is a bad thing about your brother. Race riots. God."

I nodded.

"I told the children." Isaac paused. "Told them Johnny had an accident. It's better that way."

"Yes," I said. The other way would scare them.

"I know you want to see your mother. Times like this—" Isaac stopped. "But, Rachel, I can't let you go. Not right now."

I didn't say anything.

"It's not safe in Chicago. Whites going around killing people. Sue thinks you're lucky to be here."

I felt a quick chill of fear for my mother and for Sue and her family. Then I thought about the coming winter. I thought about running out of supplies. I thought about snowdrifts up to my shoulders. "It's not safe here, either," I said.

"Folks around here know us."

I had to think for a moment what Isaac meant by that. I said, "Doesn't mean everybody likes us. Mrs. Svenson doesn't."

"There's only one of her here. In Chicago there's hundreds."

"But what happened to Johnny, that was St. Louis, not Chicago."

"Chicago could be next. There's thousands of Negroes there. All crammed into the Black Belt, living in hole-in-the-wall apartments, the air stinking from the slaughterhouses. If whites took after them—" He paused. "And what do those people have, living like that? What about their children? They don't have anything."

"Your mother has it good."

"She has boardinghouses, Rachel. They aren't the Palmer Hotel. They're for slaughterhouse men."

"One of them's high class."

"There's no pride in it," he said. "Not for my children. Not when it comes to standing up to white people." Isaac got up from the rocker.

"My mother," I said.

"It's not safe."

I didn't say anything.

Isaac picked up the lamp and went to the doorway. He

turned back. In a voice so low that I almost didn't hear, he said, "When things are better. When I can send you in style," and then he was gone.

At first, I didn't understand him, and then all at once I did. He didn't want Chicago people—his mother—to see me in my patched-over country clothes and heavy work boots. He didn't want his mother seeing my chapped lips, my rough hands, and broken nails. He didn't want her seeing the weariness that I was sure showed in my eyes. Race riots had nothing to do with it. And I was wrong to think Isaac admired me. He was ashamed of me.

I pictured Mrs. Fills the Pipe's daughter, Inez, in her short linen dress with the pink sash. That dress belonged on Mary. John should have a gray suit and a crisp white shirt. The little girls should have blue dresses with white starched petticoats. They were the children of a Dakota rancher, one of the biggest land-owners in the Badlands. And me? I should be like the Circle of Eight ladies with a cream-colored blouse, a black skirt, and a brooch at my throat.

Last spring there was money to buy Mabel Walker's place. This coming winter, Isaac was going off to work in the mine. He was doing it to raise money for more cattle, for grazing rights, for that bull of Al McKee's. Isaac wasn't doing it to buy linen dresses with sashes and a boy's suit with a white shirt. He was doing it to buy Al McKee's land.

Anger welled up inside of me. Land was a measure of a person's worth. I couldn't count the number of times Isaac had said that. But there'd never be enough land to satisfy Isaac. There'd always be another patch just right for grazing, or there'd be a corner with a wash that never ran dry, or there'd be a stretch of flatlands made for raising winter wheat. It'd never end.

I squeezed my eyes shut. Fourteen years ago I lived in fear of Isaac sending me back to Chicago. I had worked hard to please him; I had done everything he'd asked of me just to see a shine of admiration in his eyes. Looking back, I understood that I had done it all too good. He couldn't run the ranch without me. I was never going home.

13

MARY

L ate the next day I stood in the open doorway looking out.
The air was fresh and cool; the rain had quit that morning. It
was the day after I'd read Sue's letter about Johnny. I had just put
the little girls to bed and had my sewing basket and mending in
my hands. The light wasn't all that good for mending, I decided.
Either that or my eyes weren't up to it.

"Fall finally got here," Isaac said to me. His rocker thumped
unevenly over a rough patch on the plank porch floor. I sat down
in the rocker beside him. "Rode in on the storm," he said. From all
sides of us, toads chirped their quick, high call. I had thought the
drought had killed them all, but I was wrong. All along they'd
been biding their time, low in the grasses, waiting for the rain so
they could do their calling and mating.

Isaac said, "I'll go to Al's tomorrow, get the horses and the
wagon. It'll be dry enough. With Mary and John's help, I'll have
the wheat in the ground in a week's time. You wait and see, Rachel.
Come spring, the fields will be green and the cattle getting fat."

My brother Johnny had been killed. That morning there'd
been more blood in my underclothes, and the baby still wasn't
kicking. There was winter to get through on low supplies and

Isaac away at the gold mine. All that to face and he was looking past it.

"Spring," I said.

"It'll be here before you know it," he said.

I held my tongue. Like yesterday, everything was still peculiarly sharp in my mind. There'd been more clouds than sunshine, but even so, the sun had seemed too harsh. The wind was overly crisp and the children's voices were shrill, all of it setting my teeth on edge. And the mud. The heavy, rotten smell of it made my belly roll.

Earlier that day, right after noon dinner, the prickly sharpness in my mind made me go to the root cellar. I needed to see firsthand how it was going to be this winter. Usually by September sealed jars of tomatoes, corn, and carrots lined the cellar shelves. Usually I'd be busy putting straw on the cellar's dirt floor so I'd be ready when it came time to store the potatoes and the heads of cabbage. Most times in September, I was counting and sorting vegetable seeds so I'd know what I had for the spring planting.

But this was a different September. The canning jars on the cellar shelves were empty, and there was no need to line the dirt floor.

Sitting on the porch in the twilight, I pulled my shawl closer. I thought about Johnny in some potter's field far from home. I hoped that someone had prayed over him. I wanted to think there was a cross to show where he rested. I hoped that his fingernails were clean and that someone had thought to fold his hands on his chest. Isaac stood up, jarring my thoughts. He whistled for Mary and John, and the shrillness of it ran clear through me. I tensed, my back arching.

John and Rounder bobbed out of the wash that now had a stream running through it. They loped up the rise, both of them muddy, John's hands pressed together making a cupped circle.

John spun to a quick stop in front of Isaac and me. "Look," he said, darting a nervous look at me. The children had been careful around me all day. In their eyes, Johnny's death made me a stranger. It turned me into a woman what hollered at them for no good reason. I forced a smile.

He opened his dirty hands just enough to show the head of a green-speckled toad he'd captured. "He's a jumper. Watch." John fell to his knees on the porch, and I heard something give way in his pants. One more thing to mend, I thought. John put his cupped hands on the ground. "Get back, Rounder," he said.

With his finger, John poked the toad. Rounder let out a great woof of excitement. Startled, the toad jumped a short length of the porch, its back legs dangling high in the air. It plopped into a sudden landing, folding its spotted legs beneath itself.

John sprang forward, scooped up the toad, and turned to me, waiting for me to say something. "My," I said. He grinned, and in that instant he looked just like Isaac.

"That's some toad," Isaac said. "Must have gone a good foot and a half, maybe even two. And he's a little fellow. Let's see for sure. Get your ruler, John. I'll hold your toad."

I looked toward the barn. "Call again for Mary, would you?"

Isaac did, but his whistle was not all that shrill or long. His mind was on that far-jumping toad. I got up. "I'll go get her," I said. "She must be where she can't hear."

"I'll go," Isaac said, but he was down on the porch floor with John, measuring the jump with the ruler.

"I feel like walking," I said. And I did. All of a sudden, I was restless. I felt like doing something hard. I felt the sudden urge to drag all the rag carpets from the house so I could beat the dust out of them. I even had it in me to polish the cookstove, and after that I wouldn't have minded going out in the pasture and picking up a wheelbarrow load of cow chips.

The baby, I thought, fear shooting through me. That was what had me all stirred up. I'd be giving birth any time and I didn't know how it was going to go.

"Jumped twenty-two inches, Daddy. Just look at that," John was saying as I walked down the rise toward the barn. "Isn't he some kind of jumper? Didn't I tell you?"

"You're right about that, son. Let's try him again."

Their voices faded as I made my way to the barn, mud sticking to my boots. At the barn door I stopped, taken aback by the swarms of flies and by a stink that reminded me of meat gone bad on an August day. "Mary, bedtime," I called. "Daddy's been whistling for you."

She didn't answer. Holding my shawl close, I stepped into the barn and waited for my eyes to get used to the sudden dark. My nose pinched against the stink. I swatted at the flies, sorry that I hadn't thought to bring my bandanna to keep them from my mouth and nose.

"Mary? You in here?"

"I'm over here with Jerseybell," Mary said. "She's bad."

I went to the stall. Jerseybell was down and on her side. Mary sat beside her, running her hand along the cow's flank. "I've been trying to tell her she's got to eat," Mary said. "She's got to get up, but she won't do it. It's like she doesn't care."

I found a lantern and took a match and a piece of sandpaper from my apron pocket. I struck the match; the light flared. I lit the lantern and hung it from a bent nail in the dirt wall. In the white circle of light, Jerseybell panted. Her eyes were dull and unseeing. Her ribs poked out and she looked half her size. Yesterday's castor oil treatment hadn't helped at all; maybe it had made her worse. Isaac better get over to the McKees' first thing tomorrow and get that new cow home quick.

I said, "Honey, time for bed."

"I don't want her to die."

"We've done all we can. It's bedtime."

"I can't leave her."

Oh, Mary, I thought. *You're a good girl. You help with your sisters, and without being asked, you do whatever needs doing in the kitchen. You have a way with the cattle, and you sit well on a horse. When school's in session, you do your lessons. I couldn't ask for a better girl but I wish you weren't so tenderhearted. Life is hard on such people.*

In the shadows cast by the lantern light, Mary looked near grown, even with the two little-girl braids that came close to brushing her shoulders. She was dark, like me, and she had my dimple, but she didn't look anything like me. She was more like Isaac, not that she looked all that much like him. It was how she carried herself with pride. And that made her beautiful, I realized all at once. And strong, even with a tender heart.

"All right," I said. "You can stay. But just for a little bit. Understand?"

She nodded.

"Where's your shawl? It's cold in here."

"I'm all right."

"Here, use mine." I draped it around her shoulders and let my hand stay on her back for a moment. I said, "You want some company?"

Mary gave me a surprised look.

"Go tell Daddy we're sitting with Jerseybell for a while. Tell him I said not to wait up."

Mary jumped to her feet and was out the barn, running like she was afraid I'd change my mind. But I wasn't going to. I wanted to be with Mary, and as peculiar as it was, I wanted to be with Jerseybell. No creature should be alone when it died.

I lit three oily rags in smudge pots. I got a horse blanket and wrapped it around me like a shawl. With my foot I pushed the milking stool near a stall post so I'd have a place to rest my back. Wishing for my rocker, I sat down.

When Mary got back, she sat cross-legged beside Jerseybell. We didn't say anything; we listened to the sounds of the barn as Mary rubbed the soft hair behind the cow's ears. Flies hissed and buzzed, and now that it was a little past dusk, mosquitoes whined and stung, not the least bit bothered by the smudge pots that were supposed to keep them away. Bats from the loft dipped and darted, chasing mosquitoes, their wings making soft, feathery sounds.

But the loudest sound was the rusty rattle caught in Jerseybell's throat. It was a sound that played hard on my nerves. It made me think of Johnny dying with no family to comfort him.

"Daddy wants to put Jerseybell down," Mary said. "Daddy never gives up on anything, but he's giving up on her."

"She's suffering."

"Daddy said he'll wait until morning." Mary gave me a hopeful look. "She might be better by then. Don't you think so too, Mama?"

"No. I don't."

I was sorry as soon as I said it. My mother never would have said such a thing to me. Next to Isaac, Mama was the most hopeful person I knew. At bedtime she believed in finding one good thing to say about that day. Each morning she always said to be on the lookout for a happy surprise. There was bound to be at least one in each day, maybe more.

Once, when I was a little girl still in braids, the preacher's sermon hadn't sat well with me. I couldn't work out how Jesus fed the multitudes with a handful of bread and just a few little baskets of fish. I said so to Mama. "That's too many people and not enough food."

She gave me a stern look. "It was a miracle," she said, "something you can't explain, can't even try. But all the same, Jesus worked a miracle, He surely did. There were witnesses. And you know what that means, don't you?"

I didn't.

"Means honest folks have to work hard and keep their eyes forward. When a miracle slips up on them, that way they're ready to grab hold." Mama lifted her chin. "I should know. I was born a slave, but I'm not one now."

I studied Jerseybell. I didn't look for a miracle tonight.

"Mama?"

"What, honey?"

"You think Jerseybell knows how bad off she is?"

"I expect so."

"Think if she does die, not that I think she will, but if she does, think she'll go to heaven? She's been awfully good. Especially for a cow."

I thought about that, trying to remember what the Bible said about animals and heaven, but nothing came to mind. I recalled, though, a passage, or maybe it was a poem, about all animals great and small. I wasn't sure if it was from the Bible, and I didn't want to say the wrong thing about heaven. Then I thought of Johnny and my Isaac Two and Baby Henry.

I said, "I expect there's folks up there wanting butter on their bread and cream in their coffee. There's babies in heaven without their mamas, and they'd be needing their milk. It wouldn't be much of a heaven, seems to me, without cows."

"There's big herds of cattle in heaven," Mary said. "That's what I think. And green pastures 'cause it rains every day but only at night." She slapped the back of her neck, then looked at her fingers. There was a smear of blood from a mosquito. She said, "When we're real sick, you sing to us."

I agreed.

"You sing and rock us and we get better."

Eight years ago I sang lullabies to Baby Henry as I held him to my bosom. But that hadn't kept him from passing out of this world not long after his birth.

"Mama, singing would help Jerseybell."

"Honey."

"Could you sing to her? I know it'd make her feel better."

"I'm not going to sing to a cow."

"But it's Jerseybell."

Jerseybell was Mary's friend. There were a handful of girls at school, and Louise Johnston was Mary's good friend there. But school was only for five months, and if the winter was hard, weeks at a time were missed. There were children scattered all over the Badlands, but even if they were just two or three miles apart, children old enough to walk that far had chores at home that couldn't be missed.

I knew what it was like to have friends. A handful of children lived on the sugarcane plantation in Louisiana, and in Chicago there were girls my age all up and down the street. We used to have good times. If we weren't skipping rope or playing hopscotch, we were giggling over the least little thing. No wonder Mary had had fun with Franklin, Mrs. Fills the Pipe's nephew. It'd been months since she had been with children other than her brother and sisters.

I said, "You got a particular song in mind for Jerseybell?"

"'Michael Row the Boat Ashore.'"

I blinked back my surprise. "All right then."

Mary's eyes smiled. She pulled down her bandanna, batted away some flies, and cleared her throat. When she sang, her voice was just above a whisper. I followed along, rusty and a little off-key.

My brothers and sisters are all aboard, Hallelu . . . jah.
My brothers and sisters are all aboard, Hallelu . . . jah.
Michael row the boat ashore, Hallelu . . . jah!

It had been a long spell since I'd last heard singing. I used to sing when I did my housework, but not that summer. Isaac used to whistle tunes; ragtime was his favorite. Once he spent a week practicing nothing but "Maple Leaf Rag" until he got it to suit him. "My Castle on the Nile" and "Congo Love Song" were two of my favorites, and when I told him that once, he whistled those songs just to please me. During our first summer in the Badlands, Isaac whistled while we built our barn and dugout. When pointy shoots of winter wheat broke the soil that first spring, Isaac whistled. When in April I told him he was going to be a father by early fall, he whistled as he sanded and polished the old cradle he had found at the Interior store. Then the babies came, one after another, and Isaac sent them to sleep each night with sweet whistled lullabies.

Michael row the boat ashore, Hallelu . . . jah!

Isaac didn't whistle tunes anymore, and Johnny didn't play the piano. My throat choked, taking my breath. I shook as an ache from deep within gripped my heart.

"Mama! What's wrong? You sick?"

I couldn't hold back the tears.

"I'll go get Daddy."

I shook my head no.

"Please, Mama. We'll make Jerseybell better. Sing. That makes everything better. Sing with me."

The river is deep and the river is wide, Hallelu . . . jah.
Milk and honey on the other side, Hallelu . . . jah.
Michael row the boat ashore, Hallelu . . . jah!

Mary's voice filled the barn. The music was so tender, and in my mind I saw the words drift out the barn door and float over the Badlands like a fine linen bedsheet, set loose and free. I began to say the words.

> *Jordan's river is chilly and cold, Hallelu . . . jah.*
> *Chills the body but not the soul, Hallelu . . . jah.*

My tears easing up, we sang for Jerseybell. We sang for each other, and we sang for ourselves, the music comforting like a visit with an old friend. We sang the songs from my childhood when going to church was handy.

> *What a friend we have in Jesus,*
> *all our sins and griefs to bear.*
> *What a privilege to carry*
> *everything to God in prayer.*

Other songs came from the sugarcane fields of Louisiana.

> *I looked over Jordan, what did I see*
> *Comin' for to carry me home?*
> *A band of angels comin' after me*
> *Comin' for to carry me home.*

I was the wife of a rancher and I had my own house, a wood house. But I wanted to leave. I was looking over Jordan. I wanted to go home, where everything was bound to be better. My people sang about it. Maybe they wanted to go back across the ocean to where they had come from. Or maybe they looked to heaven. *Same thing,* I thought, *once homesickness takes root.* A person wanted to be anywhere but where she was.

> *Swing low, sweet chariot,*
> *Comin' for to carry me home.*

Mary and I rested our voices while Jerseybell's breath came hard and raspy. Somewhere in the barn, crickets made their own kind of music and field mice rustled in the scattered straw.

"Mama, these songs are sad."

"Well. They're slave songs mostly. Nothing to be happy about when you're a slave."

"Oh."

"But Mary, lots of music's fun; lots of it cheers you up. You know that from school."

"Miss Elliott doesn't like us being overly happy."

"And she's right about that. School's hard work. But there's lots of music that perks you right up."

"Like which ones?"

"I don't know, honey. Lots of them." I looked over toward the open doorway. It was dark, long past bedtime. Getting up in the morning would be harder than usual. But there was something about the eager look on Mary's face that made me want to please her. I blew out some air. "All right," I said. "One more, this time a toe-tapping song."

Mary smiled.

"Let's see if I can remember some of the dance tunes that were popular."

"Dance tunes? You danced?"

"Of course I danced. Back when I was a girl. I never was all that good—it was Johnny what could dance. All the women, even the old married ones, waited in line for him. Course, he didn't do all that much dancing; he was mostly at the piano."

"Oh." Mary ducked her head. "Mama?" she said, not looking at me.

"What?"

"Daddy let me read the letter. He said I was old enough to know."

Isaac should've told me. And then I thought that he did this so Mary would think bad of big cities. He wanted her scared of places like East St. Louis. And Chicago.

Mary said, "Why'd they hurt him that way?"

"I don't know," I said. "Some people carry hate, looks like. They don't need a reason to hurt somebody; they see their chance and they take it."

"I don't like it."

"I know it."

All at once, I recalled what Mrs. Fills the Pipe had said about soldiers—buffalo soldiers—and what they had done to her and her people. I thought about the Indian squaw with the little boy and how Isaac had run them off. I took a ragged breath. "You've got Uncle Johnny's eyelashes," I said to Mary. "His eyes, too."

"I do?"

"That's right, and you can count your lucky stars."

Mary felt her eyelashes with her fingertips and then batted her eyes a few times. I smiled to myself. She said, "Was Uncle Johnny handsome?"

"Well," I said, doing my best to remember the particulars of his face. It had been fourteen years. "I wouldn't say handsome, not exactly, not like your daddy. His nose was squashed and pushed over to one side from the time he broke it falling out of a tree. That was in Louisiana—we didn't have trees in Chicago. His nose being that way set his looks off a little.

"Johnny was dark, dark as you and me, and when he was a boy, he was skinny like he was hungry, but he wasn't—we most always had enough. He was slow to fill out. But his eyes were something—deep and dark and fringed with those long lashes. I always envied him his lashes. He was smart too. He could do numbers in his head without hardly thinking. When he was a boy, he wanted to be a teacher, said he'd make his students do figures all day long. But then music took ahold of him and that was all he wanted to do, play and write music."

"And Uncle Johnny played dance songs?"

"For a while he played on Sundays at church, but Preacher Bisbee made him quit, said his playing had too many flourishes, said he turned hymns into saloon music. Shamed Mama something awful."

"What were the dances like?"

"They were a good time, something to look forward to. We had what we called the Second Street Social Club. Most everybody in the neighborhood belonged, and a few times a year we had dances at the grammar school. We got all dressed up in our Sunday best and the women served refreshments—punch and cake and such things. I liked the waltzes; it was pretty music. Most everybody could do a waltz, even if you weren't very good.

Mr. Brandon—he lived next door—he played the fiddle, except he called it a violin. If he wasn't clear-headed enough, Johnny played the piano. But if Johnny got a chance to dance, he loved doing the cakewalk."

"What's that?"

"It was the rage; even white people danced it. Johnny was such a show-off, strutting his partners around, doing that high-stepping dance." I pictured that for a moment and wondered if folks were still dancing it.

"But for me," I said, "my favorite music of all was the blues. Maybe because of Mr. Brandon. He mostly played that fiddle of his at the dances, but once in awhile he'd get out his cornet and play the blues. I could sit forever and listen to his cornet." Seeing Mary's raised eyebrows, I said, "That's a kind of horn, and with the right man handling it, it brought out a hurt you didn't even know was there."

"Does he still live by Grandma?"

"Grandma doesn't live in the same place anymore." I paused. "Don't know what's happened to Mr. Brandon. Hard to believe he'd still be living in that old falling-down shack. Every snow-storm that blew through, Mama just knew it'd come down on top of him, bury him alive. It was a disgrace how his landlord didn't keep it up. But maybe that was Mr. Brandon's doing. He used all his money for whiskey. Least that's what Dad always said. There was talk that when he was a young man he went off to Europe somewhere to learn music and that he even played in an orches-tra there. I don't see how; he was a fair-skinned man, but he couldn't pass—anybody could see he was a Negro. But he's the one what taught Johnny the piano. He had an old upright in that rickety house of his, and Johnny took lessons every Saturday morning. Evenings Johnny studied his sheet music at the kitchen table, reading the notes, his fingers running up and down the table just like he was playing."

"But what about you? Didn't you get lessons?"

"I tried a few times, but I didn't have it in me. All I really wanted to do was sit and listen. That's what I did when Johnny was taking his lessons. I sat on the floor next to the piano. I'd put my hand on the back of it where it stuck out from the wall. Johnny'd play and I'd feel the music, listening all at the same time." I smiled. "Mr. Brandon's floor slanted good, I'll tell you what. One end of the piano leaned against the wall. Johnny used to joke that he couldn't play a piano unless it ran downhill. Mama wouldn't let us go to Mr. Brandon's if there was a storm; she was that afraid of his roof."

I rested the back of my head against the railing post, hearing once again the piano chords and the keyboard exercises. "Classical music, that's what Mr. Brandon made Johnny learn. People like Schumann and Chopin. Mr. Brandon talked about those people like he had grown up with them."

"Gosh."

"Isn't it something that I've remembered those names? Germans, I think, or maybe they're Frenchmen."

"They're the ones that are fighting now," Mary said. "Why're they doing that?"

"I don't know, honey. They'd be better off playing the piano." *That'd quit all the killing,* I thought. *That'd keep Al McKee, our* neighbor, from thinking he had to go over there and straighten them out.

"Anyway," I said, "on summer nights in Chicago, when it was too hot to sleep, Mr. Brandon, a little tipsy, would come out on his front stoop and play that fiddle of his. His music pulled us to him; we couldn't help ourselves no matter how tired we were. We'd get out of our sticky, hot beds, make ourselves decent, and go outside. That man made us forget who we were."

"What do you mean?"

"I mean that we'd forget what we'd done that day and what was waiting for us the next. We'd forget about the slaughterhouses or about cooking and cleaning up after other people. Mr. Brandon lifted our spirits. He got our feet tapping and our hearts pounding until someone would let out a whoop, grab themselves a girl, spin her around, and before you knew it, we had ourselves a dance. A dance on a city dirt road. Trains came through; we couldn't hear a note, but we just kept on dancing, keeping time in our heads until the trains were gone and the music came back."

"And you danced?"

"My, yes."

"But just with Daddy?"

"Oh no, honey, this was before I even knew your daddy."

"Oh," Mary said, sounding shocked. Then her voice took a lonesome turn. "Wish I could've seen you dancing."

"Those were good times."

Mary swatted at Jerseybell's nose. A knot of flies flew out.

A low feeling came over me. A young girl like Mary should know something about dancing. She should have socials and dances to go to, and she should know what it was like to have friends what lived a door or two down the street. But with Isaac working the gold mine in Lead, I'd need Mary at home. She wouldn't be going to school.

I was a few months short of fourteen when I quit school. I did it so Johnny could keep going. Mama had backed me on this, and Dad hadn't fussed all that much. He didn't see that a girl needed much schooling, and even if he never said it, Dad was proud that Johnny was smart. He might have said that he wanted Johnny in the slaughterhouse, but Dad paid for piano lessons and he let Johnny earn a high-school diploma.

Mary was smart enough to be a teacher. Or a nurse like Mrs. Fills the Pipe's daughter. Isaac's father had started a nursing school for Negroes. That was where Mary should go. It was her grandfather's school; it was where Mary belonged. I pictured her in a starched white uniform. I imagined sick people turning to Mary as she walked through a hospital ward. They'd call her Nurse DuPree.

It wasn't right that she'd have to quit school this winter. I tapped my foot. It was wrong what Isaac was doing to us, leaving for the winter. I tapped harder, willing Mr. Brandon's fiddle music to find its way to me in a barn buried in the heart of the Badlands.

"What're you doing, Mama?"

"Listening."

"To what?"

"Fiddle music." I cocked my head and put my hand behind my ear. "Hear?"

Puzzled, Mary drew her eyebrows together. I sang.

Get out the way for old Dan Tucker
He's too late to get his supper.

She grinned, her fingers keeping time on Jerseybell's flank.

Supper's over, dishes washed,
Nothin' left but a piece of squash.

"Sing it again, Mama. Please?"

"Only if you'll dance."

"Dance? By myself?"

"No." I used the stall rail to pull myself up. "With me."

"But we're both girls."

"Nobody's looking."

Mary giggled and stood up.

"Come over here," I said, "where we've got some room. Now, face me like this and give me your hands. When I start singing, we'll slide a few steps that way, and then we'll slide a few steps the other. Can't do like I used to, can't do much more than walk, but you'll get the idea."

Mary squeezed my hands.

Now old Dan Tucker is come to town
Swinging the ladies round and round
First to the right and then to the left
Then to the girl that he loves best.

Together we sang and danced, laughing when Mary bumped into Isaac's plow, bobbing our heads to show we were sorry when we stepped on each other's feet. Mary's glowing face gave me a special kind of pleasure, the kind of pleasure a person got from making someone else happy. Not that I wasn't happy; I was. Dancing with my daughter was a moment of such pure lightheartedness that I knew I would never forget it. I'd press the memory of it in my heart. I'd use it to get me through the coming winter.

"I've got to stop," I said a few dances later, propping up my belly with my arms. Breathing hard, I sat down on the milking stool.

Mary wasn't ready to stop. Humming, she danced on—spinning, dipping, and sashaying around the barn, her arms out before her, her hands touching a partner only she could see. When she finally stopped, she curtsied and sank down to the hard-packed floor beside Jerseybell.

"Just three months till the Schoolhouse Christmas Dance," Mary said, fanning herself with her hand.

My smile faded. We didn't go to the Schoolhouse Christmas Dance. Isaac always wanted to, but it was me what said no. I didn't like the thought of being the only Negro woman in a room crowded up with white people. That'd make me uneasy; I wouldn't know what to say. Every year Mindy McKee begged us to come to the dance with them, saying how friendly folks were, how nice it was to see neighbors all dressed up and having a good time. But I always had a reason not to. I'd remind Mindy that I was in the family way and showing too much. If that weren't so, I'd tell her that it was too cold to haul the younger children all those miles, and at night too.

It was different for Mary. She was used to white people.

We were still the only Negroes in this part of South Dakota. There were the Thompsons and the Phillipses, two other Negro families, but they were north of the Black Hills. It'd been months since Isaac had heard anything about them. Maybe they'd sold out like everybody else. But even if they hadn't, they were a good ninety miles from us.

"Honey," I said, "we don't go to that dance."

"But now that I know how to dance . . . "

I didn't say anything.

"Louise's father's going to let her dance with bigger boys this year, not just with other little kids like before."

"She's older than you."

"Just by five months."

I took a deep breath to steady my voice. "You got any boys you'd like to dance with?"

Mary pressed her lips as if embarrassed.

"Well?"

"Maybe."

"Well?"

"Joe Larson isn't so bad. When I won the spelling bee he said he wished he could spell as good as me."

"He did?"

"He gave me a cookie one time. It was round like a ball and had white powdery sugar on it. He said it was a Swedish cookie, his mama made it. That's where they're from. Sweden. Miss Elliott showed us where on the map. Joe's the first in his family born in America. He's real proud of it. He speaks English for his parents."

Lord, Lord. What would I do if a yellow-headed boy with

blue eyes came up the road carrying a spring bouquet of orange wildflowers? What would Isaac do? Or this boy's parents? Or the other ranchers?

Mary said, "Louise teases, saying how Joe Larson's sweet on me, but I don't think so. He talks to all the girls." She ran her hand along Jerseybell's shuddering side. "But I think Franklin's real nice."

An Indian. Merciful Jesus. Isaac would skin him alive.

I said, "These boys, you're best off ignoring them."

"Why?"

"Be polite, but don't be friendly."

"What?"

"Don't share lunch with the Larson boy anymore. And Franklin's an Indian, and you know what your daddy thinks about them."

Mary's mouth twisted.

"Honey," I said, not knowing how to explain this thing and wishing that I didn't have to. "People get along best if they stay with their own kind."

"Their own kind?"

"That's right. Negroes with Negroes and whites with whites. And Indians . . . well, it works best this way."

"What about Louise?"

"That's all right. It's just with boys, well, it's different. You stay with your own kind when it comes to boys."

"But they're my classmates."

"You heard me. Stay away from the boys. Understand?"

She nodded. In the flickering lantern light, I saw tears standing in her eyes. I put out my hand to her. "Come here."

"Ma'am?"

"Just wanting to gives you a hug, that's all. It's been a good while."

Mary came to me and wrapped her arms around my swollen middle and rested the side of her face on top of my belly. I patted her head, feeling the springy hair that had worked loose from her braids.

I wanted to tell her I was sorry. When we first came out to the Badlands, Isaac was sure the country would fill up with Negroes. That hadn't happened.

The barn was quiet. Even the crickets had stopped their chirping. But the biggest quiet came from Jerseybell. Her breathing had stilled and her chest wasn't shuddering. I pulled my handkerchief from my sleeve. "Honey," I said. "Jerseybell's dead."

"Oh no," she said. "Oh no." She went to Jerseybell, laid down, and put her head on Jerseybell's neck and an arm around her. I let Mary cry for a while before telling her it was time for bed. She wiped her eyes on my handkerchief and helped me up from the milking stool.

I unhooked the lantern, blew out the oil rags, and put my arm around Mary's shoulders, feeling the sharpness of them. "You've been to your first dance," I said. "There'll be more." I forced my voice to be strong. "With boys. Negro boys."

14

THE MANDOLIN PLAYER

Isaac?" I said when I came into our bedroom after coming up from the barn with Mary. "You awake?"

"Some."

"Jerseybell's dead."

The mattress crackled as he turned onto his back. "Mary all right?"

"She will be."

"At least this way I don't have to put Jerseybell down."

I put on my nightdress, sat on the edge of the bed, and wiped the bottom of my feet with a rag. "You going to bring Al's milk cow home tomorrow?"

"I'll go as soon as I take care of Jerseybell."

I got in bed beside him, lying on my side, my back aching. My earlier spell of restlessness was gone now, washed out by all the dancing. Maybe the baby was a few days off. That'd give Isaac time to get the new cow. That'd give the baby time to perk up and start kicking. I said, "Mary's growing up."

"They all are."

"She's noticing boys."

"She's only twelve."

"She'll be thirteen in a few weeks. Lots of girls from around here start courting by fourteen."

"Not Mary."

"I'm just saying she's noticing boys. Boys from around here." I felt Isaac looking at me. "White boys."

"Good God."

I said, "Mary needs to meet some Negro boys."

He didn't say anything.

"She needs to meet some nice Negro boys before she thinks the only boys what count are white." Or Indians, I almost said.

"What are you saying?"

I paused. "There's going to come a time when our children'll have to go home."

"This is home."

"Chicago," I said.

"There's no need for that. Zeb Butler will help. Him and Iris."

"What?"

"They know most of the Negroes in the Dakotas, Nebraska and Iowa too. They'll know who's right for Mary. And for John, when it comes time."

Zeb Butler and Isaac had served together at Fort Robinson. He had quit the army a year or so before Isaac and had gone to Sioux Falls. Him and his wife, Iris, rented rooms in their house to Negroes passing through town. Me and Isaac had stayed at their home on our way from Chicago to the Badlands. They were rough people. Zeb Butler drank too much to suit me. I didn't want them having anything to do with our children.

"But not before Mary's sixteen," Isaac was saying. "She's not getting married before then. We need her here." He paused. "I'll find her a rancher, a good man who knows what he's doing, someone proud to have her."

"Maybe that's not what Mary has in mind. Maybe she wants to be a teacher, maybe even a nurse."

"She's a rancher's daughter. She'll want her own land."

It would never be hers, I thought. It'd always be her husband's. But Isaac was right. Mary was born to the life. Someday she'd want her own house, and marrying was the only way our girls would have anything. I'd been taken aback when Isaac first told me how it worked. "This will all be his," he had said a day or so after Isaac Two, our first boy, was born.

"And Mary's," I said. She was a year and a half.

"She's a girl," Isaac said. "Ranch land always goes to the oldest boy so the land stays intact, doesn't get split up. Then it goes to his oldest boy. That way it stays in the family, keeps the family name."

"But Mary?"

"She'll marry a man with his own land. I'll see to it."

"What if we have more sons?"

"They'll work for me and Isaac Two until they're ready to go out on their own, get their own ranches."

Put that way, it seemed sensible. But it hadn't gone that way. Negroes hadn't come to the West, and Isaac Two had slipped on a pile of rocks. The ranch was going to John.

Isaac said, "Zeb Butler'll know of ranchers, Negro ranchers in need of a wife. And John'll want a woman from around here, one who has a taste for the work. He won't find that kind in Chicago."

Isaac was talking about our children like they were cattle. Their marriages would be bargains for land. Just like ours had been. Isaac would do the bargaining for his children and they'd go along with it. They'd want to please him. Grown up and married off that way, they wouldn't know the first thing about courting, about sharing ice cream sodas or about going to dances. They wouldn't know anything about falling hard in love and how that made everything easier to bear.

I said, "You've got this all worked out."

"Ever since Mary was born."

I felt sick. I saw the girls married off to men what worked them hard and treated them rough. I pictured John's wife—worn out and little more than a ranch hand. That wasn't what I wanted for them; our children should have better. I had to make Isaac see that too.

I gathered up an old memory, a favorite that I pulled out sometimes to soften the hard times. I said, "Remember when Mary was about a month old and we went to Interior?"

"No."

I had to help Isaac remember. "Well, on that day it'd turned warm again even though we had had a heavy frost just a few days before. You called it Indian summer. You said it was our last chance to go to town before the cold set in. I hadn't been in months. I was proud to go—I had Mary to take." I laid my hand on his arm and felt the hardness in his muscles. "Remember?"

"No."

"I had my shopping to do. I was in the store holding Mary; I was waiting for Mrs. Johnston to finish up with Mrs. Nelson. When she did, Mrs. Nelson came over and asked to see Mary. It surprised me; most usually she wasn't all that friendly. Then I recalled that her children were all grown up and moved off. I could see she wanted to hold Mary so I let her. She ran her finger over Mary's cheek and she put the tip of her finger to her eyelashes. She told me that a girl with such eyelashes would break every boy's heart what looked her way. Me and her smiled over that." I stopped. Mary had been such a little thing. At the time I couldn't imagine her anywhere close to grown.

I said, "You were waiting by our wagon. 'Let's find a patch of sunshine,' you said, 'and have our dinner before heading home.' But we never did. Because across the street in front of the blacksmith's was a wagon, and there was a white girl sitting on the buckboard. Remember her, Isaac?"

"No."

"I do, just like it was yesterday. She had brown hair—braids— and freckles everywhere. I'll never forget her face. She was plain, but there was something pretty about her—her eyes maybe. She couldn't have been a day over sixteen, if that. One of her horses was missing, it must have thrown a shoe. But she didn't seem to mind in the least because she sat there playing her guitar like she was home in her own parlor."

"A mandolin," Isaac said. "Somebody asked her and that's what she said."

"That's right. A mandolin. It was the prettiest music. People stood around listening, enjoying themselves. For once nobody was in a hurry to get home to their chores. The girl told somebody her and her husband were from Billings, clear over in Montana. They were on their way home. I thought, *Husband? She's too young to be married; she isn't even wearing her hair up.*

"But here's what I especially like remembering about that day. You took Mary from me—she was asleep by then. You tucked her into her basket and put her on the floor of our wagon, right under the buckboard. Then you looked right into my eyes and I remember thinking, Why, Isaac's not the least bit sorry he married me. I've made him glad. He wanted a son but he got a daughter and still he's glad. My heart nearly busted wide open, I was that happy."

Isaac turned over on his side to face me. "You never complained," he said. "As hard as I worked you, you never complained."

"You didn't either," I said. Then, "You remember what happened next?"

"No."

"You bowed, like a gentleman from a book, and said, 'Mrs. DuPree, will you do me the honor of this dance?' Before I knew it, we were dancing right there in the middle of the street in front of all those people."

"It was a waltz," Isaac said.

"That's right, it was. It was our first dance. Married a whole year—more than a year—and we had never danced. Because we'd never courted."

Isaac said, "You kept your head down. All I could see was your bonnet."

"Couldn't imagine what all those white people were thinking about us. But at the same time, I wanted that sweet music to go on forever. I knew I was the luckiest woman in the world, married to you and having Mary. It was the finest moment of my life."

It was also when things changed between me and Isaac. It was when I became his wife.

I said, "When she stopped playing, the girl tipped her head to us like we had pleased her. Then you swung me up on the buckboard, and we rode off. We were halfway home before we thought to stop for dinner."

I was quiet so we could both think about that. After a while I said, "Everybody needs a sweet time in their lives."

"I don't disagree with that."

"That's what I want for our children, a dab of sweetness mixed in with all the hard work. Because that's mostly what it is. Hard work." I put my finger on his cheek. "They need to do their own choosing." I felt the rough stubble of his beard.

"I won't hold a gun to them."

"You won't have to. They'll do anything to please you."

"I'm their father."

"And that's a big thing."

Isaac didn't say anything.

I thought about the freckle-faced girl sitting on the buckboard that long-ago day in Interior. It was the end of October, her horse had thrown a shoe, and she and her husband were far from home. Everybody needed something to fall back on when they were having hard times, and for that girl it was her mandolin.

I thought about the root cellar with its empty shelves. I thought about snowdrifts as high as a man. I thought about water frozen in buckets and white blizzards that burned people's sight away. In blizzards, grown men were known to get lost between their houses and their barns. If they were lucky and found their way home, they were grateful that the worst thing that happened to them was frostbite. They were grateful if they only lost tips of noses, fingers, or a few toes. If a winter was particularly hard, cow chips for stoves ran low and children fell sick with chest ailments. Women died too, leaving their children motherless.

Our children needed something to fall back on during hard times. Isaac thought land was enough. I knew different. During hard times a person had to be able to say that it wasn't always so hard. A person needed to say, Once I played hopscotch with girls my age, once I played baseball with boys like me, and once I sang and clapped my hands at a neighborhood dance.

Isaac's breathing told me he was asleep. Tears came to my eyes. For him, everything was settled. He was going to Lead to work the mine this winter. Me and the children were staying behind. When it came time, he'd find a hardworking woman for John and men with land for our girls. Isaac was doing it for the ranch. The ranch was his way of lifting up our children. He didn't want his daughters to cook and clean for white people. He didn't want John in a slaughterhouse or taking white people for rides on hotel elevators. But that didn't mean ranching was easy. It didn't mean that a marriage based on a bargain lifted the heart.

"They need a dab of sweetness," I whispered. "For the hard times."

I got up, went to the parlor, struck a light, and sat at the writing desk. I got out two sheets of paper and blew the grit off of them. Isaac was going to Al McKee's tomorrow, and a few days later Mindy was going to Interior to take the train home. On one sheet of paper I wrote a letter to Mindy McKee. *Good-bye.* On the other, I wrote a letter to Mama. *Can we come?*

15

EMMA

The next morning just before breakfast, Isaac came up from the barn, bare chested but wearing a fresh pair of overalls. His face, hair, and arms shined from the scrubbing he had given himself at the pump. The children, seated at their places along the kitchen table, stared at him. They knew what he'd been doing. Isaac always opened up the belly of a cow when it died of a sickness.

"Where's Mary?" he said.

"Out walking," I said, spooning mush onto our plates. "She's taking it hard. Said she can't eat."

"She'll be all right once we get the new milk cow."

Isaac was going to the McKees' for the horses and the cow. I had stayed awake most of the night thinking about the letters I had written and worrying about the baby, wanting it to kick. It hadn't, but the bleeding had quit, and I tried to take that as a good sign.

Isaac said, "Jerseybell had pneumonia like I thought. That and her front belly was full of dirt. Pebbles too. Must have licked up fifteen pounds' worth. Thank God for the rain. Maybe she'll be the last to go down."

"The good Lord willing," I said, but the words had a hollow

sound. I put my hand to the letter in my left pocket. We were bound to lose more cattle this winter. "I'll get your shirt," I said to Isaac. "So we can eat."

He nodded and then glanced at the children. Their mouths were puckered and their eyes were big with sadness. Jerseybell was dead. Isaac gave a little shake as if to gather himself. Then he pulled air deep into his lungs making a show of filling his chest up with kitchen smells. He blew the air back out, his chest collapsing to its regular size. "Fresh bread," he said. "Nothing like it in the whole world." He grinned at the children. "Know what?"

"What?" John said.

"Your mother won me over the very first time I ate some of her bread. That and her biscuits. I said to myself, This little gal's more than pretty; she knows her way around a kitchen."

"Gosh," Liz said.

"That's right, Liz. I was a confirmed bachelor till I had a bite of your mother's bread. I fell to my knees right then and there and begged Miss Rachel Reeves to be my wife. Let that be a lesson. John, you marry a girl who cooks like your mama and you'll be a happy man. And girls, you make good bread and the world's yours for the asking."

"Daddy," Mary said from the doorway. "You're making that up. It takes more than bread."

"Mary," I snapped.

She put her head down. "I'm sorry, Daddy."

Isaac let that hang for a moment and then gave a sharp nod. "Apology accepted."

Mary had it right, I said to myself, but not how she thought. Isaac was making it up, doing it to get the children's minds off of

Jerseybell. But all the same, I didn't like what he'd said. Isaac never got down on his knees for anybody, and he surely hadn't for me. I had been nothing more than the kitchen help until he figured he could stake an extra claim in my name. But that wasn't the kind of story anybody wanted to tell their children.

I said, "This bread's turning cold. I'll get your shirt."

It took the rest of the morning for Isaac and John to get Jerseybell out of the barn. Waiting made my nerves bad. I wanted Isaac to get on the road to Al McKee's and then back home with the new milk cow. But Jerseybell came first. Our barn cat had gone missing during the winter, and without him, rats would be drawn if Isaac didn't cart Jerseybell off.

It was a hard job. The horses were at Al's, and strong as Isaac was, he couldn't haul Jerseybell out of the barn without them. After breakfast, he sharpened his saw. I knew how it would go; I had helped once before when years back a cow had died all tangled up in barbwire. Isaac would likely start with Jerseybell's legs, then her head. She was big; likely he'd saw her trunk in half, maybe into thirds.

"They're coming," Mary said finally from the parlor window.

Isaac and John were pushing the wheelbarrow out of the barn. It was covered with a tarp. "All right," I said to the girls. "Go on. Emma, you're staying here."

At the corral, the girls sat on the fence watching Isaac and John push the tarp-covered wheelbarrow back and forth to a canyon about a quarter mile off. The wheelbarrow made a deep track in the soft damp soil as clouds of flies hovered. I saw how in a few days' time the ground would dry and the track harden into place, reminding us always of this bad time.

Two-year-old Emma, with me on the porch, watched the wheelbarrow. I tried not to as I scrubbed clothes on the washboard. All I could think of was how time was passing.

"Last trip," I heard Isaac tell the girls. "Come on."

I knew what Isaac had in mind. He'd have the children stand near the rim of the canyon and say a prayer of thanks for all the good things Jerseybell had done for our family. He'd done this before when our first dog, Tracker, died after a fight with a coyote.

I scrubbed all the harder at the washboard. Overhead, turkey vultures glided, dipping into the canyon where Jerseybell was, some of them shrieking when driven off by the bolder ones. Emma pulled on my skirt. "Me too," she said, poking out her lower lip and pointing at Isaac and the others. The children and Rounder were walking with Isaac as he pushed the wheelbarrow. It made me think of Louisiana and how we used to follow the dead to the cemetery as someone beat a drum, one step at a time. It made me hope that someone had followed my brother Johnny when he was taken to the potter's field. I hoped someone had said a prayer over him.

Emma pulled at my skirt, her face tight. "Me," she said. "Me too."

I told her no. I couldn't carry her the quarter mile to the canyon and Mary shouldn't have to. Not today.

"Want to."

"No."

She stomped her foot.

"You're trying me," I said.

She stomped her foot again, harder.

"Get inside," I said.

"No."

I wiped my hands on my apron and reached for her hand that wasn't burned. She jerked her arm away and frowned at me. I narrowed my eyes at her. Emma screwed up her face and screamed. The shrillness of it ran down my spine. Isaac and the children stopped and looked up at us. Gritting my teeth, I waved them on.

Emma screamed louder. I picked her up, her legs kicking at my belly. "Stop it," I said, tightening my hold. I got her inside and to her bedroom and put her down. She shrieked. "Stop that," I said.

She screamed even more, stretching my nerves tight.

She threw herself down. Flat on her back, Emma kicked the floor with her heels, screaming. My nerves on fire, I itched to throw something—anything—against the wall.

My jaw set, I hurried to the kitchen, got the soothing syrup, and went back to the bedroom. "Lookie, Emma," I said, forcing my voice to be calm. I swung the brown bottle back and forth before her twisted face. "You like this; it's good." She gulped back a scream and lifted her head. Her eyes followed the bottle, trying to focus on the picture of the smiling white woman and her little boy. Frowning but curious, Emma sat up, sniffling, snot clotting her nose.

I said, "Get up, honey, and I'll give you some."

She bunched her eyebrows together, her face wet with tears. She got to her feet.

A few drops of syrup spilled on the wood floor as I poured out a tablespoon. I put the bottle on the dresser. I leaned down and carried the spoon to Emma's open mouth. She shot me a sly look. Her hand flipped up. The spoon flew in the air, spattering syrup on my face and on her dress.

She laughed.

I raised my hand and slapped Emma on the side of her head. She fell back, landing on her bottom, her eyes going wide with fright.

"Honey," I said, shocked by what I'd done. I'd hit her hard, harder than I'd ever hit any of our children. I reached out for her to make it right, and as I did, she drew herself up and rolled under the bed. The bandage on her burned hand came undone. She shrieked with pain. "You're all right," I said, coaxing. I got down on my hands and knees. "Now come on out."

Emma whined, holding her hurt hand close to her chest. "Honey," I said. She whined louder, making my skin crawl, my nerves bad all over again. "Come out from there," I said. "Right now." She started crying. A sudden wildness rose up inside of me. Jerseybell dead, winter coming, another baby on the way. I wanted to hit something. I glared at Emma. She flinched, whining all the more. "Stop it," I hissed. Emma's face froze.

Gripping the feather mattress, I pulled myself up. I grabbed the syrup bottle from the dresser and reared back, aiming to throw it against the wall.

Emma made a funny gurgling sound; I wanted to slap her. I pulled in some air, and all at once I saw Emma's scared face and I saw what I was about to do. *Calm yourself,* I imagined my mother saying. *Calm yourself.* "Mama," I whispered, "oh, Mama," and I rushed out of the room, through the parlor, and out the front door, slamming it behind me. On the porch, I slumped against the door.

Emma shrieked. I started to cover my ears but stopped. The syrup bottle was still in my hand.

I held it up before me. The bottle sparkled in the sunlight. Calm yourself. Some of the syrup had spilled on my hand but there was a good three inches of it left. Maybe a little more. I licked my hand, liking the sweet, heavy syrup. Isaac and the children were on their way to the canyon. There was only Emma, and she was inside. There was no one to see. I put the bottle to my lips.

The heavy liquid coated my throat, and I felt the syrup slip down into my belly. It felt good. I drank the rest of it. I sat down in one of the rockers and waited for my nerves to settle as the syrup slid down my veins all the way to my ankles.

I pulled in some air and blew it out. My arms turned heavy like they weren't part of me anymore. I watched the turkey vultures float. They were the prettiest things, riding the air that way with their wings outstretched. They tilted from side to side, making the silver in their wings shine in the sunlight. In a week's time, there'd be nothing left of Jerseybell but her bones. I heard Emma crying, but she was far away. The vultures circled and dipped, swooping in and out of the canyon.

I leaned forward in my chair. Isaac and the children stood on the canyon's rim. Isaac was probably saying something uplifting about Jerseybell.

I closed my eyes, liking the looseness in my arms and legs. The house was quiet. Everything was quiet. The baby wasn't going to be born today or tonight, and Isaac had plenty of time to get to Al's. My hand found the letter in my pocket that I was waiting to send to my mother. My mind was made up. I was taking the children to Chicago for the winter. Mary was going to go to a dance. Isaac didn't know a thing about any of it, but that didn't matter. I was doing it anyway.

After a while, I got up and looked in the bedroom window. Emma had come out from under the bed and laid on the middle of the floor, sucking her thumb. She'd worn herself out.

I walked behind the house and down the rise a short way to the trash heap. With my foot, I buried the syrup bottle under a pile of rusting tin cans. Taking my time, I walked back to the house. I was the first in my family to own a house. Dad and Mama always had a landlord; so did Sue and her husband, Paul. Johnny and Pearl rented a room in East St. Louis. I was the first to own anything that meant something.

Winter would go hard on our house with nobody here to care for it. I could hardly bear to think of it. Isaac said he'd get a hired hand in, but with me gone, it'd take at least another one. I didn't know how I was going to work that all out, but no matter what, I wasn't going to let anybody live in our house. Strangers weren't going to use my things. I'd rather the house fall down than have strangers dirty it up. The hired hands would have to settle for the dugout.

I put my hand on the door latch, feeling the solid metal of it. The key was somewhere, I wasn't sure where, but I'd look for it first thing. That way I could lock the door when me and the children left the Badlands.

After a while I went inside. Emma's eyes were half closed.

Maybe I hadn't hit her as hard as I thought. Other than spanking their bottoms, I'd never hit any of our children before. It shamed me that I had done it now.

I remembered Peaches Orwell what lived behind Mrs. Du-Pree's boardinghouse. Her baby screamed day and night, and Peaches always wore a stretched-out, tight look on her face. I put my hands to my face, surprised that my cheeks were wet. I rubbed them, not wanting to carry Peaches's look.

"Honey," I said to Emma, holding out my hand. "Let's get your dolly and get that hand of yours fixed up." She looked at me as if considering. I smiled at her. She got up and put her good hand in mine.

The syrup made me feel heavy and light all at the same time. "All better now," I told Emma.

16

MARY AND JOHN

I t'll be after supper," Isaac said as me and Mary cleared the noon dinner dishes later that day. "Don't wait for us."

Just like that, the good feeling brought on by the soothing syrup left me. My hand slid over my swollen belly and went to my apron pocket. I fingered the letter I'd written Mama, remembering each word.

Mama it is time the children got to know family. There GRANDMA and AUNT. And COUSINS. If you think it is safe this winter from RACE RIOTS can we come?

The nerve of it made my knees wobbly. It wouldn't take much for Isaac to figure out what I was planning. One careful look and he'd see it on my face. I turned away from him and steadied myself against the kitchen counter. "I'll keep something warm," I heard myself say.

"Obliged," he said, and then, "Ready, son?"

John took one last gulp of water and was out the door, breathless with his good luck. Helping Isaac with Jerseybell that morning had taken the starch clean out of him, but just the idea of going to the McKees' perked him up. John admired Al almost as much as he admired Isaac. Since coming home three days ago, John had talked about nothing but Al McKee.

"He'll scare the Germans something big," John had said to me just the day before. The two of us had been on the porch; I had clothes soaking in a tub. "He's a mountain man," John said, "a real mountain man."

"That so?"

"Yeah, and he showed me his rifles. For grizzlies. Used to hunt them in the wilds of Canada. Him and his daddy, when he was my age. Showed me his gutting knife too." He held his hands out, palms facing, and stretched them further and further apart. "It was this big, that knife was. Me and Daddy, we're thinking about it."

"That so?" The water in the tub turned muddy. I took the clothes out and put them in a dry one. "Help me empty this. I'm needing fresh."

John picked up one of the handles; I got the other. He said, "Daddy said maybe before the first frost we could go hunting in the Black Hills, get ourselves a few bears. Make a good cover for the beds, Daddy said. Plenty of meat for the winter too."

Halfway down the porch steps, the water sloshing, I stopped. "What's that?"

"Daddy said bear hunting would be a fine adventure."

My mouth went dry.

"Mama?" John said. "What's wrong?"

"Nothing," I said and I got myself moving again. We went out into the yard, and I watched John from the corner of my eye. His tongue was poked out some as he held his end of the tub, careful to not flood the prairie grasses as we went from patch to patch.

John was too thin, anybody could see that, but he was tall and wiry, the muscles showing in his arms as he tilted the tub. A few days of enough water and better eating showed too. His light skin had lost its dullness; it looked alive again. But it was the shine in John's eyes that seized my heart with sadness. He was going bear hunting, one more fine adventure thought up by his daddy. I saw what would happen a few weeks after the hunting trip. "Take care of the ranch, son," Isaac was going to tell John. "It'll be an adventure; you'll make me proud," and John would want to believe that. He was only ten, but with those words behind him, he'd put his shoulders back, stand tall, and want to do it.

John was going to buck me. He wouldn't want to go to Chicago, not for anything. I looked off toward Grindstone Butte. A ten-year-old boy could run off and hide there. In the canyons too. I wouldn't know where to begin to look for him. I tightened my grip on the washtub handle. I was going to lose John.

Don't think about it, not right now, I told myself as me and the girls stood on the porch ready to see Isaac and John off to the McKees' place. I handed John the cloth sack we used for carrying lunches. I said, "Give this to Mrs. McKee." He squinted at me, the midafternoon sun in his face, his eyes only a few inches lower than mine. I wanted to put my arms around him and hold him close. Instead, I said, "It's a few biscuits for their trip east."

I took the letter from my right apron pocket and gave it to Isaac. "For Mindy. I had to say good-bye."

"When'd you write this?" he said.

"Last night. Couldn't sleep."

The other letter, the one in my left pocket, was big and heavy. My nerve buckled. If Isaac knew what my words said, he'd see me for what I was: a woman what had gone against him. He wouldn't do like most men. He wouldn't hit me; he wouldn't even yell all that much. What he'd do would be worse. He'd take on a hardness—it'd make me wither up inside. He'd turn his voice cold and tell me to go on, get out, if that was what I wanted. Go to your mama. Our bargain ended long ago. You got your year; I got my land.

I put my hand in my left pocket. My fingers froze up. Take the little girls while you're at it, I imagined Isaac saying. But not John. Or Mary. I get them, not you. Understand?

I did. But I had to try. I couldn't let our children freeze to death, I couldn't let them starve, not without a fight. I was doing right even if it felt wrong, even if it made me sick. I drew in some air and pulled out the letter. I held it out to Isaac, wishing my hand wouldn't shake so. "It's to Mama," I said. "Thought Mindy'd be willing." I stopped, my mouth filled with cotton. I worked up some spit. "Maybe she could post it. Before getting on the train."

Isaac studied the envelope, his eyebrows raised. I said, "It's about Johnny," and that was some true.

"She'll be glad to get it," he said. He put both letters in his knapsack. I let out some air, relieved. Isaac rolled his shoulders like he was trying to get rid of an ache. He was sore, I knew, from sawing Jerseybell. Then too, just three days ago, there had been the hard walk home in the rain and mud. For a moment I wanted to put my hand on his arm and tell him I was grateful for all that he did. For a moment I wanted to say I was sorry for how it was all turning out. Instead, I thought of our children, hardened my heart, and looked past him.

"Rounder," Isaac commanded. "Stay home. Be on guard." The

dog's tail drooped, but he came to my side. I put my hand behind his ears and watched Isaac and John walk off, tears coming to my eyes as the Chicago-bound letter started on its way to my mother.

Me and Mary got busy with laundry as soon as they were out of eyeshot. We made a fire outside and had just gotten the kettle of water to a strong boil when Rounder sat up, ears perked. He let out a loud bark and shot off down the rise, running toward the two people—Isaac and John, as it turned out—that were walking back up the road toward the house.

My insides went weak. Isaac had turned back. He had read my letter.

Mary and the girls ran down the rise to meet them, calling to them. I stepped back to the porch and leaned against the railing, drawing in big gasps of air. A sob rolled up from the bottom of my throat. *Isaac*, I thought. *Don't do what you mean to do.*

"Mama!" John hollered.

It was all going to end.

"Cows got out!" John hollered louder. Then Isaac was calling, "Rachel, you all right?"

I lifted my head. He was hurrying up the rise to me, the children staying at the barn. "Rachel," he called again. There was worry in Isaac's voice, not cold hardness. Maybe he hadn't read the letter. Maybe he thought the baby had started.

"You all right?" Isaac said when he got closer. Relief washed over me. I saw that he hadn't opened the letter.

"Yes," I said. "Just some tired."

"You sure? I don't have to go."

"You do," I said. "The milk cow." Then, because Isaac expected it, I said, "Some cows got out?"

"Seven of them. Came across them on the road, a few of them nicked up a fair amount from the barbwire. We rounded them up but I've got to fix that fence. Need my fencing pliers."

All at once, I saw the meaning of it. The letter wasn't meant to be posted. The cows broke out for a reason; Isaac's coming back was a second chance. I wasn't meant to go to Chicago, I wasn't supposed to take the children. "Mama's letter," I said, putting my hand out.

"Still in my pack," Isaac said. "Safe and sound."

"I—" Words jammed up in my mouth. I had to get the letter back. Isaac wasn't looking at me; he was looking off to the road that stretched west. I had to have a good reason for wanting it back.

"Damn cows," Isaac was saying.

"The letter," I said.

He shook his head. "Been fighting all summer to keep them up on their feet, and what do they do? Turn on me, trying to run off." He looked back at me; he wasn't thinking about the letter. "Like they think it'd be better somewhere else."

Heat rose to my cheeks. Isaac might not have read my letter to Mama but he knew what was in my heart. He said, "I've got to fix that fence before any more break out. I'd still like to get over to Al's today. You all right with that?"

"Yes," I said, because all at once I was. The letter was written. I was doing it for our children. I wanted it posted.

"Going through the rest of his herd will take awhile. Means

I'll likely stay the night." He nodded toward my belly and gave me a questioning look.

The bleeding from the baby had stopped. There hadn't been any pain, but neither had there been any kicking. Most usually, before going into labor, I had a day or two of twinges. That hadn't started yet. "Go on," I said, thinking how I wanted that milk cow and how I wanted the letter sent. "But I'll be looking for you early morning."

He gave me a quick smile. "I'll be on my way home first dawn." He cocked his head, looking at me. "You look all done in."

"I'm all right."

"I'll have John stay, help with the chores."

"That'll make him sorry."

Isaac scanned the sky, reading the clouds. "Place needs a man," he said. "John knows that." Then he put an arm around my shoulders and pulled me to him. "In the morning then."

"First dawn."

Isaac let go of me, nodded, and headed to the barn for his tools. It wasn't but a handful of minutes before he left again, waving good-bye to me and the children, both letters riding in his knapsack.

The rest of the afternoon passed like every other—with chores—and I was glad of it. Work was good for tamping down all my queasy feelings. I left the laundry to Mary and the little girls while me and John shoveled out Jerseybell's stall. It turned my belly but I kept at it, scrubbing Jerseybell's blood and small meaty bits from the wheelbarrow. Better me than Mary; it'd break her heart.

When we were done, John got the rake, I took the long-handled sickle, and the five of us—Rounder too—went down to the cottonwood.

"Can I?" John said, looking at the sickle.

"You're not big enough," I said.

"Daddy would let me."

"Daddy's not here."

I raked as best I could while Mary swung the sickle, cutting dried-up grass to put down in the barn for the new cow. I was slow and heavy, held down by the baby in my belly and the worry in my heart. Alise and Emma sat on the piles of cut grass, doing their best to keep it from blowing away, while John and Liz stuffed it in the hemp sacks. Above us, thin clouds stretched low across the sky. It was hot but not like before the storm. Isaac was right. The sun was losing its grip. Fall had come.

Writing the letter to my mother wasn't enough; I understood that. I had to raise money for the train trip. I had to find a way to take care of the livestock while we were gone. My hands gripped the sanded wood of the rake's pole as I followed behind Mary, the sickle swinging, cutting down the grass. The rake's prongs caught in the tough, long roots that held fast to the soil. I yanked; one of the prongs twisted. Roots had nearly worn me and Isaac raw when fourteen years ago we chopped sod bricks for the dugout and barn. I had cursed those roots—Isaac had too—but we kept on. I was younger then, I thought to myself as I bent over and worked the prong free. Fresher to it all.

I needed money. And a plan.

Nothing came to me as I kept at the raking, Emma behind me sitting on a pile of grass. I couldn't see myself past the November day when I'd hitch the horses to the wagon, load the children, and head to town and the train depot. What was I going to do if John ran off? Panic tightened my chest. *Scared,* I whispered to myself. I was scared. I had to have a plan, but I couldn't think. *Let it come to you,* I told myself, as the rake caught again in the roots. There was time. Just let your mind circle around it; a plan is sure to come.

Later that day, after supper, things went as always. The little girls played with their rag dolls until bedtime. Mary and John checked John's rabbit traps—still empty—and then wandered off to the wash to throw pebbles into the running water. I sat on the porch doing my mending, trying to come up with a plan.

I put my hand down and rubbed Rounder's ears. He looked up at me and I could hardly bear it. I'd be leaving him too.

All at once, I felt sick. I had never kept anything so big from Isaac. I had never wanted to or had a need to. But I was doing right. I was doing it for our children.

We'd only be gone a few months, I told myself. If the winter was mild, we'd be back by the end of March. Not that it would matter. Isaac was going to turn against me for leaving. He'd never forgive me; it'd never be the same between us. But if me and the children stayed the winter and things went bad, I'd have hard feelings of my own. I looked off toward Grindstone Butte, its sharp edges fading some in the twilight. There'd be hard feelings all the way around. There was no middle road on this one.

It was when I got up to call Mary and John in from evening chores that the sick feeling in my belly turned into a cramp, its sudden hardness making me suck in my breath.

I sat back down. *Nerves*, I told myself. Or maybe something I ate. I rocked slowly in my chair, cold and clammy with fear. I waited for the next cramp, and when nothing else happened, I got up again and called for Mary and John. They came on the first call, and it was later, while Mary was reading *Swiss Family Robinson* to John in the kitchen, that another cramp pulled me. This time it wasn't nerves or something I'd eaten.

My fingers drummed the rocker's armrests. The front door stood open. The lantern sitting on the kitchen table cast a small patch of wavering light on the wood-planked porch floor. I listened to Mary read but the words meant nothing to me.

It was too late to send John to get Isaac. He might get lost in the dark. The McKees didn't live on the road like we did. The last mile to their place was nothing more than two narrow grooves in the ground. And the coyotes—a ten-year-old boy on foot wouldn't stand a chance against a hungry pack. It'd be the same for Mary and anyway, I needed her with me.

Rounder nuzzled my knee with his cold, wet nose. The Milky Way, high above me, arced with the curve of the earth. It was bright with hundreds of stars.

I wasn't one for asking for Jesus' help if I could figure out a way on my own. It wasn't my place to bother Him, especially now that He'd sent rain. He was plenty busy with the war over in France and all those soldiers in trenches shooting at each other. But tonight I looked up at the Milky Way and asked Him to give me strength.

My prayer said, I gathered myself. "Mary. John. Come on out here."

"What's wrong?" Mary said when they came out.

"Sit down." She took the other rocker, and John sat at my

feet, crossing his long legs. I said, "There's something you have to know." I paused. "There's a baby coming."

One of them made a little squeaking sound. Birthing babies wasn't something I talked about with the children, not even with Mary. When there was a baby on the way, the older children just came to understand.

I said, "Daddy might not be here, not in time."

Mary drew in some air. John said, "Why not?"

"It might come sometime in the night or maybe early morning. I don't know."

"You mean tonight?" John said.

"Could be. Babies are like that, you don't ever know ahead of time." My hands shook. I tried to make them rest quiet on the armrests. "You might have to help me get this baby born. If Daddy's not back."

"I don't want to," John said.

"I know it. But you might have to."

John's face was frozen up with fear. I knew what he was thinking. He was remembering when Emma was born. It had taken all night. Isaac had made John and the girls get in Mary's bed. The four of them covered their heads with the blanket and still they heard me. I heard them too, crying.

"Listen to me, John," I said.

All at once, a cramp took hold, catching me unaware. Through watery eyes, I saw the two of them stare at me. I put my hand up to them, waiting until the cramp began to back off. I blew out some air. "I'm all right," I said.

"See there?" Mary said to John. "Mama needs us. And just think what Daddy'll say."

"What'll he say?"

"He'll say how he came home and found a baby waiting for him. He'll say how you and me did it."

"Daddy might not like that."

"No, he'll be proud."

John chewed his lower lip, turning that over in his mind.

"Real proud," Mary said.

And he"ll talk about it?"

"For years."

The tension eased in John's thin shoulders. Mary was her father's daughter, I realized. Like Isaac, Mary knew just what to say to buck up a person and make him think he could do most anything.

"That's right," I said, "Daddy'll be proud 'cause your part in this, John, is real important. We can't birth this baby without you. Even if your daddy gets home in time, there's things you need to do. Like see to your sisters."

As my hand rubbed circles on Rounder's back, I told them I'd be fine on my own for a long time, maybe most of the night, even if I got to looking a little peaked. "That's just nature's way," I said. "Getting a baby born is hard work. You two'll go on to bed tonight, like always. When I need you—if I do—I'll wake you."

"Yes, Mama," Mary said.

"All right then." I put my mind to what came next. "You've seen calves being born. It's the same way for babies." Mary and John sucked in air. I had shocked them. I said, "I'll be bearing down, pushing to get the baby out. You might have to help; you might have to pull it out some." My mouth was dry. I ran my tongue along my teeth to work up some spit. "I'll tell you what to do, and you do it even if you think you're hurting me. Because you're not. It just looks that way. Understand?"

"Yes, ma'am."

In the lantern light, their faces were drawn and their eyes were scared. They'd seen cows struggle when giving birth; they'd seen some of them die. "Come here, you two," I said. "Give me your hands." They came to me, and I smiled at them. "I'm proud of you, real proud." They smiled back, their lips wobbly.

"There's one more thing." I squeezed their hands, wanting to give them courage. "Just like with calves, there's going to be some blood. On the baby. But the baby's not bleeding, that's just nature's way. Nobody's hurt, not me, not the baby. Just wipe it up. Like with a calf, there'll be mucus. Get it out of the baby's nose and mouth, first thing."

"Yes, ma'am."

"And it's all right if you get to feeling puny. Just go outside and get yourself some fresh air. Come on back when you're feeling like yourself again. But come back. I'm counting on you."

"Yes, ma'am."

"Remember this. No matter how I get to looking, I'm still Mama. I'll be there the whole time telling you what to do. Now say it all back to me." They did, and between the two of them, they got most of it right. I made them say it again.

That done, Mary and John pressed even closer to me, and we stayed like that, holding hands. Together we listened to the night sounds of crickets and locusts calling for their mates as prairie grass rustled in the wind.

I didn't tell Mary and John that the baby hadn't kicked for a few days. I didn't tell them I'd been bleeding off and on. Saying anything more would only scare them worse. Scare me worse too. I had to buck them up. "You're going to have a new brother or sister," I said. "Won't that be something fine?"

They nodded and I wondered if they heard the hollowness behind my words. "Mama?" John said.

"What?"

"Think we could get ourselves a boy this time?"

That made me smile. "We'll see."

17

PAUL LAURENCE DUNBAR

I got ready for the birthing after the children were asleep. John had gotten two buckets of water like I had told him and had put them on the kitchen table. The small butcher knife was clean, but I washed it anyway. In the bedroom, I hung a lantern from a nail on the wall and put the knife on top of the pine dresser beside the white porcelain basin. Before going to bed, Mary had crawled under my bed to get the basin, the one used only for afterbirth. Without me asking, she washed out the layers of white dust that had pooled in it.

Mary had also gotten out the soft cotton rags, stained from birthings, from my bottom dresser drawer. I had washed, ironed, and folded them into small squares after Emma's birth two years ago. I put the rags beside the basin and as I did, I knew that this was the last time I'd ever need them.

It would be a comfort to have Isaac's gold pocket watch with me. Its ticking would fill the quiet and I could count along with it. The watch had belonged to Isaac's father, and inside the cover was a miniature of Mrs. DuPree and Isaac made when he was six months old or so. He wore a long white gown and sat on his mama's lap—a young, thin, soft Mrs. DuPree what I had never known.

The pocket watch, like Isaac, had been with me through all

my birthings. Isaac liked timing my pains; it gave him something to do when there was nothing to do but wait. But today the watch was with him. He always carried it when he left home, even to go to Al McKee's. A man, Isaac believed, needed to have a precise awareness of time when he was conducting business.

Good Lord, I thought, *I forgot to have Mary get my birthing gown.* It was in the bottom drawer of the dresser. Groaning, I bent down and ran my hand inside the drawer looking for it. Instead, my hand brushed against buttons. Like a blind woman, I traced the buttons to the broad lace collar that circled a neckline. It was my wedding dress, folded into a perfect square more than a foot tall. It'd been years since I'd last admired it; I couldn't remember when. With care, I lifted it out of the drawer and put it on the bed.

I found my birthing gown pushed back into the far corner of the drawer. I shook it out and white dust flew everywhere, making me sneeze. I expected that to bring on a pain, but it didn't.

I put the birthing gown to my nose. It smelled of soap and sunshine and grit. After each birth, I soaked it a day and a night to get out the worst of the stains. When I wore it for Mary, it scratched my skin so bad that I carried sores on my shoulder blades for a handful of days. But seven births later, the gown was soft from all the washings, even though faint brown stains still showed the birthing of every one of my children.

I put the gown on the bed beside my wedding dress. Taking a rag, I went to the kitchen and dipped it in a water bucket. Back in the bedroom, I got undressed.

The baby heaved as I washed between my legs. I gripped the bedpost and counted until I lost track.

When it was over, I put on the birthing gown and sat in the rocker. Rounder came into the room and with a grunt, settled down on the floor beside me.

"John'll mind if he wakes up and finds you gone," I said. "But I'm glad for the company." He thumped his tail. "You're a good dog. Should've named you Faithful." And then I thought about Isaac being gone when I needed him home. I thought about his plans to leave us this winter, and how I'd be doing my own leaving too.

With my foot, I pushed the rocker back and forth, trying to ease the ache in my back. Things could go bad if Mary had to deliver the baby. She had a steady hand and a stout heart, but all the same, she was just a child. Grown women had been known to panic if a birthing went wrong. If something bad happened, it'd go rough on Mary. It'd be the kind of thing she'd never forget. Or forgive herself for.

Through watery eyes, I saw my wedding dress that I'd left on the bed. I got up, picked it up, and sat back down. I blew the thin layer of gray dust that coated it. The white scalloped lace collar was so pretty, I'd nearly forgotten. And it hadn't yellowed at all. That would please Mama no end. She had made the lace.

My back throbbed. I shifted my weight some, grateful that the labor pains had stopped. *Everything is all right,* I told myself. The baby was waiting on Isaac.

I fingered the lace collar, following the scalloped edging. On the very first Saturday afternoon after Isaac had agreed to marry me, I had met Mama and Sue on the corner across the street from the Palmer Hotel. They laughed when they saw me coming. Like them, I had just gotten off work and I was nearly running with excitement, darting around knots of slow-moving people, the cloth handbag with my weekly pay in it pressed to my bosom. I smiled to think what Mrs. DuPree would do if she knew how I planned to spend the money. At the street corner, the three of us caught the trolley that carried us to Green's Fine Fabrics. There we studied books of dress patterns and fingered bolts of material.

I wanted my wedding dress to be a light blue, and Sue thought I looked best in yellow. It was Mama what settled the matter. "You'll want something dark for the train ride," she said. "The soot will be something awful, going all that way." After a while, the three of us settled on a plum-colored satin.

Every Sunday afternoon for five weeks we sewed in the front room of our two-bedroom rented house. Mama did the lace work while Sue worked the Singer machine making the skirt. I stitched by hand the bodice with its full, pleated sleeves and made the buttonholes that ran down the back. While we worked, we talked about that morning's preaching, and who was in church and who wasn't. We talked about who had the fanciest hat with the most feathers, and who was making eyes at who. We talked about the people at our jobs, and we talked about all of Sue's suitors and how Paul Anders kept asking her to marry him. We talked about what I needed for my own kitchen. But the one thing we didn't talk about was how far away I was going or how lonesome it'd be for those left behind.

On my wedding day—a Wednesday—Mama and Sue helped me get into my dress. "Just look at you," Mama told me. "You're as pretty as a picture."

"Prettier," Sue said.

They kissed me good-bye; we told each other again that we'd

write every Sunday. Mama cried some, and then they went on to work at the hotel. That left just me and Dad in the kitchen, with neither of us having much to say. My traveling trunk filled with clothes, linens, dishes, and pans sat by the back door. I was too nervous to eat the breakfast I'd cooked, but Dad's appetite was good and he ate in a hurry. After he mopped up the last of his eggs with a crust of bread, he left without saying a word and limped back to his bedroom. I washed up the dishes, wearing my apron to cover my dress. I got weepy thinking how it was the last time I'd wash Mama's dishes. I was drying the last one when Dad came in wearing his Sunday suit, his gray hair combed. "What're you looking at?" he said.

"Nothing." I swallowed. Then, "You."

"Isn't this your wedding day?" I nodded, all at once smiling, happy, not minding his gruffness. I hadn't figured on Dad coming to the wedding. He hadn't wanted me to marry Isaac DuPree. He disapproved of me going off with a man he hadn't met.

But on my wedding day Dad limped two blocks down to the main corner and hailed a horse cab to come to the house. "I'm not having my daughter meeting her groom with mud on her shoes," he said while the driver loaded my trunk. "New, too, aren't they?"

It was grand riding in that horse cab with Dad in his Sunday suit beside me. When we pulled up at the church, Isaac stood on the gravel sidewalk looking down the street like he expected me to be on foot. My breath caught as I watched him from the cab window. He wore his army uniform and was fresh shaved. He could have had any woman in Chicago. I could hardly believe he was willing to settle for me.

The cab driver opened the door, and when I got out, Isaac

took a step back. It was like he didn't know me in my satin dress, my waist pinched narrow by my corset, my face half covered by the wide-brimmed plum felt hat. The shock on his face showed that he had never thought of me in anything but patched-over dresses and aprons.

Isaac recovered enough of his wits to introduce himself to Dad, saying how pleased he was to finally meet the father of his bride. Dad only grunted. Then, still looking at me like he didn't know me, Isaac offered his arm. "No," Dad said. "She's still mine."

"Yes, sir," Isaac said. "That she is."

He followed us into the church. I felt his eyes on me, and the secret pleasure of it made heat rise to my cheeks. During the ceremony, with Dad and my brother Johnny nearby, Preacher Teller told me and Isaac to stay on Jesus' path and to always look to the Lord in times of trouble. *I will,* I told myself. And then I heard the words "for better for worse, for richer for poorer" and "till death us do part," and all I could think was, *Please, Lord, let death do the parting. Don't let it be our bargain.*

Now, sitting in my rocker, I touched the lace collar on my wedding dress. There were thirty-four pearl-shaped buttons that ran from the back of the collar clear down to the waist. Mama had paid for the buttons. They were her gift to me.

I wore the plum satin dress on the train. It had been a long trip; sitting together on the train as man and wife changed everything. We didn't know what to say. There was no boarding-house kitchen to sit in, no dishes to wash, nothing to help us talk. There was only the pleasure of our arms side by side, sharing the same armrest, our fingertips meeting by accident from time to time. But it was a pleasure so deep that there were moments when I was faint with wooziness.

The trip, a dusty journey with many stops and starts, took the day and the following night. We rode it sitting up, and we changed trains once in Omaha long after dark. On the first train, when we walked into the dining car, the other passengers stopped eating and stared. Maybe those white people were surprised that Negroes could afford the dining car. Or maybe they had never seen a Negro in an army uniform and his wife in such a fine dress. The man who took the diners to their tables gave us a peculiar look. He pursed his lips and pointed to the table closest to the kitchen. I didn't think a thing of it, but when I saw the tight look on Isaac's face, I said, "My, isn't this something? Our food'll be good and hot coming directly from the kitchen." The tightness in Isaac's face faded, and then he smiled some, making everything all right again.

We got to Sioux Falls as the sun was coming up, less than twenty-four hours since the wedding. The next train to Interior didn't leave until late evening. Zeb Butler, from Isaac's army days, met us with his buggy at the train station. Glad to see each other, Isaac and Zeb laughed and slapped each other's backs. I stood off to the side, my black cloth purse in my gloved hands as the two of them joshed. There were white people everywhere on the station platform, and I didn't know what to do with myself, so I made like I was taking in the sights.

Sioux Falls, South Dakota. Isaac had said it was the last big town east of the Missouri, and so I had pictured it the size of Chicago. But there wasn't much to the station, only four tracks, and I didn't see the first skyscraper anywhere, just low wooden buildings. There weren't any Negroes either, other than us, and that gave me a feeling of uneasiness.

Zeb said something, Isaac laughed, and then he turned to me and took my arm. "Rachel," he said to Zeb.

Zeb put his hand to his heart and bowed. "How do you do?" he said. He was older than Isaac; there was gray in his hair and he hadn't shaved in four or five days. He was almost as dark as me. His belly hung over his belt, and I thought I smelled drink on him.

"My wife can't wait to meet the bride," Zeb told me as we started toward his horses and buggy, picking our way over the dirt road. He took my hand to help me up into the buggy, and I believed that he held it longer than what was needed. I sat in the front and waited as the men strapped my trunk and Isaac's bag to the back of the buggy. Zeb Butler climbed up beside me then, and Isaac got in the backseat. I didn't like how Zeb let the side of his leg rest beside mine. I tried to make myself small.

"Yep," Zeb said after he cracked the reins and the buggy began to roll. "My wife wants to meet the woman that finally caught Isaac DuPree."

That got me to wondering just how many others had tried.

The Butler house was on the edge of town, not all that far from the train station. It was a faint yellow, it wanted fresh paint, and the yard needed trimming. The house beside it was empty and boarded up. Iris Butler, thinner and taller than her husband, came out to the alley to greet us. Her apron, I saw, was fresh, and that cheered me. She hugged Isaac and then me. "You got yourself a wild one," she whispered into my ear. "But you'll tame him. Like I did Zeb."

Startled, I tried to smile and think of something to say. "Much obliged for the hospitality," I managed to say. As soon as the words were out, I felt lost and homesick in that strange town. I didn't know the Butlers. I didn't know anybody. Isaac was a stranger; even I was a stranger in my beautiful dress. I should be cooking breakfast at the boardinghouse. I should be going home tonight to my parents. I should be sleeping beside Sue tonight, not by this man who somehow had become my husband.

Iris Butler said, "You could stand a washing up. Come on." I followed her upstairs, and she took me to a bedroom that had a damp smell. She told me that most Negroes that passed through town stayed a night or two with them but Isaac was an old friend and the room was free. The bed, I saw, sagged in the middle, and its spread might have been white a long time ago. "Got you a pitcher of water, a towel too," Iris said, nodding to the washstand beside the bed. "Breakfast'll be ready when you are." She started to turn away but then she stopped. "That's one fine dress," she said, her eyes sweeping up and down my figure. She studied me like a man might. My cheeks turned hot. "Isaac did good for himself," she said. "But he always did have an eye for such things."

"Oh," I said, and then I stumbled toward the washstand, feeling faint, not liking the meaning behind her words.

I washed up as best as I could, the cool water in the pitcher perking me up. I told myself that all men had an eye for women and that Isaac was no different. I dried my face and neck with the towel that Iris had laid out, trying not to notice that someone had used it before me. Instead, I reminded myself that I might be wearing a plum satin dress, but I was just the kitchen help. Isaac had married me only so he could stake a claim in my name. That was all I was to him, just a claim.

My hands shaking, I took off my hat and fixed my hair. I gathered my courage, went downstairs, and found the three of them at the kitchen table eating. I sat down with them and picked at the eggs and bacon. Isaac, Zeb, and Iris talked about the army days at Fort Robinson. Zeb and Iris had been married for five years when Zeb joined up, and Iris earned extra money by doing laundry for one of the officers and his family. The three of them laughed over the times that they'd had at the fort. They clicked their tongues and shook their heads when talking about the people they once knew. I felt far away from them all; I didn't belong. I kept a smile, though, and laughed when they did. But I was alone in that room with those people. I didn't like the Butlers, and I didn't know what to make of Isaac. Laughing and joshing, he had become as rough cut as Zeb and Iris.

Iris washed the dishes, and I dried as the men talked about the homesteads Isaac had staked in our names. "That's wild country out there," Zeb said. "It's going to be hard to make a go of it. Most folks don't last a winter. DuPree, you sure about this?"

"Hush," Iris said, glancing at me. "Zeb, these two are worn out, and I'll be late for work if I don't hurry up. As for you, Old Lady Chapman is sure to be looking for you with a list of chores a mile long." Her hands made a shooing motion at Isaac and me. "Now you two go on. Make yourselves at home. Me and Zeb'll be gone the better part of the day. Be close to suppertime before we get home."

When Zeb thought I weren't looking, he winked at Isaac. "That's right," he said, grinning. "Won't be nobody to bother you all day."

My belly tightened. Alone with Isaac. "I'll have supper started," I said to Iris, my voice sounding tinny in my ears, my hands gripping the dish towel.

"I bet you will," Zeb said. He laughed hard and Iris did too. The coarseness of their meaning made me burn with shame and confusion. My eyes down, I twisted the dish towel even tighter.

"Zeb," Isaac said, a note of warning in his voice. Zeb and Iris didn't seem to hear. Still laughing, they made a big show of leaving, slamming the door behind them, calling out good-bye too loud.

When they were gone, Isaac said, "Put down that towel." I did.

"You all right?" he said.

I couldn't look at him. I didn't want to be alone with him in the Butlers' house. It felt dirty to me; I wanted to scrub the floors, I wanted to wash the bedclothes, I wanted to get back on the train and go home.

"Zeb," Isaac said. "He—"

I looked up at him. His tone told me that he didn't like what Zeb had said. The sick feeling in my belly eased. Isaac was a gentleman; he was a better cut than Zeb. He understood my shame; he wasn't going to push. He was going to give me time. "Yes," I said, relieved. "I'm all right."

His eyes darted past the kitchen to the stairs that went up to the bedroom. I took it to mean that he thought I should have a little rest. I smiled my gratitude and began walking that way.

Isaac followed and that surprised me. I stopped and looked back at him.

I was wrong. There was expectation in Isaac's eyes. I was his wife, and I had told him that I was all right.

The house was quiet with the Butlers gone. The wood floors creaked and each stair step groaned as we climbed them. My dress rustled, and I held the skirt to keep from tripping. I went into the narrow bedroom where I'd washed up earlier and stared at the bright red wallpaper roses that swirled and climbed up the walls. Mama would call it trashy. Sunlight flooded in the eastward window, showing dirty streaks. The room was too bright but the window didn't have a shade. My back to him, I listened as Isaac closed the door behind him, the latch catching with a click.

He put his pocket watch on the dresser beside me. I heard him take off his jacket and work his arms out of his suspenders. I stood frozen, my back to him, my breath held.

"Turn around," Isaac said.

I couldn't get my feet to move.

"Damn," he said. He let out a whistle of air. "You don't know anything about this. Do you?"

Still not looking at him, I shook my head.

"How old are you?"

"Twenty-five."

"Twenty-five." I heard the surprise in his voice. Then he said, "You don't have to—it isn't part of our deal."

For two months I had thought about what it would be like when me and Isaac were alone. It had made me shake with excitement. But in that strange room in a strange town, I was scared. I didn't really know what to expect past a kiss. But I wanted Isaac to keep me, and I had only a year to prove myself. Every day mattered. That day most of all.

Over my shoulder, I said, "My buttons. I can't reach them."

I stood without moving while Isaac undid all thirty-four buttons. I kept my eyes fixed on his pocket watch on the dresser, my heart pounding to the jerky tick of the second hand. The shock of Isaac's touch made my skin sing. He didn't seem to notice the gooseflesh on my neck. He didn't rush; he took his time, careful not to tear the satin.

Years later, in the Badlands waiting on a baby that had to get itself born, I let myself cry. *Isaac*, I thought. *You never hurt my flesh. Only my heart.* After a while my tears ran out. I put the wedding dress away, blew out the lantern, and got into bed.

Early in the night, my water broke. It wasn't much more than a slow trickle. I got up and cleaned up as best as I could and then went back to bed. From time to time the baby pulled me awake, but not all that often and not with any kind of pattern. When the parlor clock chimed five times, I got out of bed and sat in my rocker to help ease the pinching ache in my back. I hadn't had a labor pain for a long while, and I told myself that was good. As soon as it lightened up a bit, I'd send John for Isaac. That way John could meet him halfway, hurry him along.

When I woke John an hour later and told him what I wanted him to do, he said, "I'll run the whole way to Mr. McKee's."

"No. You'll wear out too quick. Walk. Promise me."

I told him to get two cold biscuits for his breakfast and to take Rounder with him. Then I went back to my bedroom and sat in the rocker. Mary, in her white nightdress, came to my open door. "Mama?"

"The baby's holding off."

"That's good, real good."

"Go on and see to the girls. I hear Emma fussing."

She nodded.

"And close my door. Don't let anybody in." I didn't want them seeing me when the pains came.

The bedroom turned airless and dark with the door closed even though the small window above the bed was open. I stayed in my rocker, finding the bed too soft. I tried not to think about John on the road with only Rounder to give him courage. I tried not to think about why the labor pains weren't coming like they should. Instead, I listened to the morning sounds as the house woke up. It soothed me to hear the clinking of pots and crockery as Mary got breakfast. These were good sounds and as familiar as the voices of our children.

A pain kicked my belly. I buckled and bit my lip to keep from crying out. Tears ran down my cheeks and it wasn't just because of the pain. I was glad. The baby was doing what it should, and Isaac and John were likely just down the road a short ways.

I was half asleep when Mary brought me a biscuit and a cup of water. Rousing myself, I said, "The girls, they asking for me?"

"They're in the kitchen; they're being good. Told them you have a bellyache. They're getting restless, though. Think it'd be all right if I took them to get cow chips?"

"Is the wind blowing hard?"

"Some."

"Make them wear their bandannas."

"Yes, ma'am."

"Keep a tight eye on them, don't let them out of your sight."

"I won't."

"What time is it?"

"About half past eight."

What was keeping Isaac and John? I said, "When the wheel-barrow's half full, come in and see if I need you. I likely won't, but do it anyway."

The morning wore on and I kept thinking about Isaac and John, worrying about why they weren't home yet. Once a pain hit so hard that a knife twisting in my spine couldn't have hurt worse. I stuffed one of the rags in my mouth to keep from hollering. When the pain passed, I felt washed out and used up. My head ached like something was squeezing the top. Sweat ran from my hair.

Isaac, I kept thinking. *Get home.*

The pains were coming more often, and if Isaac were with me, he'd have his watch in hand. He'd know to the minute—to the very second even—the spacing of the pains. He'd be making bets on the exact time of the birth.

If he were here, Isaac would cheer up the children with a game. He'd make pebbles in his hand disappear and then show up behind their ears. "Magic," he'd say. "Just call me Merlin." Then he'd be back with me in time for the next pain, saying how every-thing was going just like it should.

I closed my eyes. My headache was searing hot. I wanted my mother. She'd hold my hand and tell me that I was doing all right. I rubbed my forehead, recalling what Mrs. Fills the Pipe said about aspirin curing headaches. "Mary," I called out. "Get me an aspirin, would you?" Then I remembered that Mary was outside and couldn't hear me.

All at once, I heard Isaac say my name. He was sitting on the unmade bed; he had his pocket watch. "You can do it," he said, his eyes shining. "You're that kind of woman."

"I don't know," I said.

And then Isaac quoted Paul Laurence Dunbar, the famous Negro poet that we both thought so much of.

> *Seen my lady home last night,*
> *Jump back, honey, jump back.*
> *Held her hand and squeezed it tight,*
> *Jump back, honey, jump back.*
> *Heard her sigh a little sigh,*
> *Seen a light gleam from her eye,*
> *And a smile go flitting by—*
> *Jump back, honey, jump back.*

I smiled at him. Isaac hadn't quoted this poem in years. He called this particular one a teasing poem. He took to reciting it after we'd danced in the street to the mandolin music. "Jump back, honey, jump back," he'd say, and the gleam in his eye made me reach for his hand and put it to my heart so he could feel that it beat fast just for him.

> *Heard the wind blow through the pine,*
> *Jump back, honey, jump back.*

I breathed in the sour smell of Isaac's sweat. I felt his hand on my arm, shaking me a little. "Mama?" somebody said. "You all right?"

Startled, I roused myself. It was Mary. "Where's Isaac?" I said.

She shook her head.

"Where'd he go? He was right here. On the bed."

"No, Mama, you've been dreaming."

I moaned.

"What's wrong?" Mary said, her voice high. "You don't look so good. Maybe you should be in the bed."

"No."

She leaned closer like she couldn't hear me.

I said, "Sitting up is best, that's what Isaac says. It's how the Indians do."

"But you're not an Indian."

I sucked in my breath, put the rag in my mouth, and bit down. "Mama!" Mary said. She patted my back, her fingers nervous as they skimmed the surface of the birthing gown like she was afraid she would hurt me even worse.

When the pain eased, I took the rag from my mouth. I tried to smile for Mary. She was scared, tears running down her cheeks, her lips pressed so tight that they had disappeared.

I licked my lips, tasting blood. My mouth was so dry. I said, "The girls?"

"Don't die, Mama." Mary was on her knees beside me trying to put her arms around me.

"The girls?"

"They're in their room; they're all right."

"Isaac?"

"He's coming, Mama. I know he is."

A stab of pain shot through my head. I heard Mary crying. "Get a pillowcase," I whispered through clenched teeth.

"What?"

"Hang it on the clothesline."

She wiped her eyes, brightening some. "I will, Mama. I'll do it right now," and then she was gone. Flying something white by itself was a call for help. All homesteaders knew that, but I had forgotten until that moment.

Mary had just left the room when the next pain came. When it passed, my head felt clearer. Gripping the rocker's armrests, I got to my feet somehow and made my way over to the dresser. I leaned against it. I worked the birthing gown up and tucked it under one of my arms. I straddled my legs as far apart as I could and with my free hand, I went looking for the baby.

I couldn't feel the head or a foot but instead felt a wet stickiness on my fingers. I let the gown drop. My hand was bright red with blood.

My heart twisted up with fear and sorrow. It was Baby Henry all over again—a long labor, bleeding, and a baby gasping for air. The room swayed. I wanted to give up right then, I wanted to cry, I wanted someone to put an end to this.

I got a rag and stuffed it between my legs to soak up the blood. I shuffled back to the rocker, wanting Isaac, wanting my mother, wanting to die.

A pain took me.

Love me, honey, love me true?
Love me well as I love you?
And she answered, "Course I do"—
Jump back, honey, jump back.

"Course I do," I said to Isaac. "Course I do."

From somewhere far off, there were kitchen sounds and children's voices.

I woke up with a jerk. I was still alive, still slumped in the rocker. I held my breath, waiting for the next tearing pain. It came; black spots floated before my eyes. "Isaac," I called out. He didn't answer.

The pain passed. I let my head rest on the back of the rocker. The house was quiet. Wind whistled around the corners and the stovepipes' metal lids rattled as they flapped up and down, but inside, the house was quiet.

"Mary?" I called.

She didn't answer.

More pain gripped my belly.

"Isaac," I heard myself say. Then all at once I knew. Everybody was at the water well. Isaac was putting Liz in it; I had to stop him. I scooted forward on the rocker. Gripping the arms, I stood up. My birthing gown, wet, stuck to me. I staggered forward, reaching a bedpost. A hot liquid ran down my legs. A pain grabbed my belly and as I held onto the post, I knew the baby was coming.

My breathing ragged, I inched my hands down the bedpost. I was tangled in my gown—it tore as I lowered myself down. When at last I was squatting, I gripped the post even tighter.

I pushed, bearing down hard, harder, wanting Isaac, wanting my mother.

"Mama!" somebody called.

"Help me get her in the bed," another voice said.

Through a haze of tears, I saw my mother. My mother with her bent back and loose strands of gray hair around her face. I could hardly believe it. "Mama," I said, but my mouth was full of dust. "Mama," I tried again.

She put both hands under my arms and pulled up. "Let go," my mother said, and I wanted to but couldn't. My fingers were locked up around the bedpost.

"I've got you," she said. Fingers pried at mine. A cramp bucked me, and I fell back. Strong arms caught me.

Then I was on the bed sinking into its softness. "Mama!" somebody said. Through a mist of stinging sweat in my eyes, I saw Mary and I saw my mother and she didn't look right to me, but before I could worry about that, I heard splashing sounds.

"Isaac," I called, trying to sit up. "Don't you go putting her in the well."

Hands pushed me back down. My mother said, "I'm getting your legs up. Have to see what this baby is doing."

Hands lifted my legs and bent them at the knees. My feet were placed flat on the bed. My legs were pulled apart.

"What's wrong?" Mary said.

"It can't push through," my mother said. "Get a knife, a small sharp one. And a needle and thread. Thick thread. And a bedsheet."

"A knife?" Mary said.

"Get it." There was a rustling sound. "And whiskey. Is there any?"

"Whiskey? I'm not allowed—"

"Get it."

"Mrs. DuPree," my mother said. Why didn't she call me Rachel? "I'm going to cut you some. Then you have to push."

I felt my hips being held up as something soft was put under me. Sweat burned my eyes. Hands lifted my head.

"Open your mouth," my mother said. "Drink this." Liquid burned my throat; I gagged some. A rag was put between my teeth.

"Hold her knees apart," my mother said. "Hold her good." From far away, someone cried.

Then the knife, held by a firm hand, cut me.

18

WANAGI CANKU

When I woke up for good, I knew the baby was dead. Nobody had to tell me. I had known it since I had fallen during the rainstorm and the baby stopped kicking.

"Can you get up?" Mrs. Fills the Pipe said.

She was the one what gave me the whiskey and cut me wider so the baby could be born. I had wanted Isaac, and when I couldn't have him, I called for my mother. Mrs. Fills the Pipe was all I had.

"Yes," I said to her.

She propped me up. Pain shot through me. She got my legs over the edge of the bed; I hunched over. The wood cradle in the corner of the room was covered with a square of cheesecloth. I turned my head away, my arms wrapped over my belly. "My husband?" I said.

"He isn't here."

"John?" I said. "My son?"

Mrs. Fills the Pipe shook her head.

"My girls?"

"With Mary."

Tears filled my eyes. I didn't know if I was crying for the baby or if I was crying because I wanted Isaac and he hadn't come home and I didn't know where he was.

"I need to bathe you," Mrs. Fills the Pipe said. I nodded and she began unbuttoning the top buttons of my birthing gown. It meant nothing to me. All I could think of was Isaac. And John. Something bad had happened to them. Isaac said he'd be home by breakfast; he knew I was close to my time. I couldn't stop the tears. Him and John must be dead.

Mrs. Fills the Pipe lifted my arms and then pulled the gown over my head. It was bloody, and I never wanted to see it again. She let it fall in a heap to the floor.

She bathed me with a clean rag and got me into my night-dress. I was numb to it all. She put her arms around me and stood me up. I cried out as a hot pain bolted up and down my legs and deep into my belly. Mrs. Fills the Pipe looked into my watering eyes. I took a shallow breath, and she walked me to the rocker.

She gave me another drink of the whiskey, and that stopped my crying. Through half-closed eyes, I watched Mrs. Fills the Pipe change the bedclothes. It was a peculiar feeling seeing another woman do my work and touch what belonged to me. I was too hollow, though, to care all that much. When she finished, she put her arms around me again and put me back to bed, this time propped up on the two pillows.

Mrs. Fills the Pipe stood at the side of the bed and gave me a long look. She said, "You need to see him."

Him. A boy. I glanced over at the covered cradle. "I can't," I said, but then I nodded yes. She went to the cradle and got the baby.

The sun had moved to the other side of the house, and the light that came through the small window over the bed was dim.

It had to be late afternoon; there was one lit lantern on the dresser. The baby was as light as a shadow in my arms. He was wrapped in a blanket, and I couldn't bear to look at him. Instead, I held him close, wanting to cry, but couldn't. I was all dried up.

"Look at him," Mrs. Fills the Pipe said.

The steel in her voice made me do it. My baby boy was a light, dusty color and there were purple bruises under his eyes. I put my curved palm over his head, feeling a dent. His skin was cold, and that chilled me, but his brown hair was soft to my touch. I put my finger to his puckered lips—they were dry—and then to his eyelashes. They were my brother Johnny's lashes, they were Mary's. Maybe the baby would've had an ear for music. Maybe he would've had an easy way with cattle, horses, and dogs.

I unwound the blanket. He wore the long white dress and the knit booties that all of my newborns, except Baby Henry, had worn.

Mrs. Fills the Pipe said, "Mary found the clothes."

The dress was too long and the booties came up to his knees. Liz and Emma had been small babies but nothing like this.

"He's ready for his journeys," Mrs. Fills the Pipe said. She was sitting in my rocker.

He had ten wrinkled fingers. I put my fingertip to each one of his. His nails were long. I would've had to wrap his hands to keep him from scratching his face.

Mrs. Fills the Pipe said, "For one year the spirit stays here, this place of his birth and his passing. Then the spirit is ready for the journey along the Wanagi Canku—the Milky Way."

I heard her voice, but I wasn't listening.

She said, "The spirit travels the Wanagi Canku to the other world. An ancestor will come and show the way to the other ancestors. And to those who are yet to come."

I took off the booties and counted his toes. Ten. He had long legs. Like Isaac. I felt myself crumpling. Isaac was dead too. Sorrow crushed my chest.

"A year from now," Mrs. Fills the Pipe said as if I had asked her a question.

After a while I said, "Did he cry?"

"No."

"Was he breathing?"

She paused, then, "No."

"Did he even try?"

She shook her head.

I unbuttoned my nightdress, parted the baby's lips, and gave him my breast. I had nothing to give and he had no reason to take, but I did it anyway. I had to. I was his mother.

Mrs. Fills the Pipe got up and gathered up my birthing gown, the rags, and the bedsheets. Without looking at me, she left the room.

After a while, I buttoned my nightdress. I put the baby on my shoulder, and my hand began patting his back. I felt myself drift. I was so tired, I just wanted to sleep. When I opened my eyes, Mrs. Fills the Pipe was in the room. Rousing myself, I said, "How did you know?"

She gave me a questioning look.

"That I needed you?"

"Mary." She sat down in my rocker. "My sister-in-law's in a

bad way. I was traveling to her; her sons are with me. Mary saw us on the road."

A handful of days ago, I gave Mrs. Fills the Pipe tea on my porch. When I realized that she was an agency squaw, I wanted her gone. And she wanted to be gone when she found out that I was an army man's wife. She could have kept going when Mary ran down to the road and begged for help. She could have, but she didn't. I wondered if I would have done the same for her.

"These boys with you," I said. "Same ones as before?"

"Yes."

A few days ago, Mary walked with Franklin and it had made her eyes dance. I hoped that she was walking with him now. I hoped that it lightened her heart. I hoped it did the same for him.

I said, "She's dying? Their mother?"

Mrs. Fills the Pipe stopped rocking. "I believe so."

"Leaving her boys," I said.

Mrs. Fills the Pipe nodded and then set the rocker going again. It wobbled some. The chair had been moved from the slight grooves in the floor that I'd worn from rocking Alise and Emma. Setting the chair right didn't matter anymore. My baby didn't need rocking.

Mrs. Fills the Pipe inclined her head toward the baby in my arms. "Some spirits, especially the little ones, play tricks. During the year before the Wanagi Canku."

I shook my head. I was tired; nothing mattered.

"You'll see," Mrs. Fills the Pipe said. "You put the salt jar on the shelf and it falls. The fire, even when there is no wind, flickers and goes out. Something tickles the back of your neck. That is the spirit playing." Smiling slightly, Mrs. Fills the Pipe pointed her chin at the baby. "You'll see."

A month after Isaac Two had slipped and fallen on the rocks, it came to me that his one toy, his red rubber ball with a white stripe, was missing. I couldn't recall when I'd last seen it. I looked everywhere for it; it was important to find it. The ball had been Isaac Two's and nobody else's. I had searched the barn, the root cellar, the outhouse. I even went to where he had died and looked in the places between the rocks.

I never found his ball. Isaac talked me into believing that Tracker, our dog then, had dug a hole and buried it.

And Baby Henry. A few nights after he was born and died, I woke hearing him crying, wanting me. Beside myself, I ran up to the cemetery thinking we'd buried him alive. There, I got down on my hands and knees and put my ear to the fresh-turned grave. Nothing. *You were dreaming,* I told myself. You saw him die; you saw the light go out of his eyes. He laid cold in the cradle a day and night before we buried him. But the crying happened more than once; it happened night after night for the longest time. It stopped about the time that I knew there was another baby on the way.

"Ghosts," I said to Mrs. Fills the Pipe.

"Spirits," she said.

A spirit wasn't something to be scared of, not like a ghost was. I said, "A year?"

"Yes," she said. "For a year you must care for the spirit. You must put out food and milk, whatever you think pleases. When the year comes full circle, you give away the spirit's possessions. Then the journey along the Wanagi Canku begins."

"And he won't get lost?"

"The ancestors will be there."

My father. Johnny. Isaac Two and Baby Henry. Oscar DuPree, Isaac's father. I couldn't bring myself to think Isaac and John.

I wrapped my baby boy up in his blanket, and as I did, a gleam of light from my gold wedding band caught my eye. On my wedding day, after Preacher Teller pronounced us man and wife, after I said good-bye to Dad and Johnny, me and Isaac got in the waiting horse cab. I had expected we'd go directly to the railroad station, but instead Isaac gave the driver an address that I didn't know. I didn't ask him about it; I was dazed from the suddenness of finding myself married to a man I didn't much know. We sat quiet in our own corners of the cab, a big place between us. We were turned away from the other, me staring out my side window, Isaac, I imagined, doing the same.

The cab stopped. Isaac told me this was the place, we were getting out. I didn't wait for him to help me; it didn't cross my mind—I was wondering why we weren't at the train station. The street was lined with shops, and the sidewalks were crowded up with white people. They hurried past us, not seeing us, not knowing it was our wedding day. Some of the men had long hair and wore beards that came down to the top button of their black suits. "This way," Isaac said, and I followed him into one of the stores.

It was the first time I had ever been in a jeweler's shop. I had walked past such places before, and a few times I had stopped long enough to admire the diamonds that sparkled in the window displays. But being inside a jeweler's and being surrounded by all that beauty was a glory all of its own. Jewels glittered in the glass cases that lined both sides of the narrow shop.

A white man with gray, thinning hair was behind one of the glass cases. He was hunched over a square of black material, and like most of the men on the street, he wore an odd black cap too small to keep out any kind of weather. He studied a pocket watch laid out on the material. He looked up at us when we came in. Pressed in one of his eye sockets was what looked to be a little telescope about an inch long. The man took it out and eyed us for a moment, surprised, I thought, to see a Negro man in uniform. Then he cleared his throat as he slipped the watch into his breast pocket. "May I help you?" he said.

"Yes, sir," Isaac said. "I want a wedding band." I looked at him, taken aback. Never for a minute did I expect a band. My mother didn't have one. Mrs. DuPree did, but she had married a doctor.

The jeweler smiled slightly. "Ah, yes. A wedding band." He looked at me and then back to Isaac. "And this is your bride?"

"Yes, sir."

"You're a lucky man," he said. I bit my lower lip, but I smiled all the same. He waved me closer to the counter; I obeyed. The jeweler said, "Will you do me the kindness of taking off your glove?"

My smile disappeared. My hands were rough and chapped even though most every night I soaked them in buttermilk and wore cotton gloves to bed. But both men were looking at me, so I put my cloth bag on the countertop and took off my left glove, my face hot with shame.

The jeweler studied my hand, his forehead drawn. I imagined him thinking that a gold band would look out of place on such a ragged hand. Instead, he said, "Long fingers. Very nice." He picked up my hand. I drew in my breath. I'd never been touched by a white person before. He ran his pasty forefinger and thumb along my ring finger. I felt faint; his touch was soft and cool, and I wanted to pull my hand away. He didn't seem to notice. He said, "Little boned and no knuckles to speak of. A size four I'd say." He let go of my hand and stepped away. I steadied myself. He got a ring of keys from his pants pocket and unlocked a case. Humming a little song to himself, he pulled out a tray. He brought it to us and, still humming, he studied the wedding bands, his eyes looking at my ring finger from time to time. Finally, he put three gold bands on the square of black material.

One band was wide—it would cover the lower third of my finger. It was the kind the ladies in Mrs. DuPree's Circle of Eight wore. It wasn't meant for work; it was for show. As pretty as it was, I didn't want it. I looked at the band beside it. It was nearly as thin as a pencil point; hard work would wear it away. It wouldn't last long. The third band was not too big, not too small. I felt a surge of desire for it. It wouldn't get in the way of hard work, and yet it would hold up. From the corner of my eye, I saw Isaac as he studied the three bands. His forehead was furrowed, and it came to me that he was embarrassed to ask how much. My face flushed; he was sorry he had brought me there. It was foolish to buy such a thing when he was giving our marriage only a year. It was foolish when there were cows and horses to buy. I turned to him and whispered, "I don't need a band."

"Yes," Isaac said, his voice snapping. "You do. You're my wife. I won't have people thinking otherwise."

Stung, I took a step back. The jeweler made a soothing sound in his throat. "If I might suggest," he said. He held up the thin band, the one that would wear out too soon, the one that looked to be the cheapest of the three.

"No," Isaac said. He pointed to the in-between band, the one that I wanted. "This one," he said to the jeweler, not looking at me.

"Yes," the jeweler said. "Excellent choice, excellent." He held it up in the light as if expecting to see something wrong with it. When he didn't, he polished it on the square of black material. He handed it to Isaac. "She's your bride," he said.

Isaac started to give me the band, and then he stopped as if understanding what the jeweler meant. He picked up my left hand. I held my breath as he worked the wedding band down my finger. It was like I was getting married for the second time that day. When the band was in place, I thought I felt Isaac give my hand a little squeeze before letting go. I stared at the band, the gold so bright that I went woozy from the beauty of it and from all that had happened that morning.

"Congratulations and best wishes," the jeweler said. I looked up and smiled at him. He didn't seem to see; he was leaning close to Isaac, saying, "Now if you'd care to step this way."

It was me what did the stepping away. I went to the front of the shop while Isaac paid. I stood by the window and looked at my hand. I hardly knew it. I felt grand; I felt like a lady. But for all that, I wished that Isaac had bought the band to please me. I wished that he bought it because he cared a little for me. But he hadn't. I put my glove back on.

Years later, my band was worn and scratched. My knuckles were swollen from all the years of hard work. It'd be hard work getting it off if the time came.

I held my baby boy to me one last time and kissed his cold cheeks and his closed eyes. I held him out to Mrs. Fills the Pipe. She took him from me and as she did, our arms tangled. She leaned closer to me over the bed to keep from dropping him. I shifted my baby's weight to her, and it was at that moment that we both looked into each other's eyes.

Her eyes were black like my mother's. Her skin was brown like Alise's. Her face was tired and sad like mine. Her sister-in-law was dying but she'd helped me because Mary asked her to. Mrs. Fills the Pipe kept my children from losing their mama. All that from an agency Indian.

Isaac hated Indians but that didn't make it right. It didn't mean that I had to. It didn't mean I had to hold on to grievances that were never mine.

I couldn't find those words, though, not to say them out loud. Instead I tried to say it with my eyes. Her eyes, looking into mine, went soft. I believed she understood.

She turned away then and put the baby in the cradle and pulled the cheesecloth over it. She went to the door and opened it.

"Mrs. Fills the Pipe?"

She stopped. I'm leaving, I wanted to say to her. For my children, the living ones. If it was just me, I'd stay the winter, I'd see to this baby. I'd put out food, I'd look for him to play tricks. But I can't let another one die here. I can't let the Badlands swallow another child.

Mrs. Fills the Pipe stood waiting in the doorway, her head turned away as if listening to something outside. She shifted her hip liked it ached. Her mind, I saw, was on the road, on her hurry to get her nephews back to their mother before she died. I said, "Thank you."

She put her hand up, her way of saying good-bye, and then she was gone.

A lantern's light jittered, throwing a nervous shadow on the bedroom wall, but it was the wind's whistle that woke me up, and in that moment all that I had lost came back to me. The hurt of it choked my chest, making it hard to breathe. Then I saw Isaac asleep in my rocker, his chin on his chest. Relief washed over me. He was all right; nothing bad had happened to him. I eased air into my lungs, pain shooting through my belly and legs, and just that quick, I was angry.

I had had a baby coming with nobody to help but Mary and John, and it took a knife to get the baby, and he wasn't breathing, and Isaac hadn't been there for any of it. He'd said he'd be home by breakfast, but he hadn't been. He'd thought I'd be all right, but I wasn't. That's what he always thought about me—it was what he wanted to think. Now he thought I could make thin supplies stretch over the coming winter. He thought a hired hand would mind me, and this hand—a white boy—would work alongside me. Me and this hand and Mary and John could upright brokendown fences and mend windmills when the snow was high and the north wind blowing hard. I could leave Liz for long stretches to mind her little sisters. He believed I could do all that.

"Isaac?" I said.

His head jerked up, awake all at once. "Rachel," he said. "Thank God."

"Where's John?"

"Asleep, in bed. He's all right. They all are." In the dim light I saw Isaac's eyes flicker toward the cradle. The muscles around his mouth pulled.

"Where were you?"

"A son," he said, his voice low. "He's—"

"Where were you?"

He put his hand to his face, pulling at the tight muscles.

I waited, looking at him hard.

"I got here as soon as I could," Isaac said. "I—" He stopped, cleared his throat, shifting in the rocker as if gathering himself. He went on. "John got lost on the way, got turned around. After he got to Al's place it took awhile for Mindy to find me. Al and me were out doing a roundup."

Yes, I thought. *While I was birthing this baby—this baby what died—you were picking out cattle, cattle that you expect me to feed and water and tend to this winter with nobody to help but children.*

Isaac said, "Mary told me about the squaw."

"Her name is Mrs. Fills the Pipe."

He didn't say anything.

"The Badlands has taken the last of my children," I said.

Isaac looked at me.

"Me and the children. If you go off to the gold mine, we're leaving. For the winter."

"Not this, Rachel. Not now."

"I can't run the ranch alone."

"You have to."

"I can't."

"Do it anyway."

I looked away. He didn't believe me. He had it fixed in his mind that I couldn't leave. I didn't have any money. This was all talk; that's what he thought. But he didn't know. I'd find a way. Like he found a way to buy more cattle.

Isaac got up, his knees popping. He stood over me for a moment, his shadow spreading across the foot of the bed. I couldn't make out his face, but I knew what he was thinking. *Stop complaining.* I heard the words as if he was saying them. *You knew what you were getting; you asked for this life. You bargained for a year, and I gave you a house and children. I took you out of another woman's kitchen; I gave you my name. I pulled you up.*

Isaac turned and went to the cradle in the corner. He pulled back the cheesecloth and picked up the baby. His back to me, he held our son. The lantern's light made Isaac's shadow tall, narrow, and jerky. Outside, the wind whistled low, making a hollow groaning sound. All at once, Isaac's shoulders slumped and shook, startling me. This man what pushed himself hard every day, what never gave up, what wouldn't let anyone else give up, this man was crying. I'd never seen him cry before, not even when Isaac Two and Baby Henry died. I didn't know that he could.

Isaac was a man of ambition; he was the kind of man I thought I'd wanted since the day I saw Ida B. Wells-Barnett in Mrs. DuPree's parlor. He hadn't just pulled me up; he'd pulled himself up. The land had done that for him. He believed it would do the same for our children. He'd never let go of it.

But I had to leave; I had to take the children. Maybe there was a time when I would have stood the winter without Isaac. Maybe I even could have gotten us through. But that was before the drought; that was before I'd birthed eight children. That was before I'd lost three boys. And that was before I understood that our children needed a dab of sweetness, that they needed to see there was a world outside of the Badlands.

Isaac put our baby back in the cradle and pulled the cheese-cloth over it. Without looking at me, he said, "The burial will be tomorrow. I'll get started on the coffin."

The burial. Then, "Isaac?"

He turned back.

The birthing, I wanted to say. It could've killed me. Tell me you were wrong to be gone. Tell me how this scared you bad. Tell me how it made you see just what I meant to you. Tell me how grateful you were to the woman what helped me. Instead, I said, "Why? Why do you hate Mrs. Fills the Pipe?"

He gave me an odd look, one that I didn't know the meaning of. He said, "Because they bowed and scraped. Because they gave up." And then he was gone.

19

RACHEL

I never said another word about leaving. Isaac didn't believe me, I knew that, but I was all out of ways that would make him see it. I had nothing left but a scrap of hope that he'd change his mind about going to the gold mine. Holding on to that hope, I got up from our bed and did my best to make like that September was no different than any other. As Isaac expected, me and the girls sorted seeds for the fall garden. Heavy with sadness for my baby and all that I might lose, I planted those seeds, thinking it might not matter that I was doing this so late in the season. I patted them into place anyway, my mouth set, not having much to say to anybody.

In late September, Isaac got two hands in—neither of them much older than sixteen—to help drive the cattle to market in Scenic. When they got back, he wore a downhearted look and that told me the cattle were worth even less than he'd hoped. The winter supplies that he brought home then, short as they were, likely took most of the money. Without Isaac saying so, I saw how those cattle prices made him all the more determined to work the mine. All the same, I hoped.

By the end of September, me and Isaac had become like strangers, polite and saying only what was needed. We stepped around each other, our eyes not meeting, our hands not touching. The days turned shorter as nights came earlier and stayed longer, carrying a chill. That chill scared me bad; it made my blood cold; I couldn't get myself warm; my teeth chattered even when I was working at the cookstove. It was only October, but for me it was January. Nights, I couldn't sleep for thinking about stories of people snowed in, going hungry, running out of cow chips, freezing in their sleep. Fixed on those stories, my heart would seize up with fear and before I could stop myself, I'd get up and hurry to the children in their beds. I'd bend over them, close, needing to hear them breathe. If Isaac noticed any of this, he didn't say anything. Likely he thought I was grieving for the baby.

I believed Isaac was worrying about the coming winter; the lines that crossed his forehead were deep. I didn't ask, though. I didn't want to say anything that might make him all the more determined to leave. So, like every fall, at night I covered the garden against the cold and uncovered it every morning for Mary and Liz to do the weeding. I worked at making food supplies stretch. Isaac, John, and the hired hands shored up the roof of the house so it'd hold against the coming snowfalls. They did the same for the barn and dugout. I picked apart the bottom hems of Mary's and John's coats and let them out. I put the porch rockers in the barn; I patched up the holes in our gloves. The girls stacked cow chips on the porch. For a week, Isaac, John, and the hands rode off each morning to check the fence lines. While they were gone, me and the girls covered the root cellar floor with straw, our way of being ready when it came time to store cabbage and pumpkins. After the fences were repaired and stood firm, Isaac let one of the hands go, keeping the yellow-haired boy called Manny Franks.

All too soon, it was the first day of the new school year. In the early morning light, me and the two little girls waved good-bye to Mary, John, and Liz. Tears came to me when the three of them, sitting on top of Star with their legs dangling loose on both sides of the horse, took the road and headed west to the schoolhouse. Two weeks later, the first hard freeze came on, turning the topsoil brittle. My resolve to leave toughened, but only, I told myself, only if Isaac goes to the mine. He might not do it, I said to myself over and over. He might not.

Then one night at bedtime, the wind gusting from the northwest, Isaac held each child to him and kissed their cheeks. One by one he told them, even Emma, that he was going to the mine, just for the winter, doing what he had to do to keep the ranch. "Remember that," he said to them, not allowing them to cry. "This land's worth sacrificing for."

I listened outside the children's bedrooms. It took everything I had to hold myself together. Isaac was going to do this thing, but even still, I held on to hope. He could change his mind during the night; he hadn't left yet.

Without a word between us, we got up the next morning well before first dawn. With a lantern on the counter, I made Isaac's breakfast while he gathered up his things. When I let Rounder out, I saw that it was snowing. Numb to it all, I packed Isaac a lunch while he ate his biscuits and gravy. When he finished, ready to leave, he didn't kiss my cheek good-bye. Instead, he put his hands on my shoulders and looked into my eyes. "I'm counting on you," he said. "We all are."

My hand found the counter behind me. "Isaac," I said. "Please. Don't—"

"You're strong," he said. "More than you know." At that, a cry rose up inside of me, and all at once, I was in his arms, a place where I hadn't been in months.

My ear to his chest, I heard his heartbeat. Isaac bent some, just enough to rest his chin on top of my head. He thought I was strong. I pulled in his smell; I put my arms around him, feeling the strength of his back. Isaac was wrong; I wasn't strong, not anymore. His hands pressed me close; through my heavy nightdress his fingers kneaded my backbone.

I knew what he was doing. He was working me, getting me to go along with what he was about to do. *Don't let him,* a voice in my head said. *Don't.* But all the same his hands felt so good on my back. I had missed his touch. His hands were broad and strong; they were hands that knew every part of me. Ridges of calluses, I knew, ran across his palms. I wanted to run my finger over them, I wanted to put his hand to my cheek and feel those calluses.

"Yes," I said, and suddenly I believed that Isaac was right. I was strong; I could run the ranch. But just as fast, I saw the short supplies on the cupboard shelf, I pictured our children's faces, pinched from the cold, their eyes flat from hunger. I saw my boys' markers in the cemetery. By winter's end there could be more. I couldn't let that happen. And then there was my promise to Mary. There will be dances, I had told her the night Jerseybell died. There will be a dab of sweetness to carry her—to carry all of our children—through the hard times sure to come.

I lifted my head from Isaac's chest, and pulling in some air, I pushed myself away. He didn't try to stop me. "That's right," I said.

Isaac cocked his head, not seeing my meaning. I said, "I'm stronger than I know."

"I've never doubted that. You'll be all right."

"You will be too."

He gave me a quick smile, his eyes not meeting mine. He took his coat from the wall peg. He worked it into place, shrugging his shoulders, buttoning up. He pulled his hat on low, covering his ears, and tightened his stampede strings. Tears came to me; I could hardly see past them. Isaac picked up his knapsack and then he stopped. "Rachel," he said.

Hope caught at my heart. I put my hand out to him. Isaac didn't seem to see it; he looked past me. I waited, wanting him to put his knapsack down, wanting him to say, Why are you crying? I'm just seeing to the cattle. I'll be back for noon dinner.

Isaac said, "I'm counting on you."

My hand dropped to my side. He shouldered his knapsack and he left me then, stepping out onto the porch in the snow. I knew that Isaac was walking to Interior to take the westbound train.

I kept the children home from school and we got through the day somehow, all of us burdened by the sad blanket of quiet that settled over the house. Over and over, the children asked, "Why? Why'd Daddy leave?" and all I could say was, "The land. He's doing it to keep the land."

The next morning, my eyes gritty from not sleeping, I packed three lunches and gathered my cloth handbag. In our bedroom, I took out Isaac's gold watch from the top dresser drawer. It had stopped; he must have forgotten to wind it before he left. I held it in my palm. Isaac always took it to town when he had business, but not this time. Likely he thought it might get stolen. I put it back in the drawer.

I told the children that I had business in town and that everybody was to mind Mary. "Mama!" they all said, their voices like howls. "What about school?" Putting on my coat, I told them to hush, I'd be back before dark and I expected all their chores to be done when I got home.

I walked down the rise, knowing my children were calling me, their scared faces pressed against the window. I had to do this, I told myself as I picked my way around the prairie-dog holes. The sun had come out and was melting the snow not caught up in drifts. Thin streams of water ran down the rise; at the bottom, it stood inches deep. Holding my coat high, I walked through the cold melt, my boots turning dark. Come night, I knew, the water would freeze, making a thick layer of ice. I walked up the next rise, slipping some in the wet snow, and then I was at the dugout.

I knocked at the door, calling to Manny Franks, the yellow-haired hired hand. He opened it. His suspenders hung down at his sides. Manny Franks had been eating his breakfast; he held a piece of bread. I stood in the doorway. "That other boy what helped with the cattle drive," I said. "Do you know if he's found work?"

"Don't know," Manny Franks said. "Last I heard, he was cleaning stalls at the livery. In Interior."

"All right, then. Let's find him."

He grinned, showing a chipped front tooth. Likely the prospect of a friend's company made him glad. Or maybe he was happy he wouldn't be the only white boy working the DuPree place. He said, "Want me to hitch up the wagon?"

"Yes."

Me and him headed to town that sunny morning, both of us sitting on the wagon's buckboard, a blanket up to my chin. We were hardly on our way when I asked him if he knew the price of a train ticket from Interior to Chicago. His light-colored eyebrows raised, he gave me a surprised look.

"Do you?" I snapped. He told me and then said, "That's why I hop freight cars."

After that, neither of us had anything to say. Manny Franks, I supposed, had his own thoughts. As for me, I worked at the price of six tickets, doing the arithmetic in my head, wishing for a piece of paper so I could be sure. Then I thought about Isaac and how I carried hard feelings against him. Yet at the same time, I missed him so bad that it felt like somebody had shot a ragged hole through my heart. Just breathing hurt.

In town, we found Pete Klegberg in the alley behind the livery, drawing hard on a cigarette. He was an easy hire—ranching jobs were hard to come by, and my promise that Isaac would pay him in the spring was good enough.

That settled, there was one more thing to do in town. I told the boys to wait with the wagon, I wouldn't be long. They nodded, standing in a patch of sun as they leaned against the wagon, short cigarettes hanging from the corners of their mouths.

I left those two white boys, knowing they were watching me as I walked down to the other end of the street. Here and there, horses were hitched to posts and there was a black automobile, mud-splattered, in front of the bank. As curious as that was, I believed there were faces in every window of every building and that it was me they were looking at. I was glad for my hat with its wide brim; it covered most of my face. It covered, I hoped, my shame.

Near the end of the street, close to the train depot, I stopped at the only two-story building in town and pushed open the door to the Interior Saloon.

It was said of Mrs. Clay, the woman what owned it, that she was the richest person in these parts of the Badlands. It was said of her that she had a taste for pretty things. That made her the only person what might buy what I had to sell.

I stood in the doorway of the saloon, letting my eyes settle to the gloom. There were a handful of round tables with chairs, and at first I believed the place to be empty of people. Then I heard the clink of dishes. A woman stood behind the high counter that ran along the side wall off to my right. Two dimly lit lanterns hung from the wall behind her. She watched me, her hands in a basin.

I went to her. Her hair was piled high and it was red, too red, and so were her lips, all painted up. She took her hands out of the basin, shook them, and then dried them on a rag. I saw that she wore rings. I told myself that Isaac had left. I made myself think about my children, and that propped up my courage.

"I'm needing to speak to Mrs. Clay," I said. In my ears, my voice sounded like it was made of tin. I looked at the basin where her hands had been. A gray washrag hung over one side; water dripped onto the counter.

"You're looking at her," the woman said.

I cleared my throat. "I have a band." I made myself raise my eyes, seeing her red lips and her eyes that were black and hard. I said, "A band I'm looking to sell."

"Didn't think you were here for a drink," she said. Her voice was hoarse and deep; it made me think of a man's voice, a man what smoked. She said, "What kind of band?"

I took off my gloves and stuffed them in my coat pocket. My fingers were like ice, but even so, I had to twist my wedding band back and forth, working it over my knuckle. When it finally came off, I put it in my palm and closed my fingers over it for a moment. Then, opening my hand, I held it out to her.

Mrs. Clay took the ring. "You Isaac DuPree's woman?" she said without looking at me.

"Yes," I said, wondering how she knew Isaac.

She held up the ring between two fingers, turning it some to catch the light from the lamps behind her. "You leaving him?"

"No."

Mrs Clay lowered my band, then threw me a look that showed she didn't believe me.

"It's not like that," I said. "It's only for the winter." She raised her eyebrows; they had been drawn on. I said, "It's my children, they—" I stopped.

Mrs. Clay was sucking at her teeth, making a clicking sound as she eyed my band. "Pure gold?" she said.

"I believe so."

She put it between her eyeteeth and bit it, looking at me to see how I was taking that. I didn't look away. A woman like her, I understood, did not need a worn-out wedding band.

She took it from her mouth and held it up to the light. "It's scratched."

"It's gold."

She smiled at that, and as she did, something changed in her eyes; they softened some, and I believed it was pity that did that. She put the band on the counter, went to the cash register behind her, and opened it, its shrill ring making me jump. She got out money, and just to the side of my wedding band, she spread the dollar bills on the counter like they were playing cards.

Without touching the bills, I counted them. "It's worth another two dollars," I said.

The corners of her painted mouth turned down. Without a word, she got the two bills from her register and put them on the counter. My nerves turned jittery then. I wanted out of the saloon before I took to telling her that I wasn't doing this for me, it was for my children, nothing else could make me part with my wedding band.

"Take it or leave it," Mrs. Clay said. "Makes me no difference."

"Yes," I said, gathering up the money, my fingers all thumbs, nearly spilling some of the bills on the floor. My wedding band, I had sold my wedding band. Somehow I folded the money and got it in my handbag. Not able to meet her eyes, I said, "Obliged, I'm much obliged," and then I was out of the saloon and on the street, walking toward the hired hands, my eyes straight ahead, wanting to get away, wanting to go home.

Three days later I was back in town, and this time it was bitter cold, the wind blowing sharp from the north. I had the children with me, but not when I went to Johnston's Dry Goods. I made them wait across the street by the barbershop. Charlie Johnston, the owner, was Louise's father, Mary's friend from school. I didn't want Mary saying anything to him. I didn't want him knowing our business.

At the store, I put a penny on the wooden counter. "A stamp, please," I said. It had been years since I'd seen Charlie Johnston, a friendly enough man even if Isaac thought he had gouged ranchers during the drought.

"Cold enough for you?" he said, giving a small smile as he pulled out a drawer from his side of the counter. There were rough patches of flaky skin on his cheeks and the end of his nose was red like he had a head cold. He found a stamp and put it on the counter.

"Yes," I said.

"Folks say it's going to be a bad winter."

A shiver ran through me. Charlie Johnston rang up the one-cent key on his cash register and put the penny in the drawer. I loosened the drawstrings that held my cloth handbag shut. I pulled out a letter. My hands fumbling some, I licked the stamp and put it on the right-hand corner of the envelope. I pressed the stamp into place and then slid the envelope across the counter to Charlie Johnston.

He looked at the address. "I'd heard about this, how Isaac's working the mine in Lead."

"Yes."

"A letter from home. A man always appreciates that."

"I expect so." *But not this one*, I thought. I had written it the night before after the children were in bed. It had taken all evening, each word harder to write than the one before, but I had to do it. It was only right that Isaac knew I'd done what I said I would do. I pictured him opening the letter as he sat in a miner's

tent late at night, holding it close to a lantern, squinting, wishing
for his magnifying glass.

Dear Husband,
Me and the Children are going to my Mother's. In Chicago. I hired
on a second Hand. Pete Klegberg. I am Sorry for this. We will be
Back in the Spring.

                                                          Your Wife

A sudden clutch of fear seized my heart. *Get it back,* I
thought. I put out my hand, but by then Charlie Johnston had
dropped the letter into a small canvas bag that hung from a peg.
There was black lettering on it—U.S. MAIL—the print a little faded
around the edges. I let my hand drop. *Isaac left us,* I told myself.
You had to do this thing.

Charlie Johnston turned to the open cabinet that hung on
the back wall behind him. It had narrow rows of pigeonholes,
some with mail in them. He said, "It's the oddest thing about letter writing. Something I've noticed. Folks go months, even years
sometimes, without getting one. Or writing one, for that matter.
Then the letters start flying back and forth. Like with you and
Isaac." I looked at him; I didn't know his meaning. He pulled out
a letter from one of the pigeonholes. "Here's another one for you
folks. Came Monday, I believe it was. Or maybe Tuesday."

All at once the store was too hot, like the stove along the
side wall had fired up a blaze too big for the room. I pulled at my
neck scarf, but loosening it didn't help. When I had written my
mother in September, I told her she didn't have to write back if
she agreed to take me and the children. Since then, I'd been un-

easy every time Isaac went to town, worried sick there'd be word from her.

Charlie Johnston put the letter on the counter. I couldn't bring myself to look at it; I fixed my eyes on the cabinet behind him. The letter, I knew, carried bad news. It was from my mother, saying it was wrong to leave the ranch. She was warning me about race riots; she was telling me she didn't have room for five children and me. Or maybe it was from Sue, my sister, telling me that something had happened to Mama. But it was too late. I'd sold my wedding band. We had to come; my children needed to. It was only for a few months.

"You all right?" Charlie Johnston said.

Not wanting to, I glanced at the letter. It was to Isaac, not me.

"Mrs. DuPree?"

Relieved, I put the letter in my handbag. "Yes," I said, stepping away from the counter. "Good-bye."

"That's it?" he said. "You've come clear to town just to post that letter of yours? The weather being what it is?"

"No," I said. "There's this and that," and then I turned and hurried out of the store before he could say anything.

Outside, the wind gusted, pulling at my coat and skirt. Across the street, the children waited for me, holding hands like I had told them. They stood close to the wall of the barbershop but held themselves tight pressed to each other as if that could break the wind. Mary held Emma, and the carpetbag was at John's feet. The supper basket was between Liz and Alise. They wore their hats pulled low, and their neck scarves were wound tight across their mouths and knotted under their chins. Their coats were buttoned high. Mary's and John's were tight across their chests, though, and I knew their knobby wrists that showed above their gloves were raw from the cold. Their boots were tight, not that either of them complained, but I had seen how they winced when they walked. *Nobody in Chicago,* I thought, *will believe that their father was a rancher.* Our children looked like orphans from the poorhouse.

Low snowdrifts lined the south side of the street. Jumping some, I got over the drift and made my way across the dirt street that was mostly blown clear of the snow. Wind, trapped between the two rows of buildings that made Interior, whipped my clothes. I couldn't imagine who had written Isaac. My coat and skirt caught around my legs, pulling me. I staggered, stumbling, sure that I would fall, the wind bigger than me. *Put the letter behind you,* I told myself. There were enough worries without taking on another one. I steadied myself and kept going, stepping around the street's ruts that were covered with ice.

I stepped up onto the plank walk where the children waited. "Mama?" Mary said as I came near. "What're we doing?"

I ignored her as I took Emma. "Come on," I said, settling Emma on my hip.

John pulled my arm. "Where're we going?"

"Home," I said. That was what I had told them that morning when they heard me tell Manny Franks to hitch the wagon. That was what I said after I told Manny Franks he was taking me and the children to town.

John said, "But you sent Manny back home, back without us."

"Never mind that. Come on." I started walking, the children

hurrying to catch up. Our boots clattered on the wooden walk as we went past the Lutheran church, the bank, and the empty lot where the Interior Hotel stood before it burned down. We were the only people out. We walked past the Interior Saloon, and as we did, I put my hand to Emma's head and tucked her face against the wool of my coat's collar. I thought about our wood house, about how for the last three days I had worked harder than I ever had before, washing, polishing, and cleaning, getting it ready for the winter. Carrying Mrs. Fills the Pipe's words about the dead in my mind, I had gotten the cradle from the barn and put it by my bed. I put the baby quilt in it, tucking in the corners. Feeling foolish but willing to do it anyway, I took a scrap piece of paper and wrote "Chicago" in big letters. I put it on top of the baby quilt. "That's where I'll be," I had whispered, "should you come looking."

Me and the children were at the depot office by then. "John," I said, nodding my head toward the door, my way of telling him to open it.

He looked at me. "What're we doing?"

"Mama," Mary said. "Tell us. Please tell us."

I couldn't. There were no words for what I was doing.

"The door," I said. John hesitated, working up an argument. I gave him my hardest look. Wincing some, he opened the door; it nearly flew when a gust of wind caught it. I put my spare hand to it and we went inside.

A man with yellow hair stood by the open stove. He held a bucket under one arm. I didn't know him. I nodded a greeting. He nodded back, then reached into the bucket, getting a handful of cow chips. "Well," he said, "you must be DuPree's family." He threw the chips into the stove. Small red flames jumped and crackled. "You meeting up in Lead?"

For a moment it startled me that this stranger knew about Isaac, but then I remembered that Isaac had been to the depot five days before us.

"No," I said. The children pulled in their breaths; I didn't look at them. Instead I looked at the chalkboard behind the counter. The train to Sioux Falls left at 1:19 P.M. A wash of memories came over me. Sioux Falls was where Zeb and Iris Butler lived. Sioux Falls was where me and Isaac first came to know each other. It was where I had my first chance at pleasing him.

I pulled in some air, willing myself to study the prices printed on the chalkboard. A ticket to Chicago was thirty cents more than Manny Franks had said. I worked out the arithmetic, my mind almost too jumpy to hold on to the figures. I did the arithmetic again and went weak with relief. I had enough money.

I kept my eyes fixed on the chalkboard, needing next to work out the trip. From Sioux Falls me and the children would get the Chicago-bound train. I said, "Six tickets, please."

"Where to?" the depot man said, coming around to the back side of the counter.

"Chicago."

One of the little girls giggled. "Mama," I heard Mary whisper. "Mama."

"It ain't cheap," the man said.

Heat rose to my cheeks. This white man, the corners of his mouth lifted in a narrow grin, was taking in our rough, ill-fitting clothes. This man was thinking that Isaac DuPree was land rich and cash poor, so poor he had to leave his ranch and work a gold mine. Isaac DuPree's wife couldn't have money for train tickets clear to Chicago. I flushed with anger. This man was taking pleasure in the idea that Isaac DuPree had fallen on hard times.

Without looking at Mary, I handed Emma to her. I took off my gloves and opened my handbag, seeing the letter that Charlie Johnston had given me. Keeping my hands in my bag so nobody could see, I counted out the dollar bills and some change. Like Mrs. Clay had done a few days before, I laid the bills out on the counter, and as I did, I saw the emptiness of my left hand.

The bills were worn and thin. I didn't let myself think about how Mrs. Clay had earned that money. Or how I had.

The depot man looked at the bills on the counter, and I saw his surprise. He turned to the ticket cabinet on the wall beside the chalkboard, the key in the lock.

"Rounder?" John said. "What about Rounder?"

The depot man turned the key; the lock made a clicking sound. Inside the cabinet, stacks of tickets showed in the rows of pigeonholes. He studied the rows and then pulled out some tickets.

"Mama!" John said, his hand on my arm. "Who's going to see to Rounder?"

"Manny Franks and Pete Klegberg," I said.

The depot man flicked the tickets with his thumb as if counting. He laid them beside my money and stamped each ticket, the sound of it as loud as the heartbeat in my ears.

"They won't know how," John said. "They don't know anything about Rounder."

"That's enough," I said, my voice low.

The depot man gave me a few coins in change, and then he

slid the train tickets across the counter to me. I put them in my cloth handbag so that they rested beside the letter Charlie Johnston had given me. The train was twenty minutes away. "Come on," I said to the children, heading for the door.

"Hold up," the depot man said. I turned back. He said, "It's all right by me if you wait here." He inclined his head toward the stove. "It's a tad breezy out there."

"Obliged," I said. "But outside is just fine."

"Suit yourself."

I saw what he was thinking: that Negro woman was a hard one, making her children stand out on such a bitter day. My lips pressed tight, I nodded good-bye to him as I took Emma from Mary. The depot man already knew enough of our business; I didn't want him knowing more.

Outside, we stood close to the clapboard depot office wall, trying to stay out of the wind. It had begun to snow a little but it didn't stick. It just skittered in the wind, sometimes getting trapped for a few moments against the rough-cut depot wall before being lifted up and carried on. We stood there, Mary and John saying, "But Mama? But Mama?" I hung my head, thinking what to say. "A visit," I managed. "A short visit."

"But Mama," John said, standing in front of me, his eyes nearly level with mine. He pulled his scarf down below his chin. "Daddy told me to see to the ranch; that's what he said. Daddy didn't say anything about going to Chicago. I promised him."

I shook my head.

"Mama! I promised! I can't go, I don't want to!"

A knot tightened my throat so I couldn't hardly swallow. Mary said, "Where are we going to sleep, Mama, when we get there?"

"Family," I said. "We'll stay with family."

"Grandma Reeves?" she said.

"Yes."

John said, "And Grandma DuPree?" I started to shake my head but saw that the troubled look in John's eyes had changed to excitement. This was the grandmother what sent a book after the birth of each baby. This was the one what owned property. This was his daddy's mother.

"Her too," I said, not meeting his eyes.

Then all at once, Liz and Alise got excited about getting on a train, and everybody was talking too loud and I told them, my voice harsh, "That's enough!" They backed away from me, stung, and I thought of the letter I had written Isaac and how that meant I couldn't back out now. And what about the letter Charlie Johnston gave me? I put Emma down and drew open the drawstrings to my handbag. Making sure the children couldn't see, I pulled the letter out a few inches. I didn't know the hand. I angled the letter a little. The postmark was blurry.

I tucked the letter back in my handbag and drew the strings. I cocked my head; I didn't hear the train. I didn't know what to make of the letter, but I did know that it wasn't mine to keep. I would have Charlie Johnston send it on to Isaac in Lead. There was time, the train was still minutes away.

"Wait here," I told the children. "Don't any of you move. I'll be back."

"Mama!" Liz said.

"I'll be back," and I walked away from them, heading back to the dry-goods store, my eyes straight ahead, pretending the saloon wasn't there, pretending that people weren't watching me from their windows. With each step I thought about how I was leaving, how I was doing right by my children, how I was giving them a chance to see that there was something bigger than the Badlands. I thought about the six tickets in my handbag and how they were next to the letter somebody had written Isaac. The letter couldn't be from his mother; she never answered Isaac's letters. She only sent a book when a child was born, and Baby Ralph had been born dead. I couldn't begin to think who had written Isaac. Charlie Johnston had said something about letters flying back and forth. All at once that struck me as peculiar.

Just before getting to the dry-goods store, I stepped into the tight alley that ran between it and the bank. There was something odd about the letter. The wind, trapped between the low buildings, blew all the harder. My dress and coat flapped; the brim of my hat lifted. I put my back to the wind. I tightened the hat strings under my chin and inched off my gloves and put them in my pocket, afraid they might blow away. The letter wasn't my business; I shouldn't be doing this, I told myself as I carefully opened my handbag, scared the wind might catch the tickets. I got out the letter, gripping it hard, and drew the bag's strings tight. The letter wasn't mine to read. Isaac wouldn't like it. I almost laughed. Reading Isaac's letter was a small thing when put alongside of me selling my wedding band and using that money to take the children to Chicago.

The sky was gray and low, and the light was dim in the alley. I ran my fingernail under the flap of the envelope, thinking that I could open it and then reseal it. I worked the flap loose, tearing it just a little on one end. With both hands, I held out the letter. I skipped down to the signature. Zeb Butler. My heart pounded.

Zeb Butler in Sioux Falls what rented rooms, Zeb Butler what knew most of the Negroes in the Dakotas and beyond.

Isaac DuPree

It is nevr to soon. Lincoln Phillips in N.Dakota is willing to meet you. He has no wife living. Two dautrs but no sons.

Has better luck with land. Nearly 900 acrs. Says he can come mid sumr to see about your girl.

Zeb Butler

I leaned against the side of the dry-goods store, dizzy with disbelief. I read the letter again, the words spinning. I turned my face to the wind to clear my mind.

My hands folded the letter and put it in the envelope. Isaac had taken it to heart when on the night that Jerseybell died, I told him Mary was noticing boys, white boys. My hands tucked the flap inside the envelope. Isaac had said she was too young for such things. But he must have thought that over; it must have worried him to think of her admiring white boys. Like it had worried me. Only we had both seen it different. I wanted Mary to go to dances with Negro boys. Isaac wanted her married.

Mary had just turned thirteen. It was all I could think of. She was hardly thirteen. I put the letter in the bottom of my handbag. Come spring, I'd need it to prop up my courage.

I found my children where I'd left them by the depot office. Ignoring their questions, I picked up the carpetbag. "Come on," I said, my voice hollow in my ears.

"Mama?" Mary said, holding Emma close to her. "What's wrong?"

I waved her off and started walking, my footsteps loud on the planked boards. We went around the corner of the office and to the back where the tracks ran and where the water tank stood. There, on the backside of Interior, the whistling wind blew face-on with nothing for miles to break it.

I had written Mama and made it a secret. Isaac had written Zeb Butler and done the same.

"I'm cold," Alise whined above the wind. "My feet are cold, Mama."

Remember this, I thought but did not say. All of you, remember the cold of the Badlands, how it's a lonesome cold, one that you can't get away from. Feel the ache in your lungs, feel how that ache turns into a burn. Feel your toes, your ears, and your fingers, feel how they sting with the cold. Feel how the cold turns you brittle.

And remember how it was when your bellies were empty, when your mouths were dry, how you cried from it. But don't remember the well. Don't remember what we did to Liz.

"Stomp your feet," I said. "That'll warm you some." Alise did and Liz did too. But not Mary and John. They were looking at me, their eyes puzzled and worried.

Likely they thought me cruel, making them stand out in the cold that way. But I had to. That way when the train showed up, blowing its black smoke, they'd be glad. That way in the spring when they started thinking about coming back to the Badlands, their last memory would be of the cold. And the wind.

"Mama," Mary said, coming close to me, Emma's face tucked into Mary's neck scarf. "You're crying."

"No," I said, shaking my head. "It's the wind." Married at thirteen, fourteen at best. Married to a man come down from North Dakota to look her over. Married to a man what needed someone to raise his children. Married to a man what didn't care anything for her, what just needed another pair of hands to work his ranch. Married to a man what might not ever smile at her or touch her in a way to make her glad. I couldn't bear to think of how it would be for Mary. I looked past her.

Spread out before me was the Badlands. When I was new to it, its bigness scared me. There wasn't any end to it. There was nothing but canyons that cut the earth, knee-high prairie grasses that rippled and swayed like they were alive, and ranges of buttes rising sharp against the sky. The Badlands scared me, but as long as I was with Isaac, I was where I wanted to be. When the Indian squaw showed up with her boy and her swollen belly, I believed those children were Isaac's but I had looked away from it. I forgave all things because I loved him. But not this.

If Isaac wanted to marry Mary off next summer, he was going to have to come to Chicago to get her. He was going to have to face me. And if Mary went back to the Badlands with him, she had to go knowing his plans for her. But I wasn't leading her to it; I wasn't leading any of my children to that.

I felt the train before hearing or seeing it. I felt it in my feet. *There will be dances for my children*, I told myself. I gathered myself and pinched the corners of my eyes with my gloved fingers. Then I straightened my shoulders as best I could and looked west, a trail of black smoke starting to show in the gray sky.

ACKNOWLEDGMENTS

Few people write a novel alone. I certainly didn't.

I am indebted to Judithe Little, Julie C. Kemper, Lloyd E. Elliott, Pam Barton, Laura Siller, Lois F. Stark, and Bryan Jamison for their careful readings, meaningful suggestions, and for pushing me to do better; to Marianne Mills with the U.S. National Park Service for granting me a writing residency at the Badlands National Park; to the staff and instructors at Houston's Inprint, Salt Lake City's Writers @ Work, and San Antonio's Gemini Ink for their belief in writers; and to the Sewanee Writers' Conference for its community of writers.

I am grateful to Margaret Halton for her support and counsel and to all the people at Viking who worked so hard to make this book shine. And last, my heartfelt thanks go to John Siciliano, my savvy editor, whose guidance and enthusiasm were invaluable.